CAPTURED EARTH

the complete trilogy

TJ NICHOLS

Resist

Capture is a soldier's worst fear, but all his training couldn't prepare Sergeant Josh Rayne for what it meant to be caught by the alien invaders, who have claimed the desert in Western Australia.

Josh believes he is the only man left alive from the teams sent out to spy on the aliens, but in the alien prison, he is reunited with his lover and fellow soldier Xavier Fisher. There is no time to celebrate though as Xavier is gravely injured and in need of medical care.

With the exfil date fast approaching, they have to escape before the ship leaves without them.

Book one in the Captured Earth trilogy. For readers who like action, explosions, and don't mind a little gore with their gay romance.

Chapter One

"THE SIMPSON LINE HAS BEEN DECLARED." Danny lowered the radio. He ripped the battered hat off his head and tossed it to the ground in frustration. The gray stockman's hat had seen better days. After over a month and a half in the scrub and desert, all of the six-man team had been better. Their uniforms and boots were scuffed, ripped, or just missing and replaced with whatever they could scrounge in the deserted towns. They were all rough around the edges, gritty with sand, and doing their best to follow the mission to the end when every instinct told them to run.

Or maybe that was just Josh.

He scratched at his beard, then took a swig from the bottle of rum they'd found in the house. Another empty town, not even a dog left behind. Most of the time, there wasn't even a possum left up a tree. The silence was unnerving. He took another drink, then passed the bottle to Beau.

Beau accepted the bottle and paused from repacking his gear. "What does that mean?"

"We left home without our passports." Josh Rayne glanced up at the pink and orange hued sky. Another gorgeous sunset, the kind tourists had once written home about. There would be no more campaigns trying to bring tourists to Western Australia. Western Australia no longer existed. Which meant they were no longer in Australia. It was a damn waste to hand it over to the Geckos—what the humans had started calling the tall, tailed, and lizard-like invaders.

The aliens had landed and set up without asking for permission. Satellites had gone down the same day. He'd been recalled from leave, and here he was. His gaze tracked the blood stain over the porch and down the steps. The drag marks in the dirt were faint but still there. He wanted the bottle of rum back just so he could drink to oblivion and pretend this wasn't happening but given that he was in charge, he had to act like it. "Any word on the mission and exfil?"

Danny picked up the hat he'd stolen at the first homestead they stopped at and jammed it back on. He wore it all the time, even though they only moved at night. "That was a courtesy call. Nothing has changed."

"It's all fucking changed. We haven't been able to raise the other two teams in over a month. Don't they give a shit?" Did the Army understand what they were finding, or not finding, out here?

And now this.

Australia had called it quits on defending half the country. What the hell was happening in the rest of the world? If not for a weekly check in from HQ, it would be easy to believe there were no other humans left on the planet.

Josh closed his eyes and tried not to remember the echo of the screaming and yelling in the middle of the fire fight. Then nothing. He'd hoped it was because Bravo's radio had been shot to pieces.

Xavier was dead, and Josh had to keep going like it didn't matter.

He opened his eyes and drew in a breath. This time, he avoided looking at the blood stain. It was harder to ignore the bullet holes and scorch marks where the occupants had tried to fight off the invaders.

"Apparently not." Danny licked his peeling lips but didn't say anything else. He didn't need to. The way he looked at Josh was enough. They hadn't looked at him the same after that last call they'd received from Bravo.

For the first night, he'd held himself together, focused on walking and refused to let grief consume him. He hadn't wanted to believe that Xavier was dead.

Then they'd reached what had been a settlement. Three small houses and a whole lot of blood. There'd been so much blood but not a single body.

It wasn't where Bravo team had been killed, but it might as well have been.

He'd broken and cried and wished he was dead too.

Since then, the other five men in his team had kept an eye on him. They couldn't afford a weak link out here. He'd never been that man before. He'd done three tours in the Middle East, and he wasn't going to let any gunned-up Gecko stop him from getting home—was Perth still home when it wasn't part of Australia?

He breathed out; he'd peel open the hurt when he was on the ship with a cold beer in his hand and Xavier's personal effects in the other. He ran his fingertips over the grip of his pistol.

Geckos died and bled like any enemy. And now each one that he killed was for Xavier.

"Where are we, Chris?" Josh asked. For the moment, he was still in charge. They hadn't removed him, and they were still a team. But now they knew their boss had been screwing another soldier in his spare time, and they just looked at him like he was a head case.

Maybe he was.

He'd known it was a bad idea to get involved with a soldier—hell, he knew he was no catch—but it had happened anyway. Xavier was a survivor, same as all of them.

Had been a survivor.

Fucking Geckos.

Chris held the map that had plotted their course through the outback, they were supposed to round up civilians and get them headed toward the coast, toward the waiting Navy ship. Perth was too far south for them to walk to, and Geraldton no longer existed.

It had been bombed to little more than a crater the week before they'd been deployed.

"Five days from Gecko Base One," Chris said. "I think we've got enough fuel to get there. There should be an Aboriginal community on the way."

Danny groaned.

Josh pressed his lips together. They all knew there would be no one there. "There's no point in stopping there."

The closer they'd gotten to the base, the older the signs of life had been. They'd stopped hoping to find survivors after the first two homesteads. It had gone from rescue and recon to recon only. The last part of their orders was to get eyes on the base and report back.

Then pray the promised ship would still be there when they reached the coast for extraction from what was now Gecko country.

"Right then. Let's pack up and head out. The sooner we get eyes on the base, the sooner we can go get that cold beer."

They'd spent the day at this once nice homestead. They'd raided the cupboards, had made damper, and eaten cereal with long life milk. They'd thrown tins of fruit and baked beans in the ute for later. The ute was borrowed from the first empty town. No one was going to report it missing.

After securing the site, they'd filled up all their water containers from the nice full tank and siphoned off fuel into their stolen jerry cans. Then they'd slept in beds and showered.

A small reprieve from what was waiting for them. Knowing that the government had ceded half the country to the invaders just made it all that much more futile.

Eyes on the base. Since the Geckos shot down anything that could fly, it had to be done the old-fashioned way. They had to creep up on the base. But it was so fucking quiet some nights, it was hard to believe the Geckos didn't hear them coming.

Maybe they were already preparing a welcome committee.

Josh climbed into the tray. Danny joined him while the other four sat in the cab. Rolling around the back of the ute were some of the metal bits Josh had pulled off two dead Geckos. There was what looked like a robotic arm and something that had been on another's stomach. The two Geckos scouts had gone down pretty easy, and it had been nice to see them bleed.

When the blood had stopped flowing, the metal parts had been easy to lift off. Beneath the metal had been a raw stump of an arm and what appeared to be an open gut wound, something that should've required major surgery, not robotics.

Tomorrow, they'd hide the ute and make sure it was ready for the drive to the coast, the ship, and then home…or at least safety. They were on schedule to get eyes on the base.

So far, the Geckos hadn't worried about ships. Drones, missiles, planes, satellites—anything that flew—were all gone with in the first couple of days. And Australia wasn't the only country to be invaded. Josh had seen that on the news before getting the recall to base.

He'd argued with Xavier on the drive back. The knife in his heart twisted. He shouldn't have.

"What are you thinking about?" Danny nudged Josh's boot.

Josh lifted his gaze. Moonlight glinted off the metal cab. Tonight didn't feel like a good night to be out. "Do you think the rest of the world is still out there?"

Danny nodded. He had a wife and two kids back in Perth. "They'd have sent everyone east."

"Evacuated Perth and stuck'em all on the train before cutting us off," Josh agreed even though he wasn't sure it was the truth.

"Yeah." Danny nodded again. "You think they kicked the Geckos out of Nevada?"

"Of course." There was no Vegas anymore. The lights had been turned off the day the Geckos had landed. Last he'd heard, the US was fighting hard for Nevada, but that had been six weeks ago. Had the US given up? Was that why Australia had given up? There wasn't much out here, but that wasn't the point. Now the Geckos had a toehold. What happened when more arrived?

The ute bounced, making his teeth rattle.

The short burst of radio comms they got wasn't enough to ask for a global update. What about North Africa? And Saudi Arabia? It was pretty clear that anywhere with a decent hot desert was now hosting intergalactic pests.

Aliens.

No amount of training had prepared anyone for this. Those whi said it had were lying.

Danny narrowed his gaze, and it looked like he wanted to say something. Josh looked away. He didn't want to talk about it. He'd fucked up. He shouldn't have gotten involved with Xavier, but they were on different teams and they'd been ignoring the attraction for well over a year before they'd given in while in Afghanistan. They'd kept it quiet for three years.

"Bravo disappeared when they got eyes on," Danny said.

"I know. Don't think about it unless you want to join them." Three teams. They were supposed to take it in shifts to get close. They all had different areas of civilians to clear out.

"I can't stop thinking about it. I want to go home, boss."

"We're going to get home. We'll sweep the base and head for the coast. It'll be fine, mate." Josh didn't believe his own damn lies.

Danny nodded, but Josh could already see that he was no longer thinking about the job. He was thinking of home.

He kicked Danny's boot. "Get your head on."

"How do you do it?"

Josh closed his eyes. By not thinking about it. By pretending that Xavier was still alive and waiting for him. He'd deal with the reality later. That one crack had been all he could show, and it had been enough for the others to treat him like glass for a week, watching and waiting for him to lose it.

The ute stopped with a jerk. Josh opened his eyes and scanned the dark.

Danny moved, searching for a target through the scope of his rifle. Josh would have to watch him…and himself.

Silence. The engine ticked as it cooled.

Josh jumped out and walked around to the driver's side door. Crickets chirped as though all was right with the world. "What did you see?"

He hadn't seen anything, but he hadn't been paying attention. They'd only seen one scouting party and that had been near a settlement. If Danny hadn't been talking, he'd have been sleeping.

"I thought I saw a flash," Chris said.

"Gecko fire?" Or dingo eyes?

Danny jumped out of the back, rifle in his hands, still watchful. "Blue flash."

"We'll check it out." Getting closer to the base, there would be more of the almost see-through skinned freaks roaming around. "How far to the settlement?"

"Five klicks, north." Chris pointed to his right, orientating Josh. "Base is two hundred west."

"You and Linc stay with the vehicle."

"Yes, boss." They were both already moving to defend the vehicle and their supplies. While they could hunt for food, the lack of water would kill them first.

The four of them slid away from the ute and into the scrub. The stars weren't this bright in the city, and he'd always hated coming home for that reason. Now when he looked at the stars, he wondered how many other aliens were waiting to claim a piece of Earth.

They moved quickly, weapons ready in case they got the chance to kill a few more Geckos. He'd never fancied a pair of lizard skin boots before; now, he wouldn't mind a whole fucking coat. A trench coat made of their pearly white skin. Fuck it, he'd have a whole outfit and travel accessories.

Josh held his hand up. Ahead, black armor gleaming in the starlight, was a Gecko. Tall and lean with a tail like a whip, the Gecko moved much like they did, sweeping the area, gun ready, creeping with soft steps.

Josh's breathing was too loud in his ears.

They didn't know enough about the aliens. The helmet hid the head, their large dark eyes, and a mouthful of pointed teeth. That much they did know. How well they saw or heard was a mystery. How their tech worked was another unsolved mystery. Maybe some boffin on the east coast had it all figured out.

If the people at the top knew more, they hadn't shared it. His team needed to get some good intel to make this whole botched up mission worthwhile.

He watched the Gecko. Why was there only one of them? They never travelled alone.

Clicks and whistles filled the air. The Gecko he could see made a hand gesture. Telling the other to shut up? Josh almost smiled.

Beau pointed to the left. Crouching down was another Gecko, only ten meters away.

The smell of fresh blood drifted through the night.

The aliens looked trained, like they knew what they were doing. They weren't the animals that the movies of his youth had promised. Though those movies didn't hold up to inspection. How could a mindless animal intent on only eating create and fly a ship capable of space travel?

Even though Josh was standing in the shadows, the standing Gecko seemed to stare right at him.

Josh exhaled slowly. For all he knew that helmet could read heat signatures. Whatever it saw, something had given them away; they'd been made. He was sure of that.

He indicated for Beau to take the crouching Gecko to the side, then Josh opened fire on the one that was staring at him.

The body armor protected the invader. He staggered back, then returned fire with his silent gun. The only give away was the blue muzzle flash. Heat singed the hair on Josh's arm. He took a breath, steadied himself, then aimed straight for the face plate. It shattered, and the Gecko fell.

Josh searched for the other Gecko and saw him flat on the ground, unmoving.

Was there just the two? His heart was pounding as he scanned the scrub. Only his team moved. Danny clutched at his gut. His fingers came away dark in the moonlight.

"Danny's hit." Josh moved closer, relying on Beau to cover him if one of the lizards twitched. He got Danny on the ground and ripped open his body armor and shirt, exposing the wound. The scent of cooked meat assaulted him. The Geckos' guns weren't anything like what he'd seen, and the injury they left wasn't a bullet wound as much as a burned hole. He cut the bottom of Danny's pocket open, knowing where he kept his emergency kit. What good was any of it out here? But he still went through the motions, pouring on the wound sealer and placing a bandage over the top like help would arrive in the next hour.

Danny grabbed his wrist. "Don't let me die."

"You'll be right, mate." He jabbed Danny with morphine. He was fucked. There was no medivac out of here. Any helicopter that tried would be shot down by the Geckos.

Two shots punctuated the night. Beau had ripped off the helmets and put a bullet through each of the lizards' heads. Not even they could make a metal mod to recover from that.

The mods.

"I need the ute," Josh called out.

"How bad is it?" Danny asked.

Josh squeezed Danny's hand. "Help's on its way."

The rumble of the engine filled the air. Beau came over to help lift Danny.

Josh shook his head. "You know the tech we lifted? I want the plate." While it was a square plate, it was segmented like an armadillo. They'd pulled it off a Gecko with a gut wound. Hopefully it would help Danny.

Beau hesitated. "You're not going to—"

"Just get it," Josh snapped. Danny was dead if he did nothing.

This time, Beau obeyed and came back with the metal plate. He held it out like it was a dead thing. Maybe it was as it had no blood supply. Maybe it was dormant. Josh had no idea. He should. He was the medic.

"You'll kill him," Beau said.

"Or save him. What would you do? I can't do nothing." He glanced over his shoulder at the ute and his other team members. "Anyone else voting no?"

"You do what you need to, to get Danny on his feet," Chris said, but he didn't sound sure.

"What if he becomes one of them? We don't know what it will do."

"Only one way to find out." Josh lined up the plate over Danny's stomach, getting it central over the wound. He hesitated. The mods only came off when the blood stopped flowing. This would be permanent. If it worked.

And if it did wake up and turn Danny against them?

Fuck

He wasn't going to lose a man.

The others were watching.

Would he do this if it were Xavier who was wounded and dying? Risk using the alien tech?

He pressed it to Danny's skin, holding it there waiting for the metal to do something.

For several heartbeats, nothing happened. The tech was useless. Why had he even expected it to work?

Then Danny started screaming. Josh clamped his hand over Danny's mouth. Fear that there were other Geckos around to find them made him hold his friend down. The other's watched, rifles at the ready, scanning the night. Danny twitched and writhed beneath him as though being electrocuted. What had he done?

He shouldn't have used the untried tech. But he wasn't letting the Geckos take any more lives.

The screams became a groan, and the twitching subsided.

"No more Geckos?" Josh asked.

"Clear."

Josh eased his hand off Danny's mouth; there were teeth marks on his palm. "I guess it was just two."

"Or if there was a third, they ran home."

No one lowered their weapon.

Josh's heart was beating hard, but he knew the adrenaline rush would fade soon. "Strip the bodies, and let's get out of here."

Danny groaned again. He was alive, so Josh took that as a good sign.

He fingered the edge of the plate, but it wouldn't lift. Was that a good thing?

With Beau's help, they lifted Danny into the tray of the ute.

"There's three dead roos. I think they were hunting. Do we want a roast?"

"Yeah, why not? One last hot feed at the rendezvous point."

Then it would be a few days of walking to the base and a week of watching. As far as he knew, no other team had made it that far. He shoved down the memory of Xavier's death as it would do him no good.

Chris put a roo in the tray with them. "All good?"

"Yeah. Travelling in style." Josh gave him the thumbs up.

"You'll have that skinned and ready to be roasted by the time we get there, right?" Chris's gaze was on Danny, his face serious despite his light tone.

Josh patted Danny's shoulder. "Don't drive too rough. Don't want to damage the meat."

Chapter Two

THEY MADE it to the rendezvous point without seeing another alien. Danny was awake and a little confused, but he wasn't bleeding or screaming so that was an improvement. Josh didn't want to believe that the Gecko tech had worked. That seemed a little too easy.

The other men unloaded what they needed to take and then hid the ute. The netting would be enough from a distance, and it was parked in some dense shrubs. He didn't want to leave Danny with the ute because that would mean leaving another man with him and then they'd be down to four. But he wasn't sure if Danny was up to getting close to the base.

No one said it, but they were all wondering what they should do now and waiting for Josh to give directions. He gave each man a quick glance and hoped they were up to the job ahead. While they were all grim faced, the doubts and worry flickered in their eyes.

Linc glared at him and flicked his pocketknife. The blade opened and closed. "Why don't we just drive for the coast and get the fuck out of here?"

For a moment, Josh considered it. He could call off this last part and make a run for the coast. He doubted anyone would argue with him. The other teams were dead. Could they really be expected to follow?

Xavier's accusations that Josh was a coward for not wanting to jump into a fight with the aliens rang in his ears. Their last words, spoken in anger. Josh shook his head. He was here now, and it was too late to back out.

When they reached the ship, he'd be in trouble for disobeying orders and the deaths of the other two teams would be for nothing. They needed to know what the Gecko base was like. They needed to find a weakness they could exploit.

"We can't. We have to get a visual." The more they knew the sooner they could kick the aliens off Earth. "We'll move out together."

Everyone gave Danny a quick glance.

"I'm fine." Danny adjusted his hat. "I could take the ute and get reinforcements."

"Ain't going to happen. We're just going to have a look." Josh sighed. Would Danny be safer if he stayed here? Would everyone else be safer if Danny stayed behind? It was clear Danny had lost his nerve, but if he took off with the ute, it was going to be a long walk out with aliens on their six. "You'll be all right. We'll get you home to the missus in no time."

Danny glanced at him as though not sure what was the right answer. They both knew there wasn't one. The others were carefully not watching them.

A small part of Josh was glad that it was no longer him they were assessing from the corner of their eyes.

Danny nodded.

"Good. Nothing like a brisk walk to get the blood moving." Josh checked Danny's pulse. It was quick but steady, and the tech was holding him together. At least externally. God knew how his cooked insides were coping. The tech might have bought him a few days, long enough to reach the coast if they weren't stopping for a little sightseeing.

They took turns to help Danny or carry his pack. When they were several klicks away from the base, they stopped to set up camp.

The moonlight bleached the desert to silver, and the base was a tiny wart in the distance. If he could see the Geckos, they might be able to see him.

He turned away.

Chris started cooking a chunk of the roo; the rest had been kicked off the tray as they were travelling—no point in leading scavengers to the ute. The smell of the cooking meat turned Josh's stomach, but he needed to eat, and it would be days before he ate something other than cold, ready to eat meals. They'd been saving them for this part of the operation, making do with what they scavenged from farms and towns.

They'd eat, then sleep, taking turns to keep watch.

"Danny, can I check your dressing?" Danny seemed fine, but Josh wanted to know what was going on inside.

He lifted the edge of the ripped and blood-stained shirt to examine the wound. Danny hadn't asked about the metal; maybe he hadn't realized what was holding him together. The drugs would've worn off by now, and he hadn't complained about the pain. Or anything really. There was dried blood around the edges of the metal armadillo, but nothing fresh. When Josh tried to grab the edge to peel it off, he found that it was stuck fast.

Danny closed his eyes. "Is it bad? It doesn't hurt. Not much anyway."

"What kind of pain is it?" Josh frowned. He should have been in agony. He should have been dying. Had the tech healed the burn hole and fixed his guts or was Danny already rotting from the inside out?

"Warm? A bit of pulling?" Danny propped himself up on his elbow. He tugged his shirt trying to get a look, but Josh didn't let go. "Let me see."

Josh winced and let go. "You were hit pretty bad. It was all I could do."

Danny gasped and jerked back, scrabbling away as though he could escape his own stomach. "Get it off me!"

"I can't. They only come off when the heart stops." He grabbed Danny's leg to hold him still. "Take a few breaths and settle down."

"Fuck." His fingers gripped the edges, gouging at his flesh, but not harming the metal.

Josh captured his hands and pinned him down. "Listen. They can work it out on the ship, stop your heart in surgery or something, but that is all that's keeping your guts in."

"It's Gecko tech. What if it takes over?" He panted, eyes wide and filled with horror.

Josh couldn't hold his stare. He'd done this to him, saved him, but was this worse? What would the Army do to Danny? Let him go or keep him for inspection? Josh closed his eyes for a moment. Better to be alive, right?

Beau came over. He knelt at Danny's side and gripped his chin. "Calm the fuck down. We are too close to the base for this shit. We're going to take a look, and then we are going home. You are not fucking this up for us."

"Everyone else was killed when they took a look. We're going to die. Where's the ute?" Danny turned his head, arching his neck to try and find it.

"Hidden," Josh said. Danny hadn't even paid attention to where it was. He wasn't ready to do anything more complicated than sit still, and even then, Josh wasn't sure he trusted Danny to do right. "You can stay here or help us. You're still one of us. But get your shit together."

"You should be thanking him for thinking quick or you'd already be dead." Beau stood. "Roo's ready."

"You want a cooked breakfast?" Josh offered Danny his hand.

Danny didn't take it.

"Suit yourself." A meal and a sleep and then they'd move out. They had some sleeping tablets from one of the houses they'd raided. Josh had pinched all kinds of medication, not knowing what they'd need out here. He gave two to Danny who swallowed them dry. He'd never thought alien tech would save a life. He wasn't sure it had.

———

JOSH SLEPT through the heat of the day after taking first watch. This close to the Gecko base, they weren't taking any chances. Like the others, he was damn good at sleeping anywhere because they never knew when they were going to get the opportunity again.

He was shaken awake when it was almost time to leave. He took a piss, then made a final ammo check, planning to shoot every damn Gecko he saw before they got him. They'd survived two encounters with Geckos. Despite the alien's weapons and their tech they could still be killed.

That was all he needed to know.

Danny came with them; no one had wanted to leave him behind…but no one really wanted him with them either. If this were a normal mission, he'd have been choppered out. They'd been told that wouldn't be possible before they'd left Perth, though. Since then, they'd been on their own. After the first two teams went silent, they had started to realize exactly what that meant. This wasn't an extreme camping trip. Now they weren't even in Australia. Was what they were doing even legal? Or had they invaded another country?

They moved through the dusk toward the base. The night was quiet and still. Too beautiful for the occasion.

He'd always thought that. The night was theirs, and they should be doing more than scoping targets. They should be calling them in. The Air Force had tried to bomb Gecko Base One and Two which were occupying territory in the Simpson Desert. Short of a nuke, he wasn't sure anything would destroy the bases—he wasn't sure a nuke would even get close enough. Nothing else had.

They moved slowly and silently through the night, not knowing what kind of security the base had or what tech the aliens had scanning the desert. In the predawn gray, the base grew larger. It could've been another rock formation, but everyone knew what they were looking at wasn't natural.

It had a gleam if he looked at it in just the right way. The shape was wrong too.

As far as Josh knew no one else had gotten this close. If they had, they hadn't lived to radio what they'd seen. Prickles of cold spread across his back. How close had Xavier's team been? They'd have been approaching from the north.

Josh glanced at the sky. They wouldn't be able to complete a lap before it got light. He wasn't sure if the light level even mattered. The Geckos they'd encountered had no trouble seeing them during day or night.

He indicated for Beau and Chris to head left. The rest of them would head right. Fifteen minutes, then they'd pull back, debrief, and work out what the hell to do next. Just looking at the building wouldn't be enough. They needed a weakness. Something they could use. They'd been warned not to engage or try and take it out. Just recon.

Josh moved quickly over the dry, rocky ground, edging slowly closer to the structures. It wasn't just one. It was many buildings and there was no sign of the ship that had carried them and dropped them in the desert. Like most other people, he'd seen the footage of the ships and thought it a trailer for a new movie. When his phone had started buzzing with the orders that his leave was cancelled and to get back to base, he'd known it was real but had still struggled to believe. When all the satellites went dark was when he'd understood what it meant: Earth was under attack.

Now as he watched through the scope of his gun, he tried to work out what he was seeing. Had the Geckos pulled the ship apart to build their settlement? If that was the case, they had no plans to leave.

He dropped and froze. There was movement around the edges of the building. Guards. Their dark clothing almost made them invisible; only their ghostly tail showed. Hips, face mask, underarm and tail were the weak points. They'd worked that out through trial and error and by studying the armor on the bodies. A few bits of that rattled around the ute too.

Gunfire echoed from the other side of the compound.

"Fuck," Josh muttered. Even if they ran, they'd be too late. They had to go. He motioned to the others and ran toward the rest of their team.

They were too late. Everything fell quiet before they got there.

He slithered into position behind some rocks and surveyed the scene. His heart was beating hard, but he calmed his breathing. The Geckos picked over the bodies, much like they had picked over the dead Geckos, and then tossed the bodies onto what looked like a sled.

He wanted to look away but couldn't. Is this what those bastards had done to Xavier? Treated him like a piece of meat? Had they eaten him?

Bile rose in the back of his throat. Two quick shots. He could take his time to get them lined up. While he wasn't as good a shot as Xavier, he was good enough to kill those two. No one would know that he'd broken the orders. No one here would report him.

But he'd know. Watch. Only engage if fired on first.

It was a stupid rule. These were aliens. They would have their own rules of engagement, and that seemed to be kill everything warm blooded.

Danny squirmed next to him. He clutched his stomach. "Something…" He gasped.

One Gecko turned and looked straight at them as though the metal was sending a signal. *Shit.*

Danny grunted, then was up and running away as though there was some place to go.

A flash of blue lit up the night.

"Get down!" Josh yelled.

But even as the words were leaving his mouth, Danny stumbled and fell.

"Fuck," Linc muttered as he stared at the dirt. "Fuck," he said again with more emphasis.

Josh breathed through gritted teeth. He pulled a grenade. Beau and Chance were dead. Danny may not be. And there was still Linc, Matt, and him. Between the three of them they could lay down cover, haul Danny to the ute, and flee for the coast. They'd seen the base and could report that getting within two hundred meters was fatal. That was a report, though not the kind the brass wanted.

He nudged Linc and showed him the grenade. "Yeah? Then we'll head home."

The Geckos were talking, clicking and whirring like machines made flesh, not flesh with robotic parts to heal their wounds. The sounds carried across the landscape, making the desert alien. It was clearly inhospitable to human life.

Linc grimaced. "Do it."

Josh yanked the pin and threw the grenade before the Geckos could get any closer. Why hadn't they just shot them where they lay? He didn't have time to ponder that as the rock and sand erupted, and the world started ringing. He sprang up and ran for Danny, knowing they didn't have long before more Geckos came to see what was going on.

The back of Danny's head was gone. No point in stopping to take a pulse.

The rocks had stopped raining, and the dust was settling. He needed to find cover or keep running. Matt streaked past him; a flash of blue struck him in the back. Where was Linc?

Josh skidded behind a rock that was barely big enough to hide him. Out of the dust came three figures. Two tall, lean aliens and Linc.

Josh closed his eyes for a moment, his mind repeating a litany of curse words he'd picked up from various deployments. None of them conveyed the desperation, the hopelessness and panic. Why wasn't there a word for that? He risked another glance.

Linc was on his knees, shaking his head as if he knew Josh was watching.

Josh studied the Geckos. He'd be able to kill one. Maybe, but then it would all be over. More Geckos were coming out of the base, their long legs covering the distance fast.

He was not going to die from a blast to his back.

He didn't want to surrender either.

One of the Geckos put his gun to Linc's head. Linc closed his eyes.

Josh yanked another grenade free and tossed it toward the Geckos. This time, he didn't run. He stayed where he was hoping the Geckos would think he'd fled, while he got comfy with his rifle and waited for the dust to settle.

When he could see, Linc wasn't moving, but neither were the two Geckos that had been holding him. They were all crumpled on the ground.

Josh waited. Not moving. He could taste the sand in his mouth, feel it gathering on the sweat on his face. All he had to do was wait them out and then head for the ute. There was no one left to report back if he didn't get out. This whole mission would be a waste of lives. Would they send more?

Did the brass even care anymore? They'd given up this part of the country.

Maybe Danny was right and they should've just headed for the coast and forgotten all about this. But their orders hadn't changed even though they hadn't found a single person. Not even a corpse the whole time they'd been out here. The Gecko's had swept the area clean around their base for several hundred klicks. They knew what they were doing.

The hairs on the back of his neck drew tight. He turned in time to see the muzzle of a weapon pointed at his head. With his ears chiming like cathedral bells, he hadn't heard the Gecko sneak up on him. The blue flash was the last thing he saw.

Chapter Three

JOSH'S BODY ACHED. The ground beneath him was moving, and the air was filled with alien chirps. His heart stuttered, and it took everything he had not to open his eyes and sit up. He was alive.

That didn't feel like a good thing.

He wriggled his toes in his boots, relieved that he could feel the movement. He twitched his fingers. They moved too. Aside from feeling lethargic and a little nauseous, he didn't feel too bad. Something bounced into him, the brush of skin against his arm. Human skin.

Slowly, he cracked his eyes open. The sun was high overhead, bleaching the blue from the sky. He counted six Geckos around him, their black visors offering no clues about what they were looking at. Their language was foreign in his ears. He slid his gaze to the man next to him on the Gecko sled, and the gaping back of Danny's head glared at him, blood and brain leaking out onto his cams.

Josh's stomach bucked. He drew in a sharp breath and closed his eyes.

Was he the only one alive?

Yes. He'd seen them all die.

They were all dead, and he was on his own. Panic flooded him, swiftly followed by bone hollowing loss. The men he trusted with his life, who'd trusted him with theirs, were gone. He'd failed them. He should've died with them. Why hadn't the Geckos killed him? In that breath, all he wanted to do was die. Hundreds of klicks from exfil, and with no help coming. It would be better if he were dead.

Did the Geckos think he was dead?

Where did they take the dead?

In all the settlements they'd been to, they'd found no one alive. The four Geckos they'd killed were left to rot where they lay. The Geckos didn't leave the dead behind, of any species, and that bothered him. They had no reason to bury or burn the dead of their enemy.

Did the Geckos eat dead humans?

No, there would've been no humans on the planet where they'd come from. But humans were just meat like any animal.

The tightness in his chest wouldn't leave no matter how many slow breaths he took.

The sled stopped, and he risked another glance around but couldn't see anything of the buildings. He felt more than heard a hiss and then the sled was moving again, passing through some kind of barrier. Then he was in the compound. It wasn't a solid wall that ringed the base, though. There appeared to be only posts, not even wire strung between them. He was sure that he wasn't supposed to get inside the base, but if he got out, that would make for some good intel.

So far, all three teams had failed. Had any team anywhere in the world been successful? If they had, this base wouldn't be here. The hollowness and futility consumed him. He wanted to close his eyes and will death to come, but he had to memorize the layout of the buildings they passed. His training ran through his mind.

He'd failed to avoid the enemy. Now all he could do was follow procedure for after capture—but that assumed the captors were human. Doing anything while surrounded by Geckos would not be smart. He'd have to wait. But wait for what? No one even knew he was here. There was no one for hundreds of kilometers; the ship waiting off the coast might as well have been on the moon.

He couldn't feel his gun at his hip or his knife. Had they gone through his pockets or just taken the obvious weapons? It was hard to tell without moving, but he knew his vest was gone. His shoes were still on, so they hadn't gotten everything. He was lying on and surrounded by the bodies of his men. They all had weapons. On the next bump, he let his body jerk, trying to work out who was who. Danny's gear would be too hard to reach without being noticed. But the body he was on—he swallowed hard refusing to drown in hopelessness—might have something he could use.

On the next bounce he let his hand fall further down so he could run his fingers over the pockets. There was something there. It took a few moments for him to figure out what it was. Linc's pocketknife. Josh shoved it into his pocket.

The sled stopped before he could do anymore searches. A metal hand closed around his arm, hauling him up. His first instinct was to struggle, but he fought it down.

Wait.

Josh was dragged to his feet, and the lizard said something to him, cuffing him on the head when he didn't respond fast enough. Josh opened his eyes fully. A Gecko in what could be a black uniform but no helmet studied him. Its dark eyes were unreadable. Josh straightened, still much shorter than the alien, waiting for questions or shackles or punishment. Something.

The seconds ticked by.

Apprehension tightened his body with every breath. He didn't want to die, not like this.

The Gecko said something to the others, and they responded. He was sure from the tone and tail flick it was something like "I don't give a fuck." They'd done their job, and now he was this alien's problem.

The Gecko reached for him, its long pale fingers catching his shirt and tugging. The ones that had caught him had already stripped him of anything useful, not that his weapons were as good as theirs.

The Gecko tugged again; this time the buttons gave and flew off into the sand. The Gecko clicked at him, still pulling at the shirt. He wanted the shirt too? Fine.

Josh shrugged out of it, and the shirt dropped to the sand.

The alien put its hands on his face. The fingertips sucked at his skin as it peered into his eyes. Josh tried to pull away. He wasn't a horse for inspection. The cold press of metal against his spine made him still. But his captor seemed happy; its mouth opened, revealing rows of small, pointed teeth that looked like they could do some serious damage if it were to bite him.

It didn't bite, though. It finished its inspection, studying his eyes then forcing his mouth open, and Josh complied. He had to survive to escape. Escape wasn't impossible…just improbable. Completely different things.

But he didn't believe his own lies.

His captor spun him like a top, so he faced the sled filled with the bodies of his team. Dark red blood stained their sandy uniforms. He'd never again hear Danny talk about his kids or listen to Linc bitch about the heat. Their bodies blurred as his eyes burned.

Two quick whistles were all the warning he got, then something burned across his shoulders. He hissed and was turned so more of the stuff sprayed over his chest. Lurid green stained his skin and burned like the sunburn he'd had as a kid that had blistered up bad. No blisters formed though, and the pain lessened with each breath.

The alien gripped Josh's arm hard and dragged him away from the sled. Josh glanced back, but the sled was already moving, disappearing between two buildings.

"Where are they going?" He couldn't keep the fear from his voice. He knew they were dead, but they were his dead. Not theirs.

His captor clicked and whistled at him but didn't slow. Because of the height difference, Josh had to move quickly to keep up. He kept track of the buildings; not one of them was square, the angles were too obtuse. They finally stopped, and he heard human voices. Hope lifted for a moment before he realized the truth. The aliens had captives.

The Gecko put his wide, ghostly palm to the door. It opened as smoothly as any door on the stupid sci-fi movies he'd liked to watch. In the movies, the aliens never took over outback Australia.

He was walked down a short corridor before being stopped at a cell. There was a small window in the door at Gecko height. There were at least two other cell doors before the corridor bent away and became too dark.

"Fresh meat," a man called out.

Cheers and groans went up.

If he knew the alien language, Josh would've been tempted to say the Gecko laughed. The cell door was unlocked. No one charged through and attacked even though they had the numbers. They all stood there waiting for him to enter and for the alien to lock the door.

It was only when the alien had left the building, exiting out the door they'd entered through, that all eyes turned to him.

One man stood in the center of the cell and crossed his arms. "I've been here the longest, so I'll be taking your boots."

Josh gave the man a slow head to toe. He was bulky, but it wasn't all muscle. There was no definition on his stomach.

"Did they hit you in the head? I said give me your boots."

Josh lifted his gaze and shifted his feet to something closer to a fighting stance, but he kept his hands down and fingers loose. "Your feet are bigger than mine; you won't be able to wear them."

"I don't care. I want your boots."

Josh took in the cell with a glance. The other four men were sitting on the ground, watching. This guy was the cell bully, establishing his dominance. If Josh handed over his boots, he'd only be propping up this wanker. "No. I only have what I'm wearing, and I'm not giving to you."

"Then I'll take them from you." The man charged.

Josh waited until the last second and side stepped. The man crashed into the door, which only angered him.

"You think you're fucking smart? What are you? Fancy yourself a soldier in those pants?" The man had his hands up in fists, ready for Josh to throw a punch.

"Well, I've survived out there longer than you. As you said, you've been here the longest. Must have been easy to capture you." His hands were still loose by his sides. His heart was jittering with adrenaline and about ready to take flight.

The man charged again. Again, Josh sidestepped, this time following up with an elbow between the shoulder blades, dropping the man. He had him in an arm bar before he'd hit the floor. The man writhed and groaned.

"Don't break his arm." One of the other men inched closer.

"I'm not breaking anything. I just want him to understand that my boots are mine. If he touches me or my things, I will rip his fucking arms off." He pushed the shoulder joint to tearing point. "Clear?"

"Be careful. The farm!"

"Are we clear?" Josh said.

"Clear," the bully gasped.

Josh didn't believe him, but for the moment, it was good enough. He let the man go and moved out of range.

"You'll do well in the arena," an Aboriginal man said. He held out his hand. "Clarence."

Josh shook his hand, glad to have found some survivors. "Josh. What the hell is the arena and why are we here?"

Chapter Four

FOR SEVERAL HEARTBEATS no one said anything. Their gazes darted to each other and the floor.

The man who'd attacked him got up from the floor. "You're so fucking smart, work it out yourself."

Josh made sure that he could see the man just in case he did something dumb like attack again. He didn't want an enemy, but he wasn't going to let this guy grind him down either.

"Cut it out, Frank," someone from another cell yelled.

How many men were here? One thing was clear: the Geckos weren't interested in interrogating him. He wasn't bound and being tortured. Not yet anyway. This wasn't the way it was supposed to be, and he wasn't sure what was going on.

"That my bed?" He pointed to an unoccupied pile of blankets.

"Yeah. Maybe you'll last longer than the last guy," Frank said with a grin. "Maybe you won't."

Josh sat on the blankets. They looked like they'd been taken from someone's house. A nice blanket and what appeared to be a homemade quilt, the kind his grandmother had made him and that he'd hated at the time. It was only after the crash two years later that he'd appreciated having something. He ran his finger over the cloth shapes. Was it still on the sofa in his house? Did he still have a house and a sofa, or had Perth been bombed flat in his absence?

Clarence squatted opposite him. "Don't worry about Frank. He's a good guy, just been here too long."

"Haven't we all…except Josh. Did you arrive alone?" one of the others asked. They all had the smear of bright green across their chests and backs.

"Yeah." Fresh pain bloomed at the loss of his team, but he didn't feed it. He wasn't going to take it out and examine it until he was on the ship and safe. And then what? He'd be assigned to another team, and the Army would send him somewhere else or back here again. Maybe they'd figure out a way to fight the aliens. He wanted to kill them all for what they'd done, not just to his team but to the others. To Xavier.

First, he had to survive and escape.

Frank glared at Josh like he was never going to be forgiven for embarrassing him. He'd embarrassed himself by trying to be the tough guy.

A blond-haired man swore. "Why isn't anyone coming to rescue us? Why aren't they shooting up some lizards."

No one knew they were here for a start. All the brass knew was that the towns were empty. No souls found. No bodies either. Did everyone end up here?

Josh scratched at his beard, not willing to answer when no one would like the taste of the truth. "What's the arena?"

"What do you think it is?" Frank said with a gleam in his eye.

"I'm guessing there's no rock concerts or football games out here." He should've gone to more of both while he could. He hadn't realized how quickly it could be gone.

"We're the entertainment," Clarence said. "When it's our turn, they open the side of the cell. There's more cells on the other side of the arena, and then we pair off and fight."

Josh considered this for a moment. "With weapons?"

"If they put them out," Clarence confirmed.

If he got his hands on some weapons, that could be useful.

However, he didn't want to be fighting other prisoners. "How long have you been here, Frank?"

"A month," he said as he crossed his arms.

Not that long at all, but long enough to know how things worked. "They feed us?"

Frank kept his mouth closed.

It was Clarence who answered. "Yeah. Food comes twice a day. There's a tap for water over there, and on the opposite side, a hole."

Josh noted the location of both. "And when they let us out, what's the arena like?" He couldn't unlock the cell, but maybe there was a way out of the arena. No prison was watertight. There had to be a way out, and he'd find it. He wasn't going to sit tight and become boss of the cell because he had nothing better to do. He had a date with an HMAS off the coast and he was keeping it. Which mean he was on the clock.

"You'll find out tomorrow," Clarence said with a sigh. "They always make the cells with fresh meat fight sooner."

"Stop talking to him. He'll find out soon enough," Frank snapped.

Clarence scowled at Frank then stood and went back to his blankets.

Somewhere in the cellblock, someone was singing.

Josh leaned back and closed his eyes. The old habit of stealing sleep when he had the chance wasn't one he was willing to fight.

He woke to the tugging of his boot and lashed out with a kick before coming fully awake. The thief yelped and scuttled back.

Josh's laces were undone. He glared at each of the men in turn. "Is it every man for himself, or do you work as a team?" He re-tied the laces, making sure they were firm. When he got out, he'd need them.

Three of the men were barefoot. Frank had boots, of course.

"What's the point in working as a team when people come and go just as fast?" Frank lifted his hands as though there was nothing more to be said.

Josh shook his head.

"Tell us a story. What's it like out there now? How long until they blow the lizards up?" Clarence grinned.

Josh couldn't raise a smile. There'd be no blowing up of anything; nothing had gotten through the Geckos' defenses. Last he'd heard, the EU was planning on nuking the Sahara, but not everyone agreed, and the surrounding African nations had been concerned about the fallout. Josh didn't blame them.

"I've been out in the bush for over a month, so I have no idea." The partial lie stuck in his teeth, but he forced it out.

He needed to give them a reason to want out instead of sitting here like trained fighting dogs waiting for a chance to draw blood before being re-kenneled. "I heard there's a ship off the coast, waiting to take refugees. That's where I was heading with my…my friends."

"And they got away?"

Josh closed his eyes. "No."

He should've died with them. Instead, he was alive, so he had to make it count. He had to get out and make a report. Their deaths had to be for something. He was a survivor and could get through anything.

At what point did he stop surviving and actually live?

Or was that living?

No one spoke. There wasn't even a deck of cards to pass the time, so he watched the way the sunlight moved across the floor. When sleep wouldn't come, he got up and walked over to the window. It was too high up for him to see out of, so he hauled himself up using the bars, then braced his feet on the wall.

It wasn't comfortable, but he'd been in worse positions. Xavier had held him down one time. It had been a desperate scrabble as they hadn't seen each other in six months, and they'd about five minutes to get reacquainted before having to go their separate ways again. His knuckles whitened. He'd give his kidney for those five minutes, concrete grazes and all.

They should've been open, admitted they were together, and maybe they'd have got their schedules synched. Or maybe they'd have been pushed out. Maybe Xavier would still be alive, and he wouldn't be here. He drew in a breath and focused on what was outside the cell.

The arena was a sandy area between this row of cells and another. It wasn't rectangular but six sided. The buildings looked modular. The lip of the roof was higher than he'd be able to run at and climb. If he had a boost, maybe. The roofline had been lower on the outside. All the buildings that he'd seen had angled roofs.

"There is no escape. It's been tried," Frank said as though he knew everything about the place.

There was a difference between civilians trying and him trying. If he had a team, that would've changed things in his favor. Get out, get weapons, get to the ute.

Not a plan, more of an idea.

And not a good one.

He lowered himself down. "So what? We sit here all day staring at the walls, waiting for them to invite us out to fight? To die?"

"We try not to kill each other." That was the first good thing Josh had heard since waking up in the sled. Frank grinned. "But accidents happen."

Josh could feel the target being painted on his back as Frank studied him.

———

PEOPLE, men from the sounds of it, in other cells were telling stories about fishing trips. Someone was quietly crying. Josh kept his eyes closed. It was morning; he could tell from the light behind his eyelids. He needed to piss, but he wasn't ready to get up yet. He wanted to pretend that he was somewhere else for just a little longer.

Anywhere else.

If he kept his eyes closed, maybe the voices could be the members of his team or other soldiers. Not a bunch of civilians who'd decided this was it and were happy to play by the rules until rescue came. He could pretend it was yesterday morning again. He'd listen to Danny this time and they'd drive for the coast. Fuck the mission and the Geckos. Fuck the brass and their desire for intel. They could get it themselves if they wanted it so bad.

His throat swelled, and his eyes became hot.

He forced out a breath between his clenched teeth.

Survive. Escape. Report.

He opened his eyes, blinked a few times to clear the water from his lashes, and then got up. His boots had stayed on all night, but he wanted to wash. He should wash and change his socks at the very least.

He used the hole. It was too small to escape through, but it was plumbed as it was a pipe not a dirt hole. These cells had been either made when the Geckos landed, or they'd been part of the ship. He remembered hearing something about the ships separating before landing.

Why the hell would they have cells with them? His empty stomach knotted. Maybe they'd planned to take prisoners? He checked out the window again, but there was nothing new to draw his attention.

Frank's know-it-all voice broke the silence of the cell. "You'll get out there soon enough. They'll want to see what you're like."

"Good. I want to see who else is here." He wanted to see how many Geckos came to watch the fights. The more he could find out the better.

"You can't escape."

Josh gripped the bars and did a few pull ups. He was going to have to do something to stay in shape. Lying around all day wouldn't help his chances. He could feel eyes on his back as he worked. It was only when he dropped down that he saw they were all watching him.

"You're Army," Clarence said, his expression becoming calculating. "That's how you know there is a ship."

"Well, we're all screwed if even the Army guy gets captured," Frank muttered.

Wasn't that the truth?

Josh was supposed to be an expert in not getting caught. But if he admitted that, Frank would be happy, and everyone else would lose even that thread of hope. If he got out, he needed to get them all out. He didn't know how he was going to manage that miracle.

"You call it capture; the Army calls it inside information." The lies were building up around him.

"What?" Frank wasn't as dumb as he often sounded. He knew Josh was spreading bullshit thick and fast. He needed to slow down and not mess up his story.

"We knew something was going on—all those cleared out towns and cattle stations—but without satellite, we couldn't see much. There are boots on the ground and a ship on the coast." But the men who'd been wearing those boots were gone. Had Xavier been brought here in a sled?

The screaming of that last transmission still haunted his sleep.

"So you're here to do what?" Frank glared at him.

"Find out what's going on and orchestrate a breakout."

Frank laughed again, but there was no joy in it. He was only laughing to make Josh appear the fool. The others joined in after a moment of confusion. "That's the best story yet. Good one."

He stood, throwing off his blankets and scratched before making for the hole, pulling down his pants and squatting.

Josh moved as far away as he could, but the smell wasn't as easily defeated.

Clarence came over, a bowl in his hand full of water. He offered it to Josh. "I believe you. You have a look in your eyes."

Josh accepted the water but didn't drink it all, instead handing it back to Clarence so he could have some. "And the other three?"

"They are afraid."

"You aren't?"

Clarence nodded. "Only a mad man wouldn't be." His head tilted to where Frank grunted over the hole. Frank needed more fiber in his diet.

A door in the prison opened.

"Room service!" a man in another cell hollered.

Sure enough, cell doors started opening.

Last night's meal had been a chunk of kangaroo delivered by two aliens. Nothing else. If that was all he was going to be fed, his health was going to deteriorate fast. Josh had sat quietly and watched how everyone had behaved, from the men to the Geckos.

Their cell door opened.

He'd watch again, searching for a pattern.

The same as last night. One alien held the food while behind them was another one, fully armed with a helmet on. The one holding the food was in uniform but had no weapons or armor that Josh could see. Even if he used the waiter as a shield, he'd need to wrestle the weapon off the guard. He couldn't do it on his own.

And then they'd still have to get out of the compound.

The waiter put a tray of food on the floor and stepped back. There were actual bowls this morning, one for each of them. It didn't look like rice. It was too yellow.

"Damn when are they going to raid some more supermarkets? We haven't had tinned fruit in ages." Clarence picked up a two bowls and handed one to Josh. "Best not to ask what it is."

He didn't need to. He could see what it was. It looked like chopped up larvae. But the larvae were thicker than his thumb.

"Anyone want to bet whether he keeps it down?" Frank sniggered as he shoveled food into his mouth. "If you don't want it, pass it on."

"Why not kangaroo again?" The squishy chopped up larvae were making the rations in the ute look good. He prodded the food and was glad it didn't prod back.

Everyone was busy eating, resigned to what they were served.

The Geckos his men had killed had been a hunting party. They'd been getting meat and possibly canned goods from the places they'd emptied out. That meant they knew enough about humans to know what they needed to eat. This was the substitute when there wasn't anything else.

He either ate or starved, and the latter wasn't an option. He was sure he was going to regret this at some point, but he could worry about it then. He squashed some of the pieces together into a ball and then ate it like it was arancini. Xavier had made shit like that when they played house on holiday. Italian cooking had been his favorite. Josh had liked the fact that one of them was actually a pretty good cook. They'd planned five days of beaches and surf and laying around the house, drinking wine in the spa and knowing they didn't have to rush or hide what was going on.

Their holiday had been cut short by three days. They'd argued about returning. Josh had wanted to wait until morning to drive back. It was an alien invasion, a few hours weren't going to matter, and he figured they were all going to be erased anyway. He'd watched far too many B-grade sci-fi movies with his stepbrother. Xavier had been the one to insist they go right away as per instruction. He'd almost been excited by the prospect of blowing up actual aliens. They should've stayed in Margaret River. The car trip back to base had been frosty. They'd barely said a word, hadn't had time before getting orders.

Xavier thought him a coward.

Josh gagged and chewed some more. The larvae were more like raw squid than arancini balls. He forced himself to swallow.

Frank watched him.

"Could do with a little garlic and a nice cold one on the side." Xavier would've slapped him for not wanting wine. He wasn't sure what wine would go with larv…arancini balls. Really bad, raw arancini balls—the kind of thing he'd have turned out if he'd been the one in the kitchen with just an apron on. He grinned as he shoveled in another mouthful. Frank's eyes narrowed. He'd expected more of a show.

Fuckwit Frank wasn't going to get one from him.

He finished his bowl and washed it down with some water. There was no way he was sticking around for a month of eating that. He tossed his bowl on the tray, hard enough that if it had been crockery, it would've broken. It spun and settled. No sharp edges but it could still be used as a weapon if needed. He picked something out of his teeth, missing his toothbrush back at the ute. "I'm only giving this place a one-star review; there's no condiments on the tray."

"I'll be sure to let the lizards know," Frank drawled.

Would he? As far as Josh knew, no one could speak Gecko. And the Geckos had never tried to communicate. Their ships had at first appeared like asteroids on a collision course. There had been panic. Then the various space agencies had confirmed that they were alien ships. Someone had heard Earth's message to the universe and decided to visit. More panic, more religious dooms-dayers, and a recall of all military personnel on leave.

The Geckos hadn't responded to any communications attempts. They hadn't fired any shots as they'd orbited. It was only when they entered the atmosphere that a trigger-happy politician had decided Earth had to attack first.

The Geckos had destroyed the missile launch site—he'd heard that driving back to Perth, radio turned up loud so he didn't have to talk to Xavier. What had followed had been a classic clusterfuck of humans shooting and aliens obliterating. The satellites were destroyed as were aircraft carriers, planes, and several cities. It had taken three days of heavy losses before the people in charge had worked out that fighting wasn't working. A cease fire was called, and the aliens landed in desert areas, still completely silent.

With no way of watching the aliens, military personnel had been deployed to watch and report. That was the last he knew about what was happening in the world. Since dropping into the outback, his life had been sand, sun, and stars.

He'd be happier sharing his sleeping bag with a scorpion than sharing a cell with Frank. Josh didn't know if Frank was serious about talking to the Geckos or just making sure he had the last word. He didn't have time to respond as the wall with the barred widow lifted, letting the harsh sunlight stream in. He held up his hand and blinked.

For several moments, no one moved.

One of the other men grumbled that they were having to fight because of him. He didn't want to be here either; he could've been at the ship by now if the Geckos hadn't caught him. He winced but pushed the memory of the dead down. Later.

He'd learn how to keep painful memories buried at twelve. Now he was bloody good at it. Surviving meant moving on. There was no time to wallow. After his parent's death, his stepbrother had suggested they watch movies together. They didn't have to talk.

They didn't have to discuss what had happened or how they were going to manage.

And so, they never had. They'd just gotten on with it.

At eighteen, Josh had joined the Army.

He rubbed his hands on his thigh, feeling the hard edge of Linc's pocketknife in his pocket. The aliens weren't as smart as they thought they were. He still had weapons, and he still had his shoelaces.

He was shoved forward into the arena. Frank laughed. "It's your debut. Enjoy it."

Josh let him enjoy the moment. He was more focused on what was outside the cell than what was inside of it. He stepped out into the light. Several armed aliens stood at one end. People from a different cell walked toward the center. Green was smeared on their bare chests and back, like his, but theirs was darker.

It should be totally different colors…unless the Geckos didn't see colors the way humans did. He saw two different shades of green. What did the Geckos see? What did it matter? They couldn't see anything when he shot them in the face.

Josh stood with his cell mates but appraised the others. They were all men of varying ages. Were there any women here? And if there wasn't, where were they?

Some of the men were underweight—maybe they couldn't stomach breakfast. Some were wearing shorts or jeans; one guy had on what looked like pajama pants. Most had shoes.

There was no one he recognized.

Damnit.

He'd been hoping…

He had to stop doing that as it only led to disappointment.

More Geckos arrived, stepping out of a door behind the black clad soldiers. While he couldn't understand a sound they were making, it was clear they were betting, pointing at the humans and then at a screen.

This had not been covered in his training. There had only been one conversation about what would happen if they were captured on this deployment—there would be no rescue. He should've known then that Australia was about to be cut in half and surrendered to the aliens.

They'd been given the opportunity to step back, but because Xavier was going, so was he. He wasn't a coward, he just thought that the military needed to take a little more time to assess the situation. Make a better plan because trying to blow the Geckos up hadn't worked. Putting people on the ground when they didn't know what they were getting into didn't seem real smart either. Clearly, someone needed to show they were doing something about the alien infestation.

From the middle of the arena, he was able to get a better height assessment of the roof. It didn't seem feasible to try and scale the wall, especially not with armed soldiers ready to shoot him in the back.

A bird call tore his gaze from the roof to the closed cells. Their windows were in darkness. He'd thought his ears were lying, but it came again. He didn't want to hope when it could be broken so easily, but there was someone here that he knew. It was all he could do not to grin. They were obviously able to see him, so he ruffled his hair then tapped his ear. He'd heard.

And suddenly, he liked the odds of escaping a whole lot more.

Chapter Five

THE ALIENS LINED the men up on opposite sides of the arena. They adjusted the lineup with rough shoves and pointed weapons. No one fought back. They let themselves be herded like good little sheep.

Josh was pushed into the center first. The man opposite stepped forward without being told, but his expression was sour as though he didn't want to be fighting Josh at all.

"How does this work?" Josh asked, determined to get the most from this experience.

"We fight. You let me win," the man said as they faced off.

Josh shrugged. "We'll see."

If the aliens were placing bets and survival meant winning, Josh wasn't going to throw a fight to make someone else look good. He didn't want to be taken out the back and shot for being shit in the arena.

They circled each other a couple of times. The other man was tall and rangy like he'd been stretched out. His skin was weather-beaten, probably from working outdoors though his tan was faded. Josh knew he looked pretty rough, too. The full beard was not his best look, and he hadn't seen a shower in too many days, but no one here was sparkling clean. He'd been looking forward to swimming in the ocean.

The man lunged forward with a haymaker that Josh was able to easily evade. Old school bar brawling; he could do that if that's what was expected. He let the other man make some good swings and blocked a couple by keeping his arms up and guarding his body. The next time he swung, Josh stepped in and clipped the man on the chin before moving back.

Until that moment, there had been a feel that this was for show and just for fun. It was a love tap Josh had given him, but the man's expression hardened, and his fists tightened. The game was over.

The swings came faster and harder. And while Josh could've ended it with a couple of well-timed strikes, he didn't want to reveal too much about his fighting skills in the first round. He needed to keep something up his sleeve for later. He stuck to a simple plan of wearing a few body hits and getting under the man's guard.

"You piece of shit. Just go down," the man snarled.

"After you." Josh waited for the man to lunge and then stuck his foot out.

The man stumbled and fell.

Was that it? Fight over? He glanced at his cell mates, but they weren't giving anything away. Maybe it was timed. Sweat beaded on his skin, and his shoulders heated in the sun. He didn't want to be out here cooking until his skin was red and blistered.

The man got up, glaring. This time, he didn't lunge in with swinging fists. He waited, wanting Josh to come to him. What was he planning? The Geckos chirped—in excitement or anger? Was this a good enough show? Or were they expecting blood?

Josh danced in. He wanted this over. He was burning precious calories for the Geckos entertainment. Fuck them and the ship they came down in. He kneed the man in the thigh, corking his leg. The man dropped to his knee, murder in his eyes.

The attack came much faster than Josh expected. The man threw himself at Josh, wrapping his arms around Josh's legs and driving him to the ground. The air left his lungs as his back hit the dirt. Josh rolled and tried to kick free, but the man was on him. They scuffled in the dirt. Josh pushed under the man's jaw, trying to peel him off, but he wouldn't quit.

A knee that came far too close to Josh's balls and a hand that wanted to get a grip on his throat was the final straw. He wasn't going to kill him—which was clearly his opponents plan—but he needed to stop him. Josh grabbed the man's little finger and tore his hand away from his throat while sticking his fingers up the man's nose.

He screamed and stopped fighting. Josh threw him off and moved away, crouching just in case he wanted to try again. But he didn't. His nose was bleeding, and his finger was broken.

Guilt wormed its way up. He hadn't meant to hurt him, but he hadn't wanted to be choked out either. If he was unconscious, he didn't know what would happen to him.

The Geckos stepped in.

They shoved Josh toward his cellmates and took the other man away. He started yelling and clawing at the ground about how he didn't want to go to the farm. That he could still fight.

"You should've killed him," one of the men muttered.

"It would've been kinder," Frank said.

"What do you mean? His finger will be fine." The man could still fight, and if he hadn't gotten angry, they could've put on a good show. His pride had gotten in the way. Josh's fear had gotten in the way.

"We're nothing but fighting dogs. If we're broken, we get sent to the farm."

The farm, where all good dogs went when their time was up.

"I didn't want him to die." He didn't want that responsibility, but it was already weighing him down. The humans should all be on the same side. The aliens were the enemy. "How do the fights end?"

"When they say they're over," Clarence said. "There are no rules that we've been able to learn."

"There is only one rule," Frank corrected. "We exist to keep them happy. Doesn't matter what you want. You don't matter anymore."

Just like the Army…but not like the Army. These men weren't working as a team and clueing in the new guy. They were making it as hard as possible for him. "Why didn't you say something?"

Clarence gave him a grim smile. "Because the winning cell gets an extra ration of food. Old Sav was too bloody good. Now he's gone."

"Now we stand a chance at getting more food," Frank said. "Still don't change the fact that you could've won without sending him to the farm."

Why did they keep saying that instead of admitting that Josh had sent the man to his death?

Frank was pulled out of line next.

Josh studied each fight. Most ended with a choke where the loser regained consciousness far too quickly. The humans were playing the aliens. He almost smiled. Now he understood what Old Sav had been trying to do. If he'd said something…but no. He'd wanted to take Josh out because of his pride. He'd been the best and hadn't wanted to lose.

Shit…did that now make him the best? The fighter to watch out for?

When they'd all fought, they were herded back toward the cells. He wasn't ready to go back in, so he dawdled a little. He scanned the windows into the other cells but saw no one. An armed Gecko gave him a nudge with the gun.

Clarence shook his head.

Josh gave up hoping for another clue as to who might be out there that he knew. Or hoping that inspiration on how to get out would strike. He needed more info and wouldn't be able to get it in the arena or the cell. Maybe he should aim to get injured and taken to the farm. Less security probably and working on a farm had to be better than fighting.

He stepped into the cell. The Gecko keeping watch with his weapon ready. He was a trained soldier and knew what he was doing—which wasn't good news.

The wall of the cell lowered into place. His eyes had barely adjusted to the dark when his cell mates pounced and dragged him to the floor. He struggled, but there were four of them and one of him. They flipped him face down. Panic pinched his gut, and he expected the worst. Then someone sat on his thighs. With his hands pinned, he couldn't do anything besides waste energy struggling.

"Get off me," he said as best he could with his face mashed to the floor.

Someone fiddled with his laces.

"Are you fucking kidding me? You're taking my boots after this?"

"Yes, I am," Frank said like they were talking about swapping lunches, calm as can be. "You sent one of us to the farm."

"We aren't fucking dogs. We don't go to the farm." Was Frank five? "They're going to kill him? Is that the only way out?"

"The farm is where the Geckos grow their food," Clarence said from off the side. He hadn't joined in the attack. He was an outsider in the group, but not a threat to Frank. Not quite an ally either…

Frank pulled one boot off and then the sock. "I'll keep this to wipe my ass on. Been a while since I've had anything."

Josh could smell his feet and wouldn't wipe his own ass with that sock.

"So, he gets to be a farmer." But they hadn't seen any Gecko farms on their scouting missions, and he was sure he was missing something.

"He gets to be the farm," Frank corrected.

"Where do you think the larvae grow, genius Josh?" the man on his hands hissed.

The cold metal floor pressed against Josh's face. His stomach contracted and bile burned up his throat. His body convulsed, but he didn't throw up. He swallowed hard and breathed carefully. He wasn't going to toss his breakfast, no matter where it had come from. The thought sent his stomach into another spasm.

"Yeah, now he gets it. Now you know why some are so thin. They won't eat half their rations." Frank tore off Josh's other boot, and the concealed knife Josh had carried on every mission clattered to the floor. "What do we have here?"

The grip on his hands eased as everyone's attention shifted. Josh slipped his arm free and twisted, throwing off the man on his legs.

He jumped to his feet while the men didn't know whether to grab him or wait for Frank's orders. Josh used that time to retrieve the pocketknife out of one of his pockets. Linc's lucky knife.

Josh flicked open the blade. "You're going to push my knife over to me."

"Or what?" Frank sneered.

"I'll slit your throat. You'll be dead before you hit the floor."

"Who the fuck are you?" one of Frank's obedient assistants asked.

"I told you. Army, and I know how to use that. We don't want the Geckos getting hold of our weapons, so return it, and I'll keep it safe until it's time to get out."

"We aren't getting out, genius. This is it." Frank pulled the knife out of its sheath.

It was a good knife, and it had saved his life a few times. He wasn't handing it over to Fuckwit Frank and his merry band of Flunkies. He wanted his boots back too. "Fuck that shit. I'm not sitting here waiting to die."

"You're going to break us all out?" The blond flunky looked rather too hopeful.

"Well, I'm not going to wait around for Santa Claus to do it. The way I see it, you stay, and you fight until you get hurt and go to the…farm." His stomach rolled. "Or we break out and get to the coast."

"I vote for breaking out," Clarence added. "There's definitely a ship?"

"Yep. And there's beer." There'd better be beer. He was going to need a lot of liquor to wash away the memory of what he'd eaten… and what he'd have to eat to get through the next couple of days until he had a workable plan.

"You're full off bullshit, Army boy. This is my cell. I'm keeping your boots and knife."

"And what, trade them for cigarettes? Drugs?"

Frank grinned and grabbed his crotch. "You left one thing out. You want them that bad, there's a price."

So that was his game.

"He did that to all of you? Made you earn back your stuff?"

No one met his gaze.

"Keep them. Sleep with one eye open, though. Shoelaces have a way of strangling people, be a real shame for you to not be quite dead when you go to the farm." He flicked the knife closed.

Frank's face paled. "You wouldn't kill one of us."

"Try me. I've killed men for less." A lie, but no one here knew that. "Three tours in the Middle East, and I got pulled off leave because of the alien invasion. My patience is non-existent."

"You aren't allowed to kill people for no reason. You're Army," Frank said.

Josh put the pocketknife away, making sure it was secure. "True. But I don't give a shit about the rules anymore. What are they going to do to me that's worse than this?" He stepped closer. "Push me, and we'll see what happens. From here on, you don't play games and keep things a secret. You tell me what intel we have, and we start making plans. Does anyone speak Gecko?" He kept his gaze on Frank but could see everyone else in his peripheral.

They all shook their heads.

"Great. Does anyone know the layout of the base?"

Another round of head shakes.

"Well, you're all fucking useless, aren't you? You've been here a month and have learned nothing. How did you learn about the farm?" Maybe it wasn't real. But then what were the Geckos eating?

No one spoke.

"Well? Did I click instead of speak? Is the farm a rumor?"

Clarence stood and got a cup of water. "It might be a rumor. None of us have ever seen it, but we all know about it."

And they seemed to believe in it. "How?"

"When they first started this place, the lizards needed to make sure that everyone would fight," Frank said. "I heard they killed a few men and tossed them into the larvae breeding area. Everyone knew they had to fight, or they'd end up there. Word spread. You don't think it's real."

Josh didn't know what he thought.

Frank slashed the laces on the boots and tossed them back to Josh. "Enjoy your damn boots."

Bits of laces fell on the floor. Josh didn't bend to pick them up, nor smile at the win.

Frank still had his knife and until that was safe in his boot, he wouldn't rest easy.

Chapter Six

JOSH STRIPPED the pieces of laces from his boots. From his pocket, he pulled out a thin pair of socks. Emergency socks. Some people laughed, but no one laughed when their socks wore out and they were a hundred miles from the nearest chain store. He had no emergency shoelaces on him, though there were some in the ute.

Carefully, he sorted the pieces of shoelace by size, then he used the shorter bits for over the foot, keeping the longer lengths for at the ankle. There wasn't enough lace for every hole, but what he had was workable.

And more importantly, he'd wasted some time.

Frank was playing with the knife. The others were sitting around dozing. This wasn't living, it was waiting to die, and they'd accepted that. How long until he did?

If he were killing time at a base, he'd be using the gym or making up his own routine to tick off the hours. He'd read. Play cards. Have a wank. Some of those options were out right now. But he could do something.

As much as he'd like to go for a run around the base, that wasn't going to happen. He was going to have to do something else to keep his fitness up, because he'd need to be able to sprint when escaping.

He got up, stretched his back after sitting hunched on the floor fixing his boots, then started jogging on the spot. His shoelaces held.

Frank stopped cleaning his nails with the knife. "What are you doing?"

"Training." After a couple of minutes of jogging, he sprinted on the spot, then slowed to a jog again. Repeat about thirty times.

He had an audience now.

They watched but didn't join in.

After running, he did pushups, the cold metal floor beneath his palms. Sweat dripped off him. The Geckos had arrived with cells. That disturbed him. When he flipped onto his back for sit ups, the metal was unforgiving. He didn't care. Couldn't.

They were still watching when he went to the bars to do pull ups.

"Why are you doing all that?" Clarence asked.

"Something to do. Keep my fitness up." But he wouldn't do too much because rations were limited, and if he was going to be here for anything more than a few days, that would be his biggest concern.

"You know, for when he escapes," Frank said with a sneer.

"Yep." Josh hauled himself up, staring out the window where he could see two other cell windows. No one was looking out. He couldn't see any guards either.

He pursed his lips, then let the whistle slip out. For several moments, nothing happened. Silence blanketed the arena.

Then on the far side, a hand wrapped around the bars, and the answering whistle came. Josh couldn't see who it was…but it sounded like…

No, that was wishful thinking.

But he squinted. Were they Xavier's hands? It was hard to tell with the shadows and the distance. He whistled again. All clear?

And the responding whistle was the one for no good.

He lowered himself to the ground and rested his forehead on the cold wall.

Someone came up beside him.

Clarence reached up to the bars. "Don't know if I'll be able to manage even three."

"One is a start. Tomorrow do two." He stepped back to help Clarence get in the correct position. He managed two, then took a break for a minute or so then did the third. "Good job."

Frank came over and leaned on the wall. "Why are you whistling like a love bird?"

"Who's in the cell across the arena?"

Frank shrugged. "People."

"Just men or women too?"

"Only men…why you hoping to get lucky when you break out?"

Josh bit back the retort that formed. The aliens knew enough about them to separate them. All he could do was hope that the women and kids were somewhere else. Hopefully they hadn't been taken to the farm.

Clarence stopped doing pushups with really poor form and got to his knees. "He whistled when we were out there."

"Maybe he likes you." Frank smirked.

It hadn't been that kind of whistle. It had been the 'I'm in position' tune.

It was someone he'd worked with in Afghanistan, as those were the ones he was using. That really limited the number of men it could be. His heart wanted to hope, but Josh wouldn't let it. If he was wrong, he'd drown again.

"Or he's Army." Josh glanced at the other men in the cell. "What do you know about the guys opposite us?"

Two of the men glanced at Frank as if seeking permission before speaking. Frank stayed silent.

The sandy haired man spoke up. "They're pale pink." He touched the green staining his chest.

"Everyone is pink or green, some are pale, and some are dark," another man said.

Clarence lay on the floor. "One of them wears camo pants. Never spoken to him, but he's a good fighter."

Frank bristled next to Josh. "You don't have to tell him anything.

He's new, and we can't trust him. He's already sent one to the farm."

"Because you didn't tell me what was going on. Intel should be shared." Josh fixed Frank with an icy glare, then Josh calmly plucked the stolen knife out of his hands.

Frank tried to snatch it back but was too slow.

"You can keep the socks." Josh sheathed the knife in his boot. He tugged the frayed hem of his pants over the top. He went over to the tap, had a drink, and then washed his face even though what he really wanted to do was drop his pants and wash properly in the tepid water, but that could wait until Frank was feeling a little less disgruntled.

Josh didn't want to be exposed any more than he had to be around Frank. Eventually, Frank would realize and accept he was no longer in charge.

"Tell me about the man in cams."

"Dark skinned, wears his hair in braids. He's not a local fella, though," Clarence said.

Josh smiled and held the fragile hope close. That sounded like Xavier. His parents had moved to Australia when he was a baby. A mixed-race couple in South Africa had drawn too much attention.

"He's not Army. He's a wanna-be," Frank said.

"Nah, I think he is," the blond chimed in. "He fights all lazy, making the other trip over."

It had to be Xavier. Josh's chest wanted to burst; it was almost as painful as when he'd thought Xavier dead. But he was alive.

And they were both stuck in Gecko Base One with no way out and no way to communicate.

He wanted to ask more about Xavier, but he didn't want the others realizing it went beyond professional interest. If his team-mates hadn't reacted well to discovering there was something going on between them, Josh couldn't imagine these guys reacting any better.

"What do you know about the other people?" Who could he rely on when it came time to break out?

Clarence glanced at Frank who was scowling from his bedding. "You ask a lot of questions. Frank doesn't like that."

"I don't care what Frank likes." He rubbed his hand over his beard and wished he were back on the beach in Margaret River with Xavier. If they'd ignored the order to return to base…

Would they have been evacuated? Had Perth been evacuated or had the government just wiped their hands, called it too hard, and walked away?

This whole job had so far been pointless. It didn't matter how many times they'd reported there was no one alive out here, the mission had stayed the same. It hadn't mattered when they'd lost contact with the other teams. And it probably wouldn't matter when they reported back on what was happening here. The Geckos only defended themselves; they hadn't attacked first, and now they had land, they were defending it.

"How did you all agree to fight but not kill, and do just enough to keep the Geckos entertained?" He needed to know how this place worked. "Do we get to socialize with the others?"

Clarence shook his head. "We only see them when we fight."

The dark-haired man joined them; Frank no longer had their attention. "What's out there? You've been to the farms and towns?"

Frank muttered something that sounded like, "Who cares?"

Josh wanted to give the men hope but he didn't want to lie. He couldn't say that there was no one out there and they'd been sent to get people moving to the coast and had failed because there was no one. At first, he'd hoped it was because they'd already fled. "I went to a few places. These cells…they brought them, like they knew that they'd need them."

"Yeah. We thought they might have been watching us before they came," Clarence said.

Of course they had been. But what did they want?

"People care that we're missing, right? We're winning the war with the Geckos? They were bombing the hell out of their Nevada base last I heard."

"Yeah, they were last I heard too. I don't get told much while in the field." The aliens had fired back. No one was going to Vegas for a bang-up wedding anymore. Which was a pity, as he and Xavier had once talked about it after too many beers and too long apart.

All the might-have-beens and maybes stalked him. Whenever he thought he'd outrun one, another would appear quieter than a soldier on a black ops mission. Xavier was alive.

He looked up at the men with their hopeful expressions. "We have to focus on getting out of here."

"There is no way out," Frank said.

"There's always a way." As soon as he gave up, it would be over.

"Okay, smart ass." Frank got up and walked over. "We get out and then what? We have to get to the ship that may or not be there. How far is that?"

"Two hundred kilometers. And the ship is there." But only for the next five days. No one here was going to make a two hundred klick forced march in five days. They'd be hard pressed to make it in ten, but he couldn't leave them. They all had to get out of this.

Ten days of hard walking, possibly being pursued…definitely being pursued. How many here could shoot? They'd need to get supplies on the way as there wasn't enough food or water in the ute for two people for ten days. Or enough fire power.

He'd have to radio ahead to tell the ship to wait.

He needed a plan to get out soon. So far, he had squat.

"And if the Geckos have sunk the ship? They'll recapture us and send us to the farm," the blond said.

Josh glanced at him. "Where do you think you're headed anyway?"

They were all going to the farm, it was just a matter of when. And when the Geckos had used up all the humans…what then?

Chapter Seven

DINNER WAS MORE KANGAROO. While Josh had nothing against kangaroo, this hadn't been cooked well, and it was cold when it arrived, making it dry and stringy. It was also served with tinned fruit salad. That a mix of fruit in syrup was almost the best part of the day was more than a little tragic.

Josh picked up a small piece of pineapple that was floating it the kangaroo juice in his bowl.

"It was dog food a couple of weeks ago be glad it's fruit," Frank said before Josh could say anything.

"Fresh meat and tinned food usually means there'll be new fighters," Clarence added.

Like Josh and his team had been, the Geckos were raiding supplies. They were feeding their captives as best they could. He ate the pineapple, then ate the meat, saving the rest of the fruit for later. It was pity the Geckos hadn't picked up some long-life custard to go with it. They didn't know how to make a proper shopping list.

But they knew humans needed more than meat. They didn't want their captives to die too fast. And when there were no humans to round up to entertain them or to go to the farm, what would they do then?

Those were questions above his pay grade. He just needed to give those at the top some intel. Everything that he'd seen so far was chilling, and it didn't add up. He was missing something. Why had the Geckos even invaded? What did they want?

He didn't like the first answer, which was bodies for their farm.

He finished his meal, had a drink of water, and laydown. He ran his tongue over his furry teeth, wishing he had a toothbrush. Soap and a razor wouldn't go astray either.

Darkness crept across the cell for a second night, and he was no closer to getting out.

Once they missed their next scheduled contact, they'd be assumed dead, and the ship would probably pull anchor and sail away. He closed his eyes, knowing he shouldn't be thinking like that but finding it hard to stop.

Frank's warning that the only way out was to go to the farm rang in his ears. His fingers brushed the pocketknife. He wouldn't be taken to the farm alive.

———

THE CELL DOOR OPENED, and the unarmed Gecko stepped in and put a tray on the floor. The other men all got up and one by one and obeyed the silent order. Josh had played along last time. This time, he wanted to provoke a response and kept the bowl by his blankets. He pretended to fiddle with his fingernail. The Gecko glanced around the room and clicked at them.

"Your bowl, genius," Frank said.

"I know." Josh didn't move.

The Gecko turned to him and made impatient noises. Josh didn't look up. The waiter appeared to be unarmed, but he was in the same black uniform. If this were a human camp, even the waiter would be military and trained. Maybe the same was true of aliens. They had sent ships to Earth and set up camp, so this was no unplanned stop to see the blue planet and to restock as they went on their galactic road trip.

The guard stepped in and leveled a weapon at Josh. It was gun like, and he knew it packed a punch even when it wasn't being used to kill. He'd experienced that firsthand and didn't really want to go a second round. Who knew, maybe they'd dial it up to full and fry him where he sat.

"Don't do it, Josh," Clarence whispered. "You won't get far, and you won't be brought back here."

"Yeah, I know. I'll get sent to the farm." He wasn't planning on making a move yet. He was just testing their captors.

The Gecko with the gun whistled and clicked at him, giving orders that he couldn't understand. When he still didn't move, the guard grabbed him by the arm and pushed him face first into the floor. Heat bloomed in his cheekbone. A knee was pressed into his back. He didn't struggle; this wasn't about fighting the Geckos. The foot in front of him wasn't made of flesh. It was metal, at least up to the ankle. It had four toes like all Gecko feet, and the parts moved as the Gecko balanced. It was high tech and far beyond what humans were making to replace limbs. So far, he'd only been able to check out the metal limbs on the dead. This was more interesting. Did the Gecko have feeling through the metal?

The waiter's bare feet were both flesh. The waiter grabbed the bowl, then the tray, and hurried back toward the door. The guard expressed his displeasure by putting more pressure on Josh's back. Something gave a crack—he hadn't been to the chiropractor in a while, and it almost felt good. Josh's cellmates wouldn't look at him; their gazes were locked on the floor. They behaved like dogs who'd been hit too many times.

The guard got up, not so accidentally kicking Josh in the ribs with his metal foot. Josh took the blow, knowing he deserved it for mucking up, but he wasn't sorry. He'd gotten what he wanted. He'd seen how the waiter and guard worked together. As the guard turned, his tail smacked Josh in the face. After the initial sting faded, he had no doubt he'd have matching bruises. He didn't move until the aliens were out the door. Couldn't, or he'd be seen as a threat. For the moment, he was still the new guy. He could get away with doing dumb shit for a day or so. With a final glance, the Geckos left the cell, but they didn't leave any arancini.

He wasn't too sad about that either.

"You fucking tosser," Frank spat. "Now we don't get breakfast." He got up and took two steps toward Josh. No one got up with him.

Josh got to his knees, hands loose by his side. If Frank did anything to him today, he'd lay him out. Frank glanced at the men who'd helped him last time as though expecting them to join him. They looked away.

Frank fisted his hands and glared at Josh.

Josh held his gaze and stood smoothly. He wiped blood off his cheek where the tail had broken the skin, then wiped his hand on his pants. "Anyone for a morning workout?"

The other men got to their feet.

Josh smiled.

———

THAT AFTERNOON, the Geckos hauled a pink and green team out of their cells. Josh heard the sides of the buildings move and went to the window to watch. It wasn't the cell Xavier, if it really was him, was being held in.

Damn it.

He dropped to the ground and glanced around the cell. There was nothing for him to stand on; he was going to have to do it the hard way. He pulled himself up and braced his feet on the wall.

"Why do you want to watch?"

"There's no game on TV," he said. This way, he could say he was doing something instead of staring at the walls. He had a time limit. If they missed the ship, they'd have to walk out of here, and it was a long bloody way to Perth if it still existed.

He wasn't walking all the way to Sydney.

Geraldton was gone, but maybe there'd still be some boats. No one would mind if he borrowed one. The other option was to walk north, following the coast until they reached the tourist destination of Georgetown or one of the other mining ports, again praying for a boat.

He didn't like his odds of not being recaptured if he was dragging all the prisoners along with him.

"No beer in the fridge either," Clarence replied. "Who's playing?"

"Green next door to us and pastel pink."

"That tall man is pretty good." The blond, whose name was Ben, came over to the window to peek out. He struggled to pull himself up and only managed to hold himself for a few seconds.

"Yeah, I see him." But he was more interested in the Geckos and the way they moved. Metal foot was there, so was metal hand. They chatted and motioned at the human entertainment. In some ways, the Geckos were familiar. They were soldiers making their fun while they waited…waited for what?

His stomach grumbled.

Two humans were motioned forward to fight. Green and pink put on a bit of a show. It was obvious neither were actually going for it, and neither of the men looked like they'd put up much of a real fight if it came to it. Josh doubted they'd ever thrown a punch before being captured. They were both too thin from skipping breakfast every day.

Josh scanned the other cell windows but didn't see anyone. This was ridiculous. They should be communicating with each other, but Xavier had let him know they were compromised. How?

Did the Geckos understand English? Was one of the captured men somehow miming tales and pointing out troublemakers? Josh didn't know enough, and he needed to see Xavier with his own eyes to believe it was really him. He wanted to hold him and shake him and find out what the hell he was doing getting captured. He needed to apologize and patch over the fight. He didn't want to ever be in the situation where his last words had been spoken in anger again.

The man splashed with green stumbled.

"Come on, green!" Josh yelled.

Both fighters glanced over. Neither knew what to do, but green got to his knees and tackled his opponent's legs.

"What are you doing?" Clarence pulled himself up to peek out the window.

"Cheering them on. It's a shit job being on show, knowing the bloody Geckos could take one to go to the farm. Let's have some morale."

"Do you live in the real fucking world, genius?" Frank said from his bedding.

Someone in the next cell started singing the anthem of a football team. That team hadn't won a final in years, and Josh only knew the chorus, but never mind. It was the feeling that mattered, so he joined in.

So did a few others.

It was the worst rendition to have ever assaulted ears, but the Geckos went from lax to alert. Their bit of fun had suddenly turned sour as the humans bonded.

When the song petered out, someone on the other side of the arena started another song, a pub classic usually sung karaoke style by drunk men who thought they had a chance of pulling Sharon for a quickie behind the pub.

From the sound of it, everyone knew that one. The guys in the middle were still putting on their show, but their faces had lost the grim look and had split into a grin.

Josh was sure there'd be hell to pay later, but for the moment all the prisoners were singing. Could messages be passed through song?

They needed time they didn't have. Four days until the ship sailed.

Chapter Eight

THE GUARD POINTED the gun at Josh as soon as the door opened. Josh sat still while breakfast was delivered, eyes carefully lowered just enough to make it seem as though he'd learned his lesson but not so much he couldn't observe. There had to be a way to get the gun off the guard and kill the waiter before the alarm could be raised. Tomorrow, he was going to have to try. He was out of time.

If he didn't get to the ute, and therefore the radio before the last day, the ship would leave.

He wanted to call in air support. That's what he'd do if they were anywhere else. But nothing flew over Gecko bases. Not even a tiny drone—the military had tried.

He doubted that any more soldiers would be sent in, even if he mentioned civilian prisoners. The government had cut off this part of the country. No one had taken it seriously when they'd first been told it was a possibility. No other country had been planning to give up land to the Geckos. Or had they all decided it was the best thing to do? Just washed their hands of the problem and let the aliens build their bases. He couldn't imagine a world where that was a possibility, where chunks of land were no longer under human control.

And if this were now Gecko country, what did that mean? Would more aliens come here? Would they slowly try to take over the planet, or did they only want the deserts? Maybe they were refugees fleeing some trouble on their own planet.

Except they'd brought a prison and a farm and were heavily armed.

They were more like teams sent in to scout and settle in.

He forced down the arancini balls, vowing never to eat rice or balls again. He ate fast and then spent several minutes stabilizing his stomach with deep breaths as he concentrated on trying to remember as many brands of beer as he could—in alphabetical order. By the time he got to VB. his stomach had settled. but he could really go for a cold one. Once, as a dare, he'd eaten insects. Too many cheap beers in a Thai pub had resulted in him eating an entire plate of grasshoppers to win a bet. He'd spent an hour emptying his stomach later that night and a week picking legs out of his teeth. His stomach rolled, but he kept his breathing even.

Think of something else.

The plan...take down the guard, steal his gun, and kill the waiter.

Then they should be able to open the rest of the cells. That was the easy part.

Getting more weapons and getting out would be harder, but he'd have Xavier, and they'd be able to work something out together. Even if Xavier wasn't talking to him as a lover, he wouldn't throw a mission.

As plans went it was shit, but there was nothing else he could do besides wait to die. He looked at his cell mates, who were taking their time eating like they actually enjoyed it.

Josh's stomach bounced, and he looked away. "I have an idea."

"That will get us all killed," Frank said, his words muffled by the food in his mouth.

That was a risk, but the way Josh looked at, they were cattle already on the truck to the abattoir, so what difference did it make? Better to try to break out than to go meekly. Fucking up a few Geckos on the way would be a bonus.

"I have two knives. I should be able to take down the guard; someone else needs to take down the unarmed waiter."

"With a penknife?" Clarence wasn't convinced.

Damnit. He needed Clarence on side.

"After I kill the guard, I'll have his gun. I can't take out both Geckos on my own." That was the big flaw that he needed to plug up before he acted. "I need help."

Frank tossed his bowl toward the door. It skittered and wobbled before stopping. "And then what, genius? You think we can just walk out?"

"Then we open up the rest of the cells, I go out and onto the roof. From there I can pick off incoming Geckos. When they fall, you lot can get weapons."

"We're in the middle of their base. How do we get out?"

"Are we in the middle? Does anyone actually know where we are? When I'm on the roof, I'll be able to see." He prayed they weren't in the middle of the base.

"You want us to fight our way out." Clarence shook his head. "We aren't soldiers."

"Do you want to die here?" Why had they all given up?

"No. The Army will send more men," Ben said.

Josh leaned against the wall and sighed. "You all heard of the Simpson Line?" Surely the government had talked about it, warned people before they did it? "It's been enacted. This is no longer part of Australia. There is no help coming. When we were sent out here, we were explicitly told we would get no assistance but that the ship would wait. The ship sails in three days unless I call them and beg them to stay until we get there. I need to get out and make that call. I know where the ute and gear are hidden."

Silence smothered the cell.

"They wouldn't do that. What about all the people who live out here?" Clarence sounded like someone had just walked up and shot his dog at point blank range while it sat at his feet.

"There is no one left. We were supposed to tell civilians to head toward the coast, but we found no one. Every town and every homestead and every station was empty. At first, we thought they'd fled, but there were always signs of conflict. Never any bodies." He gave a dark laugh. "Now I know why."

"No one? How is that even possible?" Frank shook his head, refusing to believe.

"It looks like they cleared a radius around their base." A smart thing to do. Brutal and efficient and it set them up with bodies for their farm.

Clarence stood up. He put his empty bowl by the door then wiped his hands on his faded jeans. "I'll help you, but you're going to have to show me what to do."

———

A SOFT CLICK was the only warning that the side of the cell was about to lift. Josh had been trying to nap after a busy morning training and quietly planning. He had been giving the other men a crash course in tackling Geckos and disabling them. He watched the slice of sunlight widen then got to his feet, adrenaline pumping.

A fight two days in a row.

Had the Geckos somehow heard what he was planning? He didn't wait for the wall to go all the way up; he slid beneath and out into the sunlight. The wall on the opposite side was lifting.

Xavier. He'd convinced himself that it was him.

His heart squeezed tight, but he didn't cross the arena. He forced himself to wait. Why wasn't Xavier rushing out? It may not be him. If it wasn't, that was fine…it was still help. But he was tearing inside, the wound threatening to split him open. Could he re-bandage and do what needed to be done?

The men in the opposite cell stepped out. He recognized the non-standard boots sticking out of the cams. Few of them wore the standard issue boots. Then slowly he let his gaze lift as the men walked into the sunlight.

He saw Xavier's dark hands and couldn't hold back the smile as he finally looked his boyfriend in the face after what felt like years of separation. It had only been a month or so, hardly any time. Xavier gave him a half smile, but it was tight. Was he still pissed?

Then Josh noticed he wasn't holding himself with his usual ease. He was favoring one leg just a little. Most people wouldn't even notice.

"There's the wanna-be. He doesn't like to hit the dirt. Can't take a punch." Frank sneered.

Xavier was no wanna-be. But there was clearly something wrong if he was hiding an injury.

The Geckos started chirping as they took what Josh assumed to be bets and arranged the fights. He scanned the other four men from the other cell. They all looked resigned. He was going to have to spread the word about his plan and hope that the Geckos didn't understand English and that no one was a rat. He glanced at Frank. If anyone was a rat, it was him.

Xavier stared at him. Josh gave him a thumbs up with the hand the Geckos couldn't see and mouthed 'you'?

Xavier gave a very clear thumb down.

Fuck. Josh tilted his head and lifted an eyebrow.

Xavier moved as though stretching, then ran a hand over his ribs and then down the thigh on the same side.

Josh couldn't see any open wounds. Broken ribs? Was his leg hurt too? If the Geckos knew he was injured, he'd have been sent to the farm, and if Xavier thought that was a bad thing, then it definitely was.

Before he could think of the best way to signal that he had a plan to get out, the Geckos started pulling people into place. He was paired off with Xavier; they would fight second.

Josh's breath caught. For the first time since arriving, he wanted to fight. He wanted to put his hands on his lover and make sure he was real. He needed to talk to Xavier, and words were better than any signal.

The first fight was little more than two men chasing each other around before rolling in the dirt for a bit and getting up to repeat it. The aliens were unimpressed.

"They aren't even trying to make it look good," Frank muttered.

On one hand, Josh didn't blame them. Why should their lives be entertainment for the aliens. On the other, a good performance meant living. And Josh refused to let those clear-skinned bastards destroy him.

Eventually, a winner was declared, and guards beckoned Josh and Xavier toward the middle of the arena.

"I thought you were dead." Josh's fingers twitched needing to embrace him, but he didn't.

"I thought I was too. Until I woke up here. I was kinda hoping you'd be the rescue party, yet here you are."

The guards clicked at them. They were ready for the fight to start.

They faced up the way they had so many times when training and started circling.

Josh threw a punch that would be easy for Xavier to dodge. "Broken ribs?"

"Left side, three or four." His teeth were clenched, and he was sweating already. He really didn't look good. Being here had sucked the life out of him, but he attacked, favoring his left leg. "Healing up now."

Josh wore the hit and countered, barely letting his knuckles brush Xavier's skin. "What else?"

"Infected cut." Xavier lifted his leg as though to kick.

It was then Josh saw the tear in his pants. How had he been hiding that?

"How bad?"

"Let me take you to the ground, and I'll tell you."

"Always the romantic." He gave Xavier a small smile, wanting to believe that everything was fine between them, knowing that even if it wasn't, they'd work together to get out of this mess.

Xavier bared his teeth in something closer to a grimace. "I try."

When Xavier attacked Josh didn't resist. His back hit the ground. The Geckos sounded excited.

"Don't forget, you have to pretend you *want* to throw me off." Xavier pinned him down. His eyes were bright.

"Didn't know you liked an audience." Josh wiggled a hand free and turned Xavier's jaw away. They fought a careful choreograph of fight and need to touch. Xavier's skin was too hot.

"For you, anything." Sweat dripped off Xavier's nose and onto Josh's cheek. "Cut is festering. I need meds."

"I got nothing on me." Josh faked a desperate scramble while Xavier tried to get a chokehold. "You right to roll on to your back like I flipped you?"

"Yeah. Go."

Josh moved, and he straddled Xavier. "I got a plan. Tomorrow at breakfast. Be ready?"

"Don't get killed." Xavier kneed Josh in the back. Not hard enough to do damage.

"When the cells open, get to the door and get a weapon."

"I'm going to throw you over." Xavier glanced over his head.

Josh let himself get airborne. He tried not to tense, but the landing still hurt. Xavier flipped him to his stomach and got an arm lock on him. He leaned in close. "Whatever was said, I didn't mean it. I love you."

The words were too final. "This isn't it."

"But if it is, I want you to know. I'm not going to last the week without antibiotics. I'm going to the farm. I just want to be dead before I get there."

The pressure on his arm eased, and the Geckos motioned for Xavier to move away. He was the clear winner. Xavier got off him. Josh sat up, and Xavier offered his hand.

Josh took it. Their hands remained linked for a few seconds longer than needed. Gazes locked.

"Tomorrow," Xavier murmured.

"Yes." He released Xavier's hand. "I love you." The words were lost in the chirping of their captors.

He wasn't sure Xavier had heard.

Xavier gave a small nod. He barely concealed the limp as he went back to line. If Josh's plan failed, Xavier was as good as dead.

They were all fucking dead.

He should've given Xavier the pocketknife, but he needed both weapons for tomorrow. Xavier said something to the man next to him. The man looked at Josh and nodded.

He was sure that by tomorrow, everyone would be ready and waiting.

Their lives were in his hands.

He was going to get some of them killed. They weren't soldiers. They'd run cattle stations, or worked in the mines, or operated tourist excursions, or lived in remote communities. But if he did nothing, they were all dead anyway. At some point, the Geckos would tire of their fun, or they'd need more bodies.

Josh glanced around at the cell windows ringing the arena and couldn't shake the feeling that this wasn't accidental. This had all been planned. When was the rest of the Gecko invasion force arriving?

Frank nudged him. "You were chummy with the wanna-be."

"We spent years working together." What had started as a convenient fuck had become something more. He didn't even remember when it had happened. Maybe when they'd gotten home and Xavier had started coming around and sleeping over more often than going home. Neither of them had actually asked what was going on. It had just been assumed. The same way they had never spoken about keeping it a secret. They just had.

Frank snorted. "And where's the rest of your platoon? Dead. You lot are useless."

Not useless, just unprepared. There was no training for alien invasion. They were out classed by an enemy who'd been watching them and preparing their landing. He glanced at Xavier. Neither of them would go to the farm alive.

Chapter Nine

THERE WAS no lazy wake up the next day while waiting for room service to arrive. Josh was alert to every sound as he sat on the blankets. He ran through the plan and played out different possible reactions from the Geckos. Once he started, he was all in and had to hope that he had the back up from his cell mates. Last night, this had seemed like a good idea…today, the men were getting twitchy.

Frank kept muttering that it was a bad idea, and he wanted no part of it. As long as he didn't fuck it up for everyone else, that would be fine.

"And I just fake being sick?" Ben wrapped himself in his blanket and lay on the floor.

Josh nodded. He would prefer it if Ben weren't cocooned in the blanket so he could get up and fight in a hurry, but he didn't want to make the young man more anxious than he already was. "It'll be fine. We'll get a gun and go from there."

"You're going to wing it. You're putting all of us at risk on a prayer." Frank pointed at him but didn't get up.

"Yeah, I am, because I'm not going to sit around waiting to die when there is a ride out of here waiting. There will be no other help. We get ourselves out now, or we may as well take ourselves to the farm like good little lambs." He pulled the knife out of his boot. If he didn't get this right, it was all over. He'd get one chance, and the enemy was bigger and faster and just as well trained. All he had was surprise.

It wasn't good odds, but it was a chance.

The door to the prison opened. Footsteps and then another door opened as the first cell got their food. He could hear them talking but couldn't make out the words. No one knew the plan in detail except the men in this room, but someone could still be warning the Geckos to watch out.

Josh glanced at Frank. "Don't fuck this up."

"Hey, I don't want people to die." Frank held up his hands like he was innocent.

"We're dying anyway," Clarence said. "Might as well do it for our benefit instead of theirs."

"They'll add your corpse to the farm, genius," Frank said.

"Well, if I'm dead, I won't care," Josh said. But he would, because Xavier was only going to get sicker, and when the Geckos realized, they'd send him to the farm too.

"And if you aren't dead?" Frank said with a sick smile.

Josh mimed cutting his throat. He'd actually go for the femoral artery in his thigh. It wouldn't even take a minute to bleed out. He'd put far too much thought it to the best way to make sure he was dead before he got to the farm.

The lock clunked, and the door slid open. Josh hid the blade by his leg.

Clarence had the pocketknife as he was the back up and the only man Josh trusted with a knife.

Ben coughed convincingly. Huddled on the floor, he looked pathetic. Would the Geckos know what a sick human looked like? The guard's attention shifted from Josh to Ben.

The waiter entered the room. Josh motioned for Clarence to wait. The waiter wasn't far enough in for them to get the door closed.

The guard clicked at Ben, who coughed again and added a

groan for good measure. If they were being held captive by humans, Josh would've said he was overplaying it. With aliens, who knew?

This time, the waiter edged closer, clicking something to the guard.

Now. It had to be now while they discussed what to do and the guard was distracted.

Josh didn't second guess himself; he acted, training kicking in and his focus absolute on what needed to be done.

He drew in a breath then lunged forward, slashing the back of the Gecko's knees. Then, as the alien turned, he brought the knife up under the chin of the helmet. He shoved hard, then tore the blade free to cut at the hand holding the weapon. The gun clattered to the floor.

Josh panted even though it had taken only seconds.

Frank picked up the gun and grinned.

The waiter was on the ground, pinned by Clarence and Trey. Josh walked over and slit the waiter's throat. The knife and his hands were slick with blue blood. He wiped them on his pants.

For several moments, there was silence.

"We're so screwed." Ben's eyes were wide. "If we don't get out, they'll kill us all."

"Not if we hand Genius over." Frank leveled the gun at Josh.

"Give me the gun, and I'll start clearing the area."

"Nah, I think I'll keep it."

"You're going to climb up on the roof and shoot Geckos to free up some more weapons? Be my guest. Out you go." Josh pulled open the door. "If they raised the alarm via coms before dying, we've got about thirty seconds." Probably less.

"Give him the gun, Frank," Clarence said. Blood dripped from the pocketknife onto the floor, making bright blue suns.

"Or what? You'll stab me with that? I'll shoot you first." Frank was gripping the gun like he didn't have a clue what he was doing, only that it made him feel like a big man. Those kinds were always dangerous—usually getting others killed before themselves.

"Clarence, toss the knife at his feet. We'll cower in the corner.

They'll think he did it." Josh wiped his blade on the waiter's shirt and slid it into his boot and stepped away from the bodies.

"But I didn't." Frank's gaze darted around the room.

Clarence tossed the pocketknife at Frank's feet. "Sure looks like you did."

They were running out of time to get out and open the other cells. He kept his breathing even when all he wanted to do was smack Frank's head against the wall until it broke. Adrenaline only gave short bursts, and he was wasting it with chit chat. Josh sat and tried to project calm.

Frank stared at the knife then at Clarence and Josh. "Fuck you." Frank slid the gun over the floor toward Josh. "I hope you fucking die."

Josh scooped up the gun and was on his feet and moving. "Get the keys off the guard and let the others out. When I start shooting, come out and get a gun."

Josh eased out of the cell, checking the corridor for other Geckos. Nothing.

He stepped to the side of the doorway that led outside. The sunlight was bright and harsh, bouncing off the red dirt. He blinked a few times. There were a few Geckos out there, but they were doing their own thing. They wouldn't be expecting him to climb onto the roof.

He tossed the gun up first, momentarily defenseless with his back exposed, then hauled himself up, glad this side of the roof was lower. He lay flat, the metal already hot on his bare stomach. He was going to be baked alive if he had to spend the day up here.

Still better than sitting in the cell.

The gun was the same as the other he'd taken from a Gecko. Was the ute still hidden? He couldn't plan for what would happen if they got to the rendezvous point and found nothing. The gun was heavy and too big for human hands, but that wasn't going to stop him from using it. The slope of the roof made finding the right angle to lie at difficult, and he didn't want to be a standing target.

All the roofs sloped. It was an angular ocean of yellowish metal. More buildings than he'd expected, but he could see the edge of the camp and the way the buildings were laid out in an orderly fashion of hexagons. Now that he could see the pattern, it would be easier to find the edge. From the ground, it would have been a maze.

The gun was already on; he could hear the faint hum. From up here, it was easy to imagine he could be anywhere. Anywhere but here would be great. A few shots, get some more weapons, and they'd get out and the Geckos would think twice about keeping pet humans for entertainment…and the farm.

Where was the farm? What did the farm even look like? Was it even on the base? They hadn't found anything that could be called a farm while they'd been scouting.

Below him, someone rapped on the door.

"Move it along, Rayne," Xavier said. His words soft enough to carry away on the barely there breeze.

"Always so impatient for a fight," Josh muttered, glad that Xavier was out of his cell and still alive. This would've almost been easier if the Geckos had realized something was up and come running. Then he'd have had some clear targets. He raised his voice. "Camp is hexagonal. Edge is two hundred meters north from our position. This building is not central."

"How big?"

He didn't get a very long look. "Big."

"More info."

Fuck you. Xavier wasn't the one making himself a target on the roof.

Movement caught his eye. "Gecko coming around the corner at three."

The alien looked relaxed; his weapon hung across his back and he had no helmet on. Easy pickings. One shot, and it would all be on, and they'd only have two weapons.

Josh waited for the Gecko to get close, then fired. The blast was hot and bright. The need to sight the target was at odds with his desire to close his eyes and protect his vision. He needed a helmet.

Xavier darted out to get the weapon. His leg must have been aching, but he wasn't going to sit this out.

"Get up here." He put his hand down. If Xavier was on the roof, he wouldn't have to run around.

Xavier tossed his gun up, then grabbed Josh's hand and swung himself onto the roof. Neither of them said anything about the effort that took when it should've been easy. Xavier was in bad shape. He lay on his back for a moment, hand still gripping Josh's. "I should've brought a picnic."

"You should." Josh leaned over him. "I missed you." He kissed him, hoping that it wouldn't be the last one, knowing that not everyone would make it out.

"Miss me later. Let's fuck up some Geckos." Xavier gave Josh's hand a squeeze, then released him. "We're heading straight out?"

"Yes. Ute as at rendezvous B."

"That's ten clicks to cover with pursuit."

"Yeah." He knew. He'd gone through it all more times than he could count. "Geckos at nine."

Xavier rolled over, ready to shoot. "Your plans are shit."

"Unless you have a better one, this is it."

Xavier took out the two that had come running. Josh moved to slither off the roof. Xavier put his hand over Josh's. His skin was ashen, and the light had gone from his eyes. "One of us has to get out of here. No matter what."

"There's antibiotics in the ute, and I'm not going without you."

Xavier looked like he was about to argue, but Josh dropped off the side of the building. He didn't want to hear Xavier's reasons about why he wasn't going to make it. He knew. He got it, but he wasn't losing him again. He couldn't compromise the mission either.

Someone needed to get out.

Odds were, it would be him.

His boots hit the dirt and he was running, stripping the weapons from the dead aliens and handing them to the two men who'd run forward. Everyone else was hanging back in the cell block.

Josh checked that the guns were on. "Point and shoot. This is the trigger." He indicated to the pad that was just out of reach of human fingers. "Two handed weapon. They're bright, your eyes will burn, and you'll feel a flash of heat. Got it?"

The men nodded.

Josh didn't have time to make sure they really understood. Xavier was shooting, covering him. Josh needed to start clearing the way before they lost the element of surprise. He didn't want Xavier left behind, but he had to trust that Xavier would sort himself out. He'd never worried before, but Xavier was wounded, and this was different.

This was why soldiers shouldn't date each other.

Fuck them all.

They were both getting out of here.

He ran forward to the next building and glanced up at Xavier. Every Gecko that went down was mobbed for their gun. They were going to get smart soon. Get organized.

"Move it," Josh barked.

Men came running out of the cell block. The ones with guns helped herd them. Josh crept around corners, killing anything that moved. He'd sight and squint to block the worst of the flash.

Behind him, there was gun fire. He had no way of finding out if Xavier was following or if he was still on the roof. The edge of the camp was in sight. They were going to get out.

Three Gecko soldiers appeared at the fence line. Josh lifted the gun, sighted, and fired. Nothing happened. Behind him, the guns had gone silent.

Shit. Shit. Shit.

He tried again.

The Geckos lifted their weapons. He eased behind the corner as flashes burned past him, scorching his forearm and making the skin blister.

Now there was panic in the eyes of the men.

"The guns aren't working," one called.

"They've jammed them somehow." Changed the frequency? How could he do that? He looked at the gun and its unfamiliar markings.

Another blast brushed by him. "Fuck me."

If he'd had time, he probably could've worked it out. Under fire with unarmed plebs, he had no chance. He slung the gun over his shoulder and pulled out his knife. "Use them as clubs. We can't stop now. When you get out, head south, ten kilometers. There's a rock formation and a ute and supplies under netting. Radio the ship. Tell them to wait. Don't drive off and leave everyone behind. The ship will wait. Pass the message down the line."

The man stared at him, then moved.

At the back, someone screamed.

They had to move know.

Josh stuck the barrel of the gun out, and it was blasted straight away. "Change of plans."

He turned and ran past the men, around the other side of the building, hoping to surprise the Geckos when he appeared.

Chapter Ten

THE PLAN WAS SHIT.

Josh wasn't even sure it could be called a plan. A random collection of wishful thinking and half-baked ideas was more accurate. He stopped at the corner, his heart thumping as he did a sweep of the area. He could see the Geckos, but without a gun, he couldn't shoot the bastards.

He was going to have to tackle them and get a working gun off them.

Which would only last until they changed the codes or whatever it was they did to turn the human controlled guns into junk.

Someone lost patience and ran at the waiting Geckos. He was shot immediately, a screaming burned mess that wouldn't die fast enough, but Josh used the distraction to launch his own attack. He clubbed one in the arm, then under the chin. That was a weak spot. Then he ditched his dead gun and used his knife to kill. The dead Gecko became his shield and he grasped the live gun before turning it on the other two. Men ran past and out to freedom.

All he had to do was stand guard until Xavier made it.

He saw the flash before he felt the hit. It seared his shoulder with white hot pain; he was sure his bone had melted. He turned, alien held in front of him and almost fell over the tail. The gun fell from his hand as his fingers stopped working, and then a Gecko was on him. Josh struggled, but the thing slammed its tail into his thigh. He stumbled back, releasing the dead alien as his leg gave way. He reached for his knife, and it fell from his hand.

He dropped to his knees and scrabbled for the knife, needing a weapon. The second tail swipe knocked him over. His head bounced on the ground. The sky was so blue. Then his eyes closed.

———

SOMETHING WAS PRESSING INTO HIM, and it hurt. He tried to move away, but he was held firm in strong sticky fingers. The familiar clicking of the aliens jerked him further out of the half sleep he'd been in. He twisted and bucked but couldn't break free. The smell was appalling, like something had died in the roof and was now quietly rotting. The pain in his shoulder didn't stop, only now it was inside too.

He stopped trying to fight and forced his eyes open. Two helmetless Geckos had him pinned. They were chatting, probably about the breakout.

He'd been recaptured which was definitely not good. How many had gotten out?

A Gecko noticed Josh's eyes were open and touched his face. Josh drew away as much as he could. His skin was swollen and tight. Wherever he was, he doubted it was for first aid.

The farm.

He'd be at the fucking farm.

He wanted to laugh but couldn't. It felt like something was burrowing into his back. The Geckos picked him up by his arms and legs. His shoulder burned, and a scream escaped his lips. What was wrong with his shoulder?

"Put me down." He struggled, only hurting himself more, but their hands gripped him tight.

They lifted him. He saw a railing, and got a glimpse of what was below. An ocean of writhing white larvae.

He'd been afraid before. The cold brush of dread, that maybe this time his number would be up and the mission would go pear-shaped, and his brother wouldn't even get a body to bury.

But this was different.

This was the kind of terror that made him claw at his captors. He kicked one leg free. He was not going down there. That smell of death was the corpses the larvae were feeding on. He was about to be added to the pile while he still lived. He was going to be eaten alive.

Hell no.

Those whispers in the cells hadn't done this place justice.

He managed to get a hand free and a fist full of Geckos uniform. "You fucking fuckers. I'm not food for your fucking arancini."

The Gecko punched him in the face. His nose crunched. And then he was airborne.

…but not for long enough.

His back hit the writhing mass. For a moment, he couldn't breathe, but that didn't stop the larvae. They latched on to him, biting onto every exposed piece of skin. They moved over him. He brushed them off his face and away from his ears. If they got inside him, they'd eat him from the inside out.

He struggled to his feet. No one was watching. No one would help.

He tore one, the size of a sausage, off his arm. It left a bloodied circle where it had already started eating him. He could pluck them off all day, and there'd still be more. His skin would be gnawed off.

He yanked several more off, but he could feel some on his back. They were trying to get up his pants. There was no clear piece of floor. He couldn't stand here. He needed to move—not that he could outrun them as they were everywhere. Beneath his boots, things crunched. He couldn't stamp on all of them. His stomach turned.

For a moment, he stood still, the stink of decay in his lungs, the larvae gnawing on his skin trying to burrow into him. Despair washed over him and dragged him away from shore. Better to be eaten dead than alive. He wasn't sure his busted shoelaces were up to the job. Did he still have his knife?

Something moved up his calf. He shook his leg, but it was attached. The thing in his shoulder was digging in.

He'd give himself until dark to find a way out, and then if he couldn't escape, he'd find a way to top himself. Another shit plan. Xavier wouldn't be pleased.

With no one to see, he let that crack widen. Because of him, Xavier was probably dead. The Geckos wouldn't have spared him, and he was already injured. He should be here. If he'd been thrown in dead, he'd already be buried under the larvae. Tears blurred his vision. Josh wanted to start digging through their fat bodies, looking for his lover.

The urge passed as he tried to be logical. Sanity was a frayed thin rope, and it was rapidly unraveling.

He stomped through the enclosure, killing the squirming bastards, and ripping them off his body. Blood smeared his skin, painting his flesh with stinging pain. He sniffed, but his nose was broken. He wiped the blood off his face with an equally bloodied hand, then assessed his cheek. It didn't feel broken, but the skin was split open like a dropped orange.

His shoulder was full of larvae and most likely dislocated. It was a teeth-grinding ache that he didn't want to dwell on. He could still curl his fingers, but he couldn't lift his arm. Maybe the Geckos had torn something in there when they'd lifted him over the railing.

For the first time, he lifted his gaze from the floor.

The floor he'd been thrown from was about three meters high. With a run up and two working arms, he might have been able to reach it. Maybe he didn't need to reach it to get out. He waded through the writhing sea to the edge, so he'd at least have his back to a wall. The feeding tank was like an empty, hexagonal pool. The wall was only two meters high, then there was a gap between the wall of the tank and the building.

Something groaned.

Josh turned, his stomach as fragile as the rest of him. Was there someone alive in there? How long did it take the larvae to kill a man? How long could a man live while being eaten? They were still trying to get in his pants and latch onto his legs. He needed to remove the one that was on his calf.

He pulled down his pants, ripped off three of the fuckers, and made sure there were no hopefuls hiding in the cloth, thankful they were big, not tiny like fly maggots. How big was the insect they came from?

He didn't actually want to know.

Lifting one leg at a time, he carefully tucked his pants into his socks. His knife was missing from his boot. The loss hurt and reduced his options.

While his pants were down, he took the opportunity to have a leak. The larvae squirmed away from the stream. Josh stopped, yet the larvae didn't come any closer.

He pissed on his shoes, and pants then splashed a little on his skin. It stung the open wounds but it worked. He had larvae repellent—and smelled like a cheap bar that hadn't been cleaned in a week.

He was being eaten by bugs and had pissed on himself. Not how he'd imagined the day going. He tried to envisage how the debriefing would go when he eventually gave his report but was sure no one would believe him. Standing in the puddle, he was larvae free. He had a whole square foot to himself. He almost smiled, but without water to drink, he was going to run out of piss.

A door opened, and the Geckos clicked to each other on the platform above. Josh pressed himself against the wall of the tank. Even though the platform extended over the sea of bodies, he didn't want to be seen. They were probably hoping he was two feet under.

Something was dropped on the platform—another person? Were they dead or alive?

Josh tried to keep his breathing as soft as possible so he could listen to what was happening above. The person groaned. What seemed like an eternity later, they were thrown over the railing with as little care as Josh had been.

It wasn't Xavier.

That was a good thing, right? He waited for the Geckos to go silent and then for the door to close. How many more would be thrown in tonight, or did the Geckos ration out the food for their farm? His mouth soured at the thought. He wanted to burn this place down and starve the fuckers.

The man started to freak out. Screaming and flailing.

"Piss yourself, mate," Josh said as loud as he dared. For all he knew, there was still a Gecko in the farm.

The man didn't seem to hear or care. Josh took a breath, gathered up what was left of his mettle, and waded back into the mess. The larvae moved away from him. He didn't blame them; he smelled like he'd woken up in a gutter somewhere rather unsavory. He felt as though he'd been in a bar brawl and come off second best, and still had the headache and shaky stomach that went with a hangover.

He stopped a meter from the man. It was Frank. He wanted to turn around and leave him to get eaten alive, but no one deserved that.

Josh glanced up at the platform but couldn't see anyone.

Frank was still thrashing around. The larvae were drawn to him. Did they smell the blood or hear the heartbeat?

"They don't like piss," Josh said again, then realized that Frank was beyond caring. He was missing a leg and the larvae were slick and red as they burrowed into his flesh. Josh's stomach heaved. Frank wasn't going to survive. He'd probably been unconscious before being dumped. He couldn't let Frank or anyone live out their final hour, or less depending on how much blood he'd lost, like that.

"I'm sorry you didn't make it out. I'm sorry for this…but it's kinder." Josh put his hands on Frank's throat. Frank stared at him, his eyes wide with horror. "I'm sorry." Josh stretched and twisted; Frank's neck cracked, and his body went limp. His face eased into the calmness of death. The burrowing frenzy continued.

Josh wanted to step away from the mess but he could already see things that might be useful. He unbuckled the belt that had been put around Frank's leg. Military issue, the kind Xavier had always worn. Frank wouldn't miss the impromptu tourniquet, and Josh might need the noose later. There was a bloody X on one of Frank's pockets. A message? Or pure chance. Maybe Xavier was alive. Or had been alive.

Josh pushed larvae aside and put his hand in the pocket. His fingers brushed metal, then closed around the now familiar pocketknife. He smiled. So much better than a noose. He put it into his pocket and checked the rest, hoping there'd be something else he could use, but there wasn't.

He'd sell his liver for a handful of grenades. Watching the farm burn would be worth it even if he didn't make it out. Whatever happened, he wasn't spending the night in here.

Even if he got out of the farm, he still had to get out of the camp, get to the ute, and get a message to the ship. Had any of the men made it? Or had they been pursued and the ute was now in alien hands?

Despair almost got a grip, but he brushed it off.

One problem at a time was all he could deal with.

Larvae bumped and writhed against his legs. He needed to get back to his puddle.

Stamping as hard as he could, he made his way back. Halfway across, his foot skidded on something hard. Beneath the bodies, he couldn't see what it was, but beneath his boot, it felt solid enough to be a weapon. Or wishful thinking. Either way, it was worth the risk. He stuck his hand in, shuddering at the press of cold squirming against his skin. His hands closed around the object, and he pulled it free. For a moment, he stared at the thing in his hand.

A bone.

A thighbone from the length. It had been eaten clean. He swallowed hard. There were bones beneath the larvae, which meant they didn't eat everything. He was definitely not staying the night in this graveyard.

Chapter Eleven

THE BELT WAS DOING a good job of supporting his arm, which took the pressure off his shoulder. The larva was still in there, but it didn't feel like it had dug any deeper. Maybe they ate slowly.

No more bodies had arrived. Which gave him hope that they'd all gotten out.

Or had they just been rounded up and locked back up?

He'd managed one more piss, but after having no water all day, he didn't like his chances of producing another anytime soon. His mouth was dry, and a headache pulsed at the base of his skull. If he didn't act soon, he wouldn't be able to.

He'd peered over the tank wall by hanging on with one hand. On the other side was a walkway and pieces of equipment. Things for harvesting the larvae or cleaning the tank? If it ever got cleaned. He'd thought about wading around to the other side to have a look but had decided not to waste the energy.

This was it, before it got any darker and he couldn't see what he was doing. If his shoulder wasn't completely busted already, it would be after this. He eased his arm out of the makeshift sling and lifted his hand until he could reach the lip of the wall. That hurt in a really bad way. Through gritted teeth, he drew in a breath, then he pulled himself up and over. His landing wasn't what one would call careful or controlled. He bit his lip and cradled him arm, cursing silently in his head and willing the pain to stop so he could think.

It didn't.

And after what felt like half a century of searing pain, he knew he had to ignore it and get on with escaping.

He sat up, put his arm back in the sling, and moved carefully around the tank, looking for a weapon he could use with one hand and a door. He found the stairs up to the platform but little else of use.

Three raps above him made him look up. He crept up the stairs, not sure if it was Geckos or something else. Ghosts? He'd never believed in them before, but if any place were to be haunted it would be this slice of hell.

After several heart beats, the knocks came again. There was no one on the platform.

He tapped out SOS on the wall and waited, not sure he'd been loud enough or if he'd been too loud.

A quick series of taps followed.

X status

Xavier was alive. And on the roof. Had he been up there baking all day? He was a mad fuck at times. Josh couldn't help the smile that formed.

OK

He was better than OK now. He was fucking fabulous.

Dark blood stained the platform and was smeared on the railing. His blood, Frank's blood. And God only knew how many others had died down there.

Come up, came Xavier's response.

Climbing up was the last thing Josh wanted to do. The ceiling wasn't that high but getting up there was still going to be a bitch. There were no ladders that he could see. At the far end of the platform was some kind of control panel that formed part of a column which reached the roof. The same column that he'd been held against.

That was going to have to do.

He didn't know anything about the alien tech except that their mechanical bits could be used on humans and that they could change the frequency on their guns. But he was guessing that the control panel had some kind of energy source and, if he was lucky, some kind of wiring.

It was then he realized that the temperature in the farm had been constant all day when the shed-like building should've heated up in the sun. This was a climate-controlled room. Be a shame if someone were to muck it up and the larvae were to die. He pulled out his pocketknife and felt around until his fingers caught the edge of a panel. There was barely enough light to see.

Where are you, Xavier tapped out.

Josh levered the panel off and looked inside. It wasn't like any electrical circuit he'd ever seen. It appeared to have living components. If he killed it, would an alarm be triggered?

Or would it squeal and scream?

Josh held the panel in his good hand and used it to give the roof three simple taps.

He needed a torch…some matches or a few F-18s to rain hell.

He'd settle for starlight and a bit of luck.

Something moved over the roof. A slide, and a scuffle and then the tap was over his head.

If he could avoid the living parts, perhaps he could short the control panel. Electricity was electricity, wasn't it?

He scraped the coating off a few of the wires.

Over his head, something scratched and twisted, but he didn't look up. He trusted Xavier.

When he was satisfied that he'd made enough of a mess, he pulled out a couple of tools from the pocketknife. It had served Linc well until this final mission. Linc's body would be under that mess of wriggling bodies. Josh kissed the red plastic. "One last job. This is for you, Linc."

Carefully, he placed the knife and the corkscrew over as many metal bits as he could. Then he put the panel back in place. The roof opened above him, a tiny triangle of sunset, then Xavier's face.

"I was expecting you to be dead," Xavier said without humor.

"The night is young. You want to help me out? My shoulder…I got a stowaway."

"Jesus."

"Just call me Josh." He forced a grin. One of them had to at least try and be positive. That wasn't usually him.

Xavier drew back, and his arm poked through the hole. "I don't know how much help I'll be."

They were both hurt. He climbed up on the control panel and clasped Xavier's hand. His palm was fever hot. The infection would be spreading, poisoning his blood, and stealing his strength. "Just hold steady; I'll do the rest."

He walked up the column until he could grasp the edge with his damaged arm. As long as he could hold on, he didn't care what tore.

The door into the farm opened.

Fuck.

Xavier pulled, and Josh forced his shoulders through the hole, used his elbows to push higher. Xavier was half dragging him. Josh wormed his way through, not caring what skin tore. He didn't want the Geckos to grab his legs and drag him back down. His shins and knees scraped the metal. As soon as he was through, he pushed the metal corner down and sat on it. He was breathing hard.

Every part of him hurt like he'd been worked over with a cheese grater. Blood trickled down his shin. His shoulder had popped, and he couldn't feel his fingers. Xavier had his fingers pressed to his lips in an unneeded warning to be quiet. Sweat ran down the sides of his face. His braids were bound back with a piece of cloth, and his eyes were dark and serious.

They were both alive.

He didn't care what gods were watching over them. This counted as a miracle.

Xavier leaned forward and rested his forehead on Josh's. "I saw you get captured."

"You should've left."

He shook his head. "If you didn't answer back, I was going to drop some IEDs and give myself a front row seat." He hooked his thumb at the things all over the roof.

Around Xavier were the pulled apart remains of several Gecko guns. Their insides glowing a faint blue.

"I hopefully shorted their control panel. We are going to have to leave."

Or should they stay?

No. They could do this.

He stared at his black-clad lover, realizing why he looked so odd. "Why are you in Gecko armor?"

"Stops their weapons."

A door opened, and clicking and chirping filled the evening air. Were the Geckos relaxing, thinking they'd sorted out the threat?

Xavier kissed him. "We're in the middle of the camp. You can't climb, and I'm running on empty."

"Where's the rendezvous?"

Xavier pointed to his right. Silently Josh, stood. This roof wasn't sloped like the others; it formed a point in the center, and it was a complete hexagon. He moved high enough that he could see the layout of the camp. From up here, it looked like so many other camps. Buildings and vehicles were everywhere, but instead of a grid, it was hexagonal like bees had planned the whole thing.

His gaze swung back to the vehicles, the flat sleds that hovered over the ground. That's what they needed. Not that he knew how to drive one. They were going to have to creep out.

Josh made his way back over. "Don't suppose you got me a change of clothes?"

"Not yet. You got another shit plan?"

"Full of them. We're going to walk out."

"That's not actually a plan."

Josh shrugged and then grunted as the pain reminded him of the mess that was his shoulder. "How about you get the critter out of my shoulder and then push it back into place." There was a small risk that Xavier would pinch a nerve and make it worse, but Josh was willing to take that chance. "I think you should put the larva on your leg wound."

Xavier shook his head. "I have limits."

"So did I." Turned out they got kind of flexible when his life was on the line.

"Turn around."

Xavier dry wretched and muttered under his breath. "It's ass is hanging out."

"Just pull; they're like remoras." Josh hissed. They couldn't even have a proper conversation. Their words had to be as soft as possible in case they carried on the night air. They were in a fairly exposed position, but the farm was the tallest building in the compound.

Something in his shoulder moved. Pain flared but then the pressure and fullness eased. It was out.

Xavier dropped the larva on the roof, and it started to slide away.

Josh grabbed it. "We should take an arancini sample to the boat."

"Arancini?"

"Did you eat breakfast?"

Xavier nodded; his lips pressed into a thin line.

"I squished it into balls and pretended it was your appalling cooking."

"I thought you liked my balls." Xavier's lips twitched.

"Attach it to your wound; maybe it will eat the dead tissue." Maggots did.

"That won't save me."

"I know. Meds are in the ute." And might as well be on Mars. There was an alien army between them and safety.

Assuming the ute was still there and the other escapees hadn't taken it.

Xavier undid his pants; his thigh was a mess of dead skin and weeping wound. It looked like he'd taken a glancing blast to the leg.

"Did you wash it?"

"Do I look stupid?" He put his hand out for the larva. Josh handed it over. Xavier swallowed hard, then put it on the area that looked the worst. He drew in a sharp breath. "I think it's attached. For the record, I object to your medical advice."

"Objection noted. After this clusterfuck, I'm sure we'll both be cleaning latrines for the next ten years." Right now, that seemed like a damn fine posting. But Josh doubted they'd get that lucky. Earth had been invaded by the scouting party. The war was yet to come.

He glanced at Xavier. Neither of them was up to fighting, but he didn't say it. He didn't want to reopen the rift.

"We're going to get demoted for not following orders and engaging the aliens, but shall we blow some shit up?" Xavier put his hand out like he was asking Josh to dance.

Josh accepted. "Thought you'd never ask. How long do those blue things have when you set them off?"

"No idea. Haven't had a chance to test them."

"And you think I have all the shit plans." The blue things were glowing too brightly now that dark had settled. "Pop my shoulder in. Then we can get started making trouble." Josh sat up straight and moved his arm into the start position. "Do you remember what to do?"

"Yeah. Nah. Quick reminder?"

"Go slow." Josh rotated his arm out as far as it could go. "Now just push forward." And if it all went well, everything would be back in place. He didn't let himself dwell on the alternative.

Xavier pushed, and Josh fought to keep his body still. Something shifted, and he brought his arm to the front.

"Did it work?"

Josh nodded. The odds of it popping out again over the course of the night were pretty high, though. "If it happens again…"

"I got it. I can walk, but I'm getting tired fast and dizzy even quicker." He drew in a breath. "I'm a liability. You'll have a better chance alone."

"I'm not going without you." He couldn't lose him again. "So why don't you tell me how these IEDs work, and then we'll start slinking through the base."

Xavier picked up one of the power sources and a stripped back gun. "When the triggers changed frequency, I knew we needed an override. Couldn't work that out in a hurry, but I did manage to remove everything but a trigger. So when this gets jammed in, it's live."

"How do we get down from here?"

"Same way I got up. Climb," Xavier said grimly. "You go first, and I'll drop one in the farm."

"No, you go. I can run." Neither of them moved. "They'll be so busy trying so save their dinner, they won't be worried about us. We'll stick to the shadows." It would be smarter to not blow anything up…but he couldn't leave that hell hole alive and wriggling.

"And the prison?"

The fates of the other men had been gnawing on his conscience. "How many were recaptured?"

"I don't know. I withdrew to wait it out. When it all calmed down, I came here because I'd seen you be brought in. I don't want to leave them, but I don't know if we can help."

He didn't know either. They were both too damaged. This had never been a rescue mission. It had been evacuate and recon. He'd tried to turn it into one and failed. "The odds of us getting out—"

"I know. This isn't how imagined it. You might have been right. I'm sorry I was so pissed at you." That was as close to an apology as Xavier was ever going to give.

Josh shook his head, refusing to accept it. "We had a job, and I was too bloody scared to do it. I shouldn't have been sent out."

"But you came even though you didn't want to."

"Someone had to be around to haul your sorry ass out of trouble." He gave Xavier's hand a squeeze. He didn't look well even in the dark. His lover was dying in front of him and there wasn't a damn thing he could do. "Shall we give them a little longer to get to bed?"

"Yeah." Xavier lay down and put his arm out. Josh lay next to him, Xavier's body radiating more heat than should have been possible.

The stars came out, bright and wild above them. The Milky Way was so clear. How many other aliens were out there?

Xavier kissed his temple. "We should've gotten married."

"We don't even live together."

"We should. What were we hiding from?"

"Possible discharge?" One of them would've had to get out. "For some reason, we like our job." Did he still? He hadn't planned on renewing next year. He hadn't told Xavier that. But if only one of them was in, it would be better. Easier.

"They can all fuck themselves. If we get out of here, the bloody ship's captain can marry us."

"That's a plan I can agree with."

They lay in silence watching the stars until it was truly night, then Josh helped Xavier up. Xavier gathered their weapons, while Josh checked the perimeter, watching for guards and looking for their patterns. Most of the guards were near the prison on the other side of the compound. The wrong way to the ute. They met back at the lifted ceiling panel. Josh squatted down and got ready to shove the power supply into the gun.

"Just walk right out?" Xavier looked at him, the Gecko helmet tucked under his arm and two guns over his shoulder.

"Yep. Nothing we haven't done before." It was nothing like anything they'd done before. Even though they'd been in some tight spots, neither of them had ever been captured. Their luck had run out on this job. Maybe it was time to pack it in for good. The words were sand on his tongue.

Xavier nodded and gave him a tight smile. "Try not to be late for the wedding."

"Try not to lose the ute."

"One time. And it was Christmas."

"Yeah, yeah. You lost the car." The car park had been huge and shopping center packed, but Xavier had still forgotten where he'd parked.

"Fuck you."

"Just get off the roof so I can do this."

Xavier flipped him off and moved quickly over the roof. He was favoring his leg, and now he had a hitchhiker. In the black Gecko uniform, he soon melted away, a dark blot on the roofline.

Josh shoved the blue energy source into the gun, lifting the metal corner he'd wriggled through not that long ago, and dropped it through the hole. He didn't wait for it to hit the platform beneath; he was already running toward the edge. Xavier had disappeared over the side.

While Josh wasn't looking forward to hanging off the roof, it was going to have to be done. He didn't give himself a chance to think about it. He glanced down, saw Xavier against the wall below, and went over the edge, pulling his shoulder out of place as he went.

His feet hit the dirt, and he almost fell. Xavier put a hand out to stabilize him, and Josh pointed at his shoulder. Without a word, Xavier shoved it back in. The hot ball of pain didn't leave, and blood trickled down his back from the open wound. Without medical treatment, they were both dead.

Xavier handed Josh a gun, then pulled the visor down on the Gecko helmet. It was all Josh could do not to step away. But while Xavier was tall, he was still over a foot shorter than a Gecko. Maybe it would be enough to fool them at a glance. Xavier pointed, and they moved to the next corner. The power source hadn't exploded yet. Josh pointed back at the farm, but Xavier just shrugged.

They worked their way around two more buildings, their progress as quick as they could manage but far too slow at the same time. He counted the seconds as they went. At ninety-three, the ground bucked beneath his feet, and Josh's ears rang. Ninety-three seconds between activation and explosion. Good to know. Xavier grabbed his arm, and they ran, crossing the next walkway and around another building.

He couldn't hear a thing. Xavier held up his hand. He slid a gun off his shoulder, shoved in a power supply, and pushed Josh in front of him like he was a captive. They turned the next corner; three Geckos were running toward the farm, but the Geckos ignored them.

They had no working weapons and a gun that would explode in seventy seconds.

When they passed the Geckos, Xavier tossed the gun onto the roof of the building. They needed to get away from this area fast.

The need to get out overtook their need for caution. They raced down the side of building and onto the next one and were almost to the edge when the second gun exploded. The flash was behind him, but it still lit up the sky like dawn. This time, Josh was ready for the ground to ripple.

They didn't pause. They ran for the final building, Xavier limping worse with every step. This close, Josh could see the perimeter. It was marked out with the alien equivalent to pickets.

Xavier took off the helmet and shoved it on Josh's head before he could argue.

There was something between the pickets. Lines of red. And there was some kind of feed on the screen, probably something about the destruction of the farm. He pulled the helmet off and used his hand to mime under.

Xavier nodded.

Like a pair of desperate snakes, they slithered beneath the fence they couldn't see.

Then they were out. They lay face down in the dirt for a moment. Not moving, just breathing.

They were free.

There were still ten klicks between them and the ute. And two hundred to the ship.

Josh squeezed his eyes shut. What he wanted was some painkillers and water. However, there was no delivery service out here, so he'd better get his ass up.

<h1 style="text-align:center">Chapter Twelve</h1>

HE CARRIED XAVIER part of the way before meeting up with the other survivors. There were only five of them including Clarence.

When they reached the ute, he forced the stolen antibiotics into Xavier and gave himself a handful of prescription painkillers.

He didn't drive, he sat in the back with a gun ready to take out anything that moved.

By the time dawn came, it was clear they'd gotten away.

It was only then that Josh let himself sleep for a bit.

He woke when the ute jerked to a stop, bogged in sand. Curses formed on his lips but were drowned out by sound of waves. He twisted around, not wanting to dislodge Xavier's head from his lap.

The ocean had never looked more welcoming.

Brilliant, blue, and with an ugly gray ship sitting just off the coast.

Xavier's eyes were still closed. The antibiotics wouldn't have started working yet, and his skin was hot, his dark cheeks flushed.

Josh smoothed a hand over Xavier's forehead. "We made it, so don't give up now."

He picked up the radio and let the ship know they'd made it.

They responded that the landing craft was underway.

Several of the men ran down to the water. They didn't bother stripping off before diving in. Josh tipped his head back to rest on the cab and closed his eyes. They'd made it.

"I see it. They're really coming for us!" someone shouted.

Josh smiled. He wanted to be on the beach to greet them. He tapped Xavier's cheek. "Come on, sleepy head. Rescue is here."

Xavier grunted but opened one eye. "I feel like shit."

"You look it too." Josh helped him out of the ute, and they hobbled over the sand together.

He could make out the people on the landing craft. There were six.

They'd been told about the injuries last night when he'd asked them to wait; hopefully, they'd come prepared.

Xavier managed a smile. "We're going to get stitched up, and I'm going to make sure they put us in the same room."

No more hiding.

Josh nodded. "Sounds good."

He was not looking forward to giving a full account of what had happened.

The landing craft nudged up onto the sand, and sailors in gray cams spilled out. Two were armed and took up position like they expected Geckos to spill over the dune any second.

The civilians were falling over themselves to get into the boat.

Josh glanced back at the dunes. He'd expected the Geckos to be following them all night, but the only life in the dunes were the birds flitting about hunting insects he couldn't see. Why hadn't they followed?

"Sergeant Josh Rayne?" a sailor said.

"Yes."

The man looked him over, then turned to Xavier. "We were expecting minor injuries."

"All limbs are attached. Anything else is minor." Dried blood covered Josh; he looked worse than he was. Xavier was the one closer to death.

The sailor reached out a hand. "Would you like some help getting aboard?"

Josh was about to say no, but he was all out of energy. "Yeah. That would be great."

A high-pitched whine filled the air.

Josh covered his ears as best he could. A flash over the ocean blinded him.

He blinked and squinted, searching for the ship.

But it was gone. Along with their way home.

Regroup

Reunited with his lover and fellow soldier, Xavier Fisher, Josh Rayne and the other survivors from the alien base watch from the shore as their rescue is blown up. Now on the run and on their own, they need to find a safe place to regroup and figure out how they are going to escape alien country and get back home.

With no military support, they are in desperate need of supplies when they make it to a seemingly abandoned tourist town. But not all is at it seems, and Josh will have to decide who runs and who has to stay and fight to give them a chance. He wants to go home, and he wants more than the vague promises he and Xavier made to each other.

Book Two in the Captured Earth trilogy. For readers who like action, explosions, and don't mind a little gore with their gay romance.

Chapter One

"NO!" Josh's legs gave way. It was Xavier who kept him upright. All Josh could see was ocean where there had just been a Navy ship. He hadn't imagined it. It had existed.

But the only reason he knew that was from the curses and cries of the survivors around him, and that there was a landing craft on the beach.

The sailors who'd arrived on the landing craft to rescue them stood open-mouthed. They would've heard of the alien's weapons but never seen them used.

"It's gone," Josh murmured, the devastation of their new reality sinking in with each breath.

"It can't be gone," Xavier said, his voice rough. "The Geckos haven't touched ships before." He used the unflattering name they'd given the aliens who had invaded Earth and taken over Australia. They looked like oversized lizards with long, whip-like tails and pale, almost see-through skin when stripped out of their black armor.

Josh closed his eyes and swallowed. He drew in a few deep breaths, then opened his eyes. There was still no sign of the ship.

One sailor was on the radio trying to raise the ship like it had somehow ducked out of sight or slid over the horizon. There'd be no answer. It would've been instant. There'd be bodies and metal fragments out there as the Geckos weapons didn't vaporize things. He didn't know how to describe the weapons aside from saying they were highly effective and deadly. As well as painful if they weren't on the kill setting.

As the shock wore off, people started asking questions.

"What are we going to do now?"

"How are we going to get home?"

The survivors of Gecko Base One who had been rejoicing in the ocean were now turning to him.

His brain was as flat and featureless as the water. His plan had stopped here. He'd promised the survivors that all they had to do was reach the coast. He'd promised them that a ship was waiting.

And it had been.

And the fucking Geckos had watched and waited.

Josh pulled free of Xavier and turned to scan the dunes, but there were no aliens hiding in the scrub to recapture them and drag them back. He gritted his teeth. He was not returning to their base alive.

Not again.

He glanced at his lover and fellow soldier, Xavier. His skin was ashen, slicked with sweat from the infection that was killing him. He needed more than a medic and the small kit they'd brought. He needed IV antibiotics and the medical team that was on the ship.

Josh needed the medical team.

"We need to get out there and look for survivors," a sailor said, attempting to take charge.

There were six of them, two well-armed, a couple of medics, and two to operate the landing craft. The two-armed ones were on the dunes, keeping watch.

He scanned the beach. The hope and glee that had been on the men's faces was gone, replaced with despair. Josh was sure his expression was similar. He had to change that, or they were all dead. He blew out a breath, knowing that he needed to direct this and come up with a new plan. They had a boat, and they had supplies, and that counted for a hell of a lot out here.

"There won't be survivors," Josh said.

"There might be. We can't leave them. There're sharks and—"

"They're gone," Josh snapped.

"You don't know that." The sailor's chin quivered. He glanced at his crew mates, wanting someone to back him up.

"No one is responding," the woman who'd been on the radio said. The badge on her uniform said her name was Marsh.

"There's no life rafts out there," Bird, the medic, said.

"There was no time," Josh said. The Geckos' weapons were undetectable until there was a visual, by which time it was too late to do anything more than draw a last breath.

Josh sank onto the sand and ran his fingers through his hair. It was full of dust and sweat. He wanted to lie on the ground and scream until his throat gave out.

Xavier leaned on Bird. "Joshy."

"Give me a fucking minute." He glanced at the rank of the sailors and their stunned faces. In his mind, he screamed. He didn't want to be responsible for all these lives. He couldn't be. Too many had already died on his watch. While a few had gotten free from the alien prison, many more had been recaptured. He had no idea how many had been killed or sent to the farm alive. He shuddered as though he could still feel the larvae in his shoulder eating him from the inside out. That grub was now in Xavier's leg; they hoped it would eat some of the infected tissue and buy him some time.

"We don't have a minute, Rayne." Xavier used his surname as though being formal would somehow flick a switch inside of him. "And I'm too fucked up."

Shut up. Just shut up.

The men on the beach were arguing about staying or going to find survivors. Xavier was dying.

"Fuck me." He forced a breath out through his teeth and stood, feeling about a hundred years old. He needed a night off, a feed, some painkillers and some time to let his body heal.

"How much fuel does that thing have?" He pointed at the landing craft. It was no good on the open sea, but that was the last place he wanted to take these people. "What supplies are on it?"

Marsh stepped forward. "A quarter of a tank of fuel. Should take us a fair way up the coast but not far enough to reach home. We have rations of one meal for everyone, thirty liters of water, and two medical kits."

Josh gave her a nod, appreciating her concise response. She knew what it was like to be in charge and no doubt had already realized they were in trouble.

"Listen up, everyone." That brought all attention to him. For a few seconds, it was blissfully silent, and he could pretend that the ship was going to come around the point at any moment. It didn't. "The Geckos have fucked up our plan. They don't like people leaving their country without getting their passports stamped or something. We are not heading into open water so they can take us out. Is that clear?"

He fixed the sailors with a glare. "You can keep trying with the radio, if it makes you feel better."

"I need four uninjured people to get the ute unbogged so it can be driven on to the landing craft. Failing that, it will be unloaded and stripped. I want every scrap of anything that might be useful. If you don't know, it goes on the boat. Volunteers?"

Two sailors put their hands up.

"Not you; you're on guard duty." Josh pointed to three of his escapees, including Clarence. That man knew how to keep his head down and survive. He was an asset where some of the others were going to be a hinderance.

"Those with medical issues will be seen to. If it's not pressing, head to the back of the line." Josh turned to Bird and nodded at Xavier. "Treat him first."

Xavier shook his head. "Don't waste your resources."

"Don't waste my time," Josh replied. He wanted to say so much more. But surrounded by so many, no words formed.

"It's only an infected cut." Xavier forced a smile.

Josh pulled the packet of antibiotics from his pocket. "He's had six of these." He handed them to Bird.

"Are we staying on the beach?"

"Will they send another ship?"

"Where are we going?"

The remaining survivors glared at him like it was his fault the ship had been destroyed. Maybe it was. If he hadn't blown up the farm on his way out…

He lifted his voice above the noise. "We're all going to get on the boat—"

"And then what? Cruise south to Perth?"

They wouldn't get that far. There was no point in heading south. "No, we'll make for Georgetown, then Darwin." Port Headland was closer, but it was the wrong direction. They had to head north and across the Simpson line that cut Australia vertically in half, ceding the west to the aliens. Darwin was on the wrong side of the line if it was drawn straight, but he knew it jagged west. Darwin was the nearest Australian city.

Josh wasn't sure they'd make it that far, but if they did, they were home.

The men nodded as though that was an acceptable plan, and Josh let himself breathe.

A yell went up from the boat. Xavier laughed. Bird had found the larvae in Xavier's leg.

"How much of that blood is yours?" the other medic, Tye, asked, pointing at Josh's bare chest.

Josh glanced down. His chest was smeared with the aliens' green paint, blood, and dirt. He was going to brush off their concern, but if he was in charge, then he had to make sure he wasn't dying. "It's my shoulder. It took a blast, got chewed out by a larva, then dislocated. Twice."

Tye stared at him. "Anything else?"

Josh shook his head. Nothing that mattered.

Did anything matter?

Chapter Two

WITH THE UTE secured on the landing craft and everyone aboard, Josh gave the order to get underway. They all scanned the ocean, searching for life rafts or people. But there was nothing out there.

They were alone.

Marsh kept the boat close to shore. It was an illusion of safety that the sailors and civilians were happy to buy into. Josh wouldn't be surprised if the aliens knew exactly where they were. They were the mouse and the cat was waiting, content to know that the prey was trapped.

He closed his eyes against the glare of the sun off the water. Behind him, some people talked, some griped about being handed out rations, others prayed—Josh was sure God didn't give a fuck. Maybe he'd decided humans had been given a chance and they'd blown it. Now it was the Geckos' turn.

Some were silent as the horrors of being captive and the loss of the ship and their way home caught up with them. All he'd wanted was a shower, a shave, a clean bed, and for someone else to take command for a few days.

Every part of him was stretched too thin. One wrong move, and he was going to break. Someone had given him a shirt, so now he wore filthy Army pants and the grey cams of the Navy.

He rested his arms on the edge of the boat, head bowed, trying to come up with a plan where they all got to live. But there wasn't one.

He knew that. In theatre, people died. That's what war was, a place of death. And he was pretty sure that most of the people here didn't think they were in the middle of a war.

Someone came and stood next to him.

Josh ignored them for several seconds as he pulled on his knew-what-he-was-doing face. If the others saw he was panicked, they'd panic, and then everything would go tits up before they had a chance.

Yeah, not everyone would get to live, but some would. And he wanted Xavier to be one of them.

Josh lifted his head and glanced over; he even forced a smile. "What's up, Marsh?"

She pulled a map out of her top pocket. It was already folded to the right part. "There's an inlet about two hours away at our current speed."

The breeze tugged at the corner of the map. "Where were we?"

She pointed to a pencil mark, and if Xavier didn't already have his heart, he might have given it away on the spot. "Has anyone ever told you, you are fucking awesome?"

She grinned, but he could see the strain. "No, Sergeant."

"Josh is fine. Can I borrow your pencil?"

Marsh handed it over, and Josh opened the map. His had been lost when he'd been captured, but he'd committed enough to memory that he could mark where the alien base was. He tried to avoid looking at how far they had to creep around the coast to reach the Simpson Line—a line that he drew in with the borrow pencil.

Marsh watched silently.

It would be quicker to drive, not that everyone would fit into the ute. There was a major road linking Georgetown to Darwin, but it took them too close to the desert and the alien base. If he was an invader, he'd be watching the major roads.

Traveling via the coast was going to take time, and that meant it was also going to take supplies. And as Marsh was suggesting, rest stops. As much as he wanted to move fast and put as much distance between him and the Geckos as possible, he couldn't drag everyone along for the ride—not unless he wanted a mutiny.

"Can you travel at night?"

"I could, but it would be risky." She kept her voice low, like she understood this wasn't a conversation that anyone else should hear.

Josh understood what she wasn't saying. If they lost the landing craft, they'd lose the ute and any supplies they weren't able to save. Worse, they'd lose lives for no good reason. "We will stop for the night then."

"We'll need to refuel in Georgetown."

"Or take a new craft." Josh had no idea what state Georgetown was in. It really depended on whether the Geckos had viewed it as a threat or not. "We'll need to resupply there, anyway. Food, water, medical…"

"I'll have the medic make a list of what he needs, now that he knows the injuries." Her gaze slid to where Xavier lay on one of the bench seats.

Josh couldn't help but follow her gaze. Xavier was so still, it seemed like he was already dead. His hands were folded over his stomach. The leg of his pants had been cut off and the wound bandaged. The white of the bandage was stark against his skin. It wasn't the first time Josh had seen Xavier hurt, but this was the worst. It wasn't the injury but the infection and the way Xavier expected to die. He'd already given up.

"Yeah, that's a good idea. We'll split into groups and hit the supermarket and hospital. You can find us a new vessel."

Marsh nodded. "You think they're up to a supply run?"

Josh turned around and scanned the faces of the men and women in the boat. Marsh and Fallon were the only women, both were sailors. Xavier was the only other soldier.

The rest were civilians who'd been captured by the Geckos. Most were too thin from the poor rations. But they'd been tough enough to survive in prison, so hopefully, they were tough enough to last a little longer.

"I guess we'll find out when we get there."

Marsh studied him. He held her gaze but knew she was wondering if he was up to the job. He'd asked himself the same question every other minute. It wasn't that long ago he would have unequivocally said yes. Now he wasn't so sure, which meant the answer should be no. He wasn't capable of leading. But there was no one else to step up. He was not putting their lives in the hands of a civvie, and none of the sailors were up to the job either.

"Any of you been to war before?" he asked her. They all looked too bloody young.

"It's not the same on a ship, is it?" She smiled as if she'd already had the same thoughts.

Josh returned her smile, knowing that he could trust her with his back. "No. While Xavier is down, you'll be my second."

Marsh lifted her gaze to the sky and sighed. "For how long do you think they will follow military command?"

"Keep them fed, keep them watered, and keep them safe, and they'll do what we say." The minute they fucked up, there would be hell to pay. "We'll split the groups tonight, find out if anybody's been there before, and make a plan. We'll reach Georgetown tomorrow, right?

"Yes. And if it no longer exists?"

"We'll take what we can from any building that survives." Josh was more worried about taking on more survivors and how they'd feed and care for them. But he didn't say that in case Marsh thought him a callous asshole. She wouldn't be wrong.

Chapter Three

WHEN THE LANDING craft nosed up onto the beach, a ripple of relief swept through the survivors. Some had looked ill all day, refusing food and water—not there was much of either.

He stepped onto the beach, and his boots sunk into the wet sand. Low dunes bracketed the thin beach. He accepted the rifle handed to him and made his way up the beach, following the river. Trees and shrubs clung to the edge of the bank. He fully expected there to be crocs lurking in the water. Crocodiles were just what he needed.

He scanned the undulating red dirt, searching for anything out of place. His heart beat a little too fast, and it took him a moment to realize he was nervous and that he couldn't brush past it like he usually did. Adrenaline and the years of experience suddenly didn't mean squat.

Josh scanned the shore again, slower this time as he tried to control his breathing. There were no fucking aliens here. They were alone...except for the mosquitoes and crocs.

The third time he took in the area, it was with an eye for a suitable place to make camp. The beach was too wet, and there'd be insects in the sand that would make a meal out of them. He slapped at his arm as a mosquito tried to steal some blood. They were going to be eaten no matter where they slept.

Josh hoped that the river had drinkable water; he'd run out of purification tablets over a week ago, so unless Marsh had some hidden in her pockets, they were going to have to boil it and hope for the best, which he really didn't want to do. Anything they burned would attract attention. Though he suspected the Geckos knew exactly where they were. Maybe they had their own satellites up there watching them. He had no fucking idea.

But it made his stomach churn and his blood cold and sluggish to know that no matter what they did or how far, or fast, they ran, they were being watched and followed, and there wasn't a damn thing they could do about it. He should have made the effort to annihilate the base. Kill every one of them. He'd have died in the process.

And there were at least another six bases scattered around the world. Taking out one achieved nothing overall.

He forced out a breath between his teeth, then made his way back to where the others were waiting. The two sailors who knew what they were doing with a weapon returned from their scouting trips north and south along the beach.

"Anything?" Josh asked even though he knew if they had seen an alien, they'd have said something already.

"All clear," they said.

Josh doubted that. The Geckos were just better. Anyone who could fly across the galaxy and land on a foreign planet, defeat all attempts to bomb the fuck out of them, and set up a working base in under twenty-four hours was a superior force. But all forces had a weakness.

They just had to find it and exploit it.

Easy.

Except it never was.

The two sailors couldn't be on duty all night. He needed to split up the watches, so it was one civilian and one military on duty at all times.

He watched as Marsh got people off the boat. She was organizing Tye to take two civilians to fetch water. Xavier was sitting up on the boat. It would be best if he stayed there.

Josh slung the rifle over his shoulder and made his way back to the survivors before they could head out on Marsh's task.

"Who knows how to use a rifle?" Half a dozen put up their hands. They didn't have the ammo to waste to see how accurate they'd be, so he was going to have to take their word for it. "Right. You will be assigned a watch. That means getting up when woken and taking up a position to keep an eye on our surroundings."

A few people looked at their feet or anxiously up the beach.

Marsh had her lips pressed together like she didn't want him killing the mood. Getting attacked by aliens would be much more of a mood kill, though.

"Do you really think they'll find us?" Dave asked. He was a short guy who'd said very little all day. He was clearly tougher than he seemed, or he wouldn't have survived being captured.

"I don't know, but it's better to be prepared. To be ready." He wasn't going to be sleeping easy until he was on the other side of the country…maybe not even then.

He tried to remember his last good night of sleep.

The memory played through his mind. He'd woken up late. Xavier had made coffee and brough it back to bed. The balcony doors were open, and he could see the waves rolling against the sand. The day was heating up already. Xavier had leaned over and kissed him awake. Neither of them had made it outside for a morning swim.

He rocked onto his heels as though every missed hour of sleep had caught up with him and wanted to drag him down.

"I think the Navy brought us some rations. Let's eat, make camp, and grab some sleep." He forced a smile like he expected everything to be fine. Maybe it would be. Maybe the Geckos would think them too much trouble, or better yet, maybe the Geckos had mistimed their blast and thought that they'd gone down with the ship and were dead.

Marsh put a hand on his arm and stopped him before he could

get on the boat to check on Xavier. "You shouldn't be worrying them."

Josh glanced at her hand, then up at her face. His jaw tightened, and she let him go as though realizing her error. "Look, you might be in charge of the boat and getting us from A to B, but on the ground, that's on me."

And he needed her to understand that and back him up.

"They're civilians," she pressed.

"I know that. But I don't see enough soldiers to set up a proper defense. So, I'm drafting volunteers," he said quietly and firmly. "We have to be united."

"That would be easier if you didn't make unilateral decisions."

Josh lifted an eyebrow. "You mean like you did? Sending people off to get water and firewood? You shouldn't have sent them without an armed guard. There'll be crocs if not aliens. No one should leave camp alone, not even to piss."

"Noted. You can let people know. Do you want to assign them buddies too?"

"Yeah, good idea." If everyone had a partner, he didn't have to keep a head count. "I'll talk to everyone over dinner, set the watches, and hopefully, we can all get some rest."

While he hadn't enjoyed being imprisoned, at least he'd had blankets. There was nothing on the boat. It was supposed to be a quick rescue, nothing more.

He sighed. "Look, I know this isn't what you'd planned for. Everyone is stressed."

She gave him a curt nod. "We're getting water, and I have enough sterilizer for a couple of days."

"Where did you hide that?"

"Medical kit." She smiled. "This might have been a rescue, but we came fully prepared."

"Tents, sleeping bags?"

"Not that prepared. What's in the ute?"

"Six swags, some tins of food, and borrowed medical supplies. You want one of yours to do a full inventory?"

"I'll do it myself. Everyone else is busy. You should eat first and get some sleep."

Josh shrugged. "I'm fine. I'll take first watch."

Marsh shook her head. "Rayne. Put my guys on first watch if that will help you sleep."

He nodded but planned on staying up anyway, even though she was right. He couldn't stay awake forever, and if he didn't sleep, he'd start making mistakes that might get them all killed. He was going to have to trust her guys.

Moving past her, he stepped up onto the boat and made his way over to Xavier. Tye finished checking the wound and got up. Josh would make a point of talking to him later to find out what kind of shape Xavier was in.

Xavier pushed himself upright. "I think I slept all day."

"Yeah. You feeling any better?" He looked better, pained, but he'd lost that clammy dullness that had marked him as a dead man. Josh sat next to him.

"I think the antibiotics are working. Apparently, five days isn't a full course, but it's a good start."

"We'll call into the chemist in Georgetown."

Xavier glanced away. "You need to not listen to me more often."

Josh stared at his hands. They could've gone AWOL instead of returning to base. But that was ancient history now. He reached out and put his hand over Xavier's. Xavier clasped it like he didn't want to let go. They sat on the boat in silence.

Eventually, Xavier leaned his head on Josh's shoulder. "I feel like shit."

Josh froze. This wasn't like Xavier, to be so open. Josh glanced to where everyone was gathered on the shore, but no one was looking at them. It was only his old fears that made him want to pull away when all he really wanted to do was pull him closer.

Josh gave into the need to touch Xavier and kissed his head. "Just means you're alive."

"I'd like to not feel like shit for a bit."

"Did you tell the medic, or did you tell him you were fine?"

"He thinks it's the infection and the antibiotics and that I need to drink more water."

"He's probably right. Do you want to stay here or eat with the others?"

Xavier glanced at his leg. "He stitched it, and I'm supposed to keep my weight off it."

"I'll bring you dinner and eat with you." Josh stood.

Xavier kept a hold of his hand. "I meant what I said on the roof."

What had he said? "That we should fuck up some Geckos?"

"That we should get married." It was Xavier's turn to look at everyone else. "I don't care what they think."

Josh wasn't that brave. He'd heard what his team had said when they thought he was asleep. And now they were dead. He pulled his hand free; he couldn't do this now. They couldn't talk about a future they may not have. "I don't want to give them a reason to stop trusting and listening to us."

He heard Xavier's muttered curse as he walked away. They'd never agreed to keep it secret; it had just happened. It had made sense. They had jobs and reputations to protect.

Still did.

But he remembered holding Xavier's hand on holiday and not caring who saw or what they thought. It had been like stepping into someone else's life. For a few days, he could pretend that he wasn't afraid of what people were saying behind his back. He hadn't cared because he was with the man he loved.

He couldn't be that person right now.

He accepted a full water canteen and the rations but didn't start eating. He'd wait to do that with Xavier. He glanced at the boat but from where he was standing, he couldn't see the bench Xavier was lying on. Everyone got half a meal, so there'd be something to eat in the morning. While the boat's medical kits were well stocked, there wasn't enough food. He was almost hoping for a croc to wander into camp. Croc steak with a side of stolen baked beans from one of the houses they'd raided would be fucking amazing.

As everyone sat to eat, Josh stood near the fire with Marsh, making it clear that they were the people in charge. Josh made three watches of three hours each. He assigned civilians to military personnel and indicated where he wanted the watches set up.

"Anything moves, shoot it. It's either the enemy or breakfast." He grinned.

A few people laughed, but no one was in the mood. He sometimes forgot that not everyone appreciated gallows humor, but then most people didn't live their lives with too much adrenaline in their blood and death as their constant companion.

"Any questions?" He hoped there were none.

"What are we meant to sleep on?"

Josh levelled a glare at the man. "This isn't a fucking glamping trip. What you have is it. You can sleep on the boat or rough it. Your choice."

He could feel Marsh's disapproval, but he wasn't handling the civvies with kid gloves. They'd either suck it up and survive or die. They were the only two options.

"When we reach Georgetown, things will get more comfortable. We'll resupply and get bedding, clothing, food and medical supplies," Marsh said. "To that end, I'd like you all to come and speak with me and tell me what you do. Anyone with medical training or cooking ability—"

"If you can shoot, you are on security. We will be also resupplying the weapons." While there wouldn't be any cattle stations in town, there would be somewhere to buy guns, not that he was going to be buying anything. He expected the town to be empty of people, the same as everywhere else.

"We will put you in teams," Marsh continued.

"Will we be stopping in Georgetown for a few days?" another of the ex-captives asked. Pink Gecko paint was smeared across his skin.

Marsh glanced at Josh.

Josh drew in a breath. "I don't want to make promises, but I'd like the chance to shower and sleep in an actual bed as much as you."

That was the truth, but from the sour expressions on the men, they didn't seem to like it. Josh didn't want to hang around on the wrong side of the country for any longer than he had to.

"We will make assessments day by day, but I think we can all agree that the sooner we get home the better," Marsh said. Then she turned to him. "Take your friend his dinner before he damages himself further. I'd feel better if both soldiers were on their feet."

Xavier was standing at the gangway like he was trying to figure out how to hop down and join everyone. Josh left the gathering and strode over. "What are you doing?"

"Listening to you make plans while I starve."

"Sit and you can eat." He helped Xavier back to the bench where he'd been lying. The medic had done his best to make him comfortable with the spare clothes from the ute fashioned into pillows.

Xavier took a drink of water, then handed it back to Josh. "So what's for dinner?"

"I didn't ask." He handed over the meal, knowing he should eat his half, but Xavier needed it more.

Xavier stared at it, then moved a bit of meat around with the fork. "I know I need to eat, but I have no appetite."

"Shovel it in. You know how it is."

Xavier nodded and ate a bite. "I can't. Have you got something less meaty in the ute?"

Josh got up, making sure his back was to the people on the beach so they couldn't see what he was doing. He pulled his bag over and slid his hand into the side pocket. There was a breakfast bar that had seen better days, a too soft chocolate bar, and fancy hip flask that someone named Robert was never going to miss. He'd been saving that for when they reached the ship. He put the alcohol away and handed over the chocolate and breakfast bar to Xavier.

His eyes brightened. "You sneaky prick."

Josh grinned. "That's why you love me."

"Damn right it is." Xavier patted the spot next to him, and Josh sat.

From here he could hear the grumbles around the fire and see the smoke but couldn't see anyone. He was glad Marsh hadn't made camp right at the end of the gangway. Sitting here in the twilight with Xavier, he could drop his guard.

Xavier ate the breakfast bar while Josh finished the ration meal. Then they split the chocolate bar. It was almost too sweet, the caramel inside too thick, clinging to his teeth and making it hard to swallow.

Xavier touched Josh's lip, and Josh licked the spot to remove any sign of the pilfered chocolate. It should have been counted in the supplies. Then Xavier leaned in and kissed him. His lips were warm and soft and sweet. And for a heartbeat, all Josh wanted to do was drown.

Forget.

Be anywhere but there.

He drew back a little, but Xavier was close enough that his breath was on Josh's skin, their thighs were pressed together. They were too close—if anyone came up to the boat, they'd see—but he couldn't bear to pull away. "You're obviously feeling better."

"I don't want to die without fucking you one last time."

No matter how much Josh wanted that, there was no way that was happening here. "Well, you'd better make it through the night."

Xavier lifted his eyebrows.

Josh softened his voice and started making up a plan that could fall apart as fast as he dreamed it. "We'll be in Georgetown tomorrow…" They could share a room. Steal a few hours and pretend that everything was fine with the world.

Or would that make it worse to come back to reality?

"And?"

"And we can take over a hotel. Get a room." What would Marsh and the others say?

"Aren't we fancy?"

"Yeah, we can be." Josh let his forehead rest against Xavier's. It had been weeks. He didn't want to waste what time they had, but at the same time, he didn't know if he was brave enough to take what he wanted.

"Mmm." Xavier's lips found his again. "Are you thinking bath and bed?"

"Yeah. Fluffy white towels. Soap." There was nothing better than getting back to running water and soap after a mission.

"You have no idea how hard you're making me," Xavier whispered against Josh's lips.

Josh's lips curved. He knew how to play this game. "A razor and a toothbrush."

"Oh, fuck yeah…" Xavier leaned back and groaned like he was coming. "I think I'd actually kill for some clean underwear."

He nodded, wanting to bask in Xavier's fantasy, but when he blinked, all he saw was the Geckos' farm and the dead men being devoured by the larvae. "You mean you're still wearing some?"

"You'll have to wait and find out. Will you stay for a bit?"

"Yeah." He'd put himself on last watch as a compromise with Marsh, but he'd sleep on the boat with Xavier until it was his turn.

They lay down head to head, cheek to cheek, toes pointing in opposite directions. He breathed in his lover. "You think we'll get out of this alive?"

"Three days ago, no. Today?" Xavier drew in a breath and stared up at the sunset. "I refuse to die." He turned his head, his nose against Josh's cheek. "I have regrets."

"Don't we all?" Death didn't care about regrets or hopes or fears. It was unfeeling.

It had claimed his parents when they'd been full of life. One drunk driver, three ruined families.

"I mean it, Joshy. Why did we never make it official?"

"It never came up." There was never time. They played house but danced around the issue. "We never even lived together."

"We did…just not officially. We could've."

Josh bit his lip and stared up at the pink streaked sky.

"Unless that's not what you want."

Josh turned, his nose banging against Xavier's. He'd go cross-eyed if he tried to look at him. He wanted Xavier, but he was scared about what that meant. He wanted to be the person who wasn't scared of getting hurt. "I don't want to lose you."

Xavier kissed his forehead. "You're never going to do that. I'm like the gum you can't get off your shoe."

He wanted to believe that, but he already wore the wound from when he'd heard Xavier's team had been attacked by the aliens. He'd thought his lover dead. Those wounds didn't heal fast, not even when it had been created by a lie.

"Get some sleep." Josh closed his eyes.

"I'm still thinking of that bath."

"You do that."

"It had better be big enough for two."

"I'll book the honeymoon suite, yeah? I'll call ahead." He didn't even have a phone.

"That sounds like a good plan." Xavier's voice softened as though sleep were dragging him under. A couple of breaths later, Josh was lying there awake on his own.

His body ached. His bones were tired.

He might sleep, but he couldn't rest until they were back in unoccupied Australia.

Chapter Four

JOSH OPENED HIS EYES. For several seconds he lay there, not sure why he was awake. Next to him, Xavier's breathing was soft and even. He let himself be lulled almost back to sleep, but something kept scratching at his brain. After a few more seconds, he eased off the bench, dropping to his knees in the landing craft to stay low. A few other people slept in the boat instead of on the sand. None of them woke.

Xavier reached out a hand, also awake. Because Josh had woken him, or because he'd heard something? Josh put a finger to his lips and motioned for Xavier to stay where he was. It was probably nothing except paranoia. But now that he was awake, he might as well check on things and make sure those on guard duty were doing their jobs.

Josh crept to the gangway, trying to stay in the shadows, and peered out into the night. The narrow beach and dunes were bleached to silvers and grays under the starlight. The fire had burned down to little more than embers. Nothing moved. He scanned the area until he spotted the sentries. All three were upright, which meant they were awake. One leaned against a tree.

Josh checked the watch one of the sailors had given him; it was nearly time for him to take over. He could relieve the man early.

He was about to get up, but he couldn't shake the feeling that something wasn't right and that if he moved, that would be the last thing he did. So he waited.

One second.

Two seconds.

The middle sentry flinched. Then something stood up next to him. Metal glinted. The sentry fell over. Replaced by a taller silhouette with a tail.

Josh bit back on the curse that wanted to tumble off his tongue. Sweat blistered on his back. He glanced at Xavier, who hadn't gone back to sleep, but was propped up as though waiting for the order. Josh mimed the sentry being killed, one hostile that he could see.

The minute Josh stood, he'd be a target. But he couldn't sit here and wait for whatever the aliens were going to do.

He felt Xavier join him rather than heard him. Even with his injury, Xavier was light on his feet.

"Go back to bed," Josh murmured.

"Hard to sleep when we're under attack."

It was a fair point. The guns they had were with the sentries, which left Josh and Xavier with a couple of knives. The alien replacement sentry hadn't moved. He stood there as if he were human. He'd even angled himself so his tail was no longer clearly visible. Josh closed his eyes. Had he imagined it?

Xavier touched his arm.

Josh opened his eyes and followed where Xavier was indicating.

Just visible in the undergrowth someone, or something, was moving. If he did nothing, another human was going to die. His heart thumped hard in his chest. Getting up would only mean his death.

He brought his fingers to his lips as though preparing to whistle and lifted an eyebrow.

Xavier glanced at the Gecko creeping up on the human sentry, then nodded.

Before Josh could whistle, the sentry started firing. Rifle shots filled the night. Josh ran along the gangway, not waiting for a better distraction. On the beach, people woke. Untrained and panicked, they added to the confusion. Josh ran for the dunes. Blue light flashed from the alien weapons, lighting up the beach.

He didn't know if the weapons were set to stun, barbecue, or kill. They were all unpleasant options. Someone screamed, and then the panic really set in.

"Get down and stay down," Josh shouted. He needed a rifle or one of the Geckos' weapons. He didn't want to let the scouts return to base, even though it was too late to stop them from reporting back.

He crouched, hoping the shrub hid him well enough, and looked up. The human sentry that Josh had thought was leaning against a tree hadn't moved. Dead. That was where he wanted to be. He crouched, ready to make a last dive over the open ground.

Aliens and humans were shooting. The night was full of pained screams, flashes, and noise. He took a couple of quick breaths before forcing himself up and running to the tree. Heat seared past him. Then the tree was at his back. He couldn't remember the name of the man staring lifelessly at the sky, neck gaping, blood staining the front of his shirt. And it didn't matter now. There'd be time for that later if they were lucky.

Josh picked up the man's rifle. He lay in the dirt and got an alien in his sights. He waited for the alien to turn, then shot him through the faceplate. With his position made, he rolled away into the dune and lay there, watching the stars as blue heat scored the ground where he'd just been.

His breath came in fast pants, and he wasn't sure he could hear anything over his heartbeat. Were there only two scouts, or were more coming?

Xavier's whistle cut through every other sound. All clear.

Josh didn't pause or wait for confirmation. He was up and moving, skidding down the dune, staying in the shadows and shrubs. The other alien wasn't far ahead. Josh was going to end him too. He crawled through the sand, hoping a snake or a scorpion wouldn't object to him joining them.

The scout fell back, dragging his fallen comrade with him.

If they were getting out of here instead of wiping out the rest of the survivors…

"Fall back to the boat. Get the boat running," Josh called, not knowing if anyone listened or cared what he was saying. "Get everyone out of here, Marsh."

Josh fired at the retreating scout. He was too far away to slot him through the faceplate, but that didn't stop him from trying to hit some other vital part. The scout dropped his buddy and returned fire.

Josh ducked as the heat washed over him.

He had to buy the others enough time to make it off the beach and out to sea. What was taking them so long?

He glanced behind; they were moving like they were at a Sunday picnic. He cursed under his breath and risked sticking his head up again. The alien had his back turned. Josh aimed for the alien's ass where the pale tail stuck out of the uniform. He fired three quick shots. The scout stumbled and fell over.

Josh was up and running before the scout could recover. He pulled his knife free and leaped onto the asshole's back. The alien rolled, squashing him. Josh didn't give a fuck. He stabbed the bastard wherever he could reach. The tail thrashed and whipped him. The Gecko lifted his head, and Josh narrowly avoided getting his face broken as the alien slammed his helmeted head against his.

Josh slashed at the alien's throat. Hot blood poured over his hands and threatened to drown him. He held his breath and shoved the body away. This time, he felt it before he saw it.

A buzz in the air.

A vibration in his bones.

Then the beach lit up.

Chapter Five

THE GROUND TREMBLED. Josh hid under the dead body of the alien as a wave of heat kissed his skin. His lungs burned from holding his breath, but he wasn't about to suck in a lungful of hot air. His limbs twitched as his body tried to override his brain. He could hold it a bit longer before he passed out.

Was the air still hot?

His skin stung.

He exhaled slowly and took a small breath that stank of blood and death. It didn't burn, so he took another slightly deeper one. Perhaps like the other weapons he'd seen, it was all flash and heat, then it was over.

Hot enough to take out an entire Navy ship.

For several seconds, he lay there listening, hoping to hear something even if it was only screaming. Screaming meant someone was alive.

Nothing.

Maybe it was his ears.

Carefully, he shoved away the body of the dead alien and sat up.

The shrubs and trees near the beach were burning. Embers scattered on the breeze before finding a new target to burn, and smoke coiled up into the sky. He scrabbled around and found his knife first and then the rifle. He half expected a third alien to appear, but there wasn't one.

The landing craft was still sitting there, wedged up on the shore. His heart sank. The beach was also empty. Not even the dead remained.

Josh slid down the now glassy dunes and skidded over sand that was like ice.

"Xavier! Marsh! Anyone?" His voice hung in the silence.

Water slapped the side of the boat.

His breath hitched like the blast had seared his lungs and he was suffocating. He wanted to drop to his knees, but he could already feel the heat seeping through the soles of his boots, and he didn't need blisters on his knees to add to his misery.

Something broke the surface of the water well out past the boat. Then another.

Josh almost sobbed with relief. He wasn't alone out here.

It was Xavier who reached the shore first. Josh met him at the waterline and pulled him into a rough hug. "What the hell?"

"There was no time. I thought you were dead." Xavier squeezed him hard, and Josh wanted to break if only so Xavier would put him back together.

Around them, the others slogged their way out of the water. The sand crunched into fine shards beneath their feet.

Xavier grabbed Josh's jaw and kissed him, not caring that they were surrounded. "Don't do that again."

Relief fled, replaced with fear. But in the dark and the confusion, no one was looking at them. He covered Xavier's hand with his own. "I'll try not to."

Marsh was calling orders about getting the boat loaded and underway.

Josh sighed and drew back. "We need to get all the alien tech off the ute."

"Why? It might be useful. The brass will want it."

But there was something about it. The wound plate that he'd put on Danny's gut had activated or something just before they'd encountered Geckos. "They might be using it to track us, so I'd rather not risk it."

Xavier considered him for a minute. "Agreed. I'll help."

Josh put his arm around Xavier and helped him hobble back to the boat. Together they dug through every pack and tossed the Gecko tech into a pile.

"What are you doing?" Marsh asked.

Josh explained, and Marsh reluctantly agreed. They all wanted to keep the alien tech in case it revealed something about their attackers and so they could make better weapons, but it wasn't worth the risk.

He gathered up the tech. A gun and a few other bits that he didn't know what they did. As much as he wanted to keep their medical metal parts, they were also too risky as once they melded to the living body, they were live and couldn't be removed. "I'll dump them on the beach. Is everyone out of the water?"

"We're missing three." Marsh's gaze flicked to the dunes where no sentries now stood.

"Fuck." Two had been killed by the aliens. Had the third made it to the water or had he been burned to death? Josh scanned the faces of the men on the boat, looking to see who was missing. They were down a sailor and two civvies. "How many rifles do we have? How much ammo?"

"Two rifles, including the one in your hand. And not enough," she said with a grim smile.

That was his estimation too. If there was a next time, they were probably dead or wishing to be.

"Water?"

"Only one container was on the boat. The others are gone. Vaporized, I assume."

Josh winced. That wasn't enough water for everyone for a day in the boat exposed to the sun and heat. But it was going to have to do.

They should've been more careful, but they'd thought they were safe. Safe-ish anyway. "From now on, supplies stay on the boat at all times."

"Unless they take out the boat next time." Marsh picked up

some of the alien tech and followed him to the beach. "We got lucky."

"They didn't miss. They knew where we were sleeping and targeted accordingly." He swept his hand out to the shiny beach.

"Why are they going to all this trouble? Do they want us dead or captured?"

Josh dropped the tech. "I don't know. But I do know we need to move faster. We need to resupply and—"

"I know. There should be a boating shop in Georgetown where I can get the maps I need to take us safely round the top."

"We're going to have to split up into pairs to gather everything we need."

"Some people aren't going anywhere." She glanced at the boat. Xavier was leaning on the side like he was waiting for them. But they both knew better. Then her gaze snapped back to him, sharp and hard. "Got anything you want to tell me?"

"No." Josh held her stare.

"Is it going to affect your ability to—"

Josh laughed. "You have no fucking idea. We've been together three years." Though much of that had been spent apart. "I thought he was dead until a week ago. He thought I was dead when I was captured during our breakout, but it is nothing that will compromise anything. I know how to do my job. I wouldn't have let the Geckos sneak up on us. Your men did." His voice was soft and the fury contained. "This isn't an exercise. This is war."

Her lip curled. "You don't think I know that? My ship is gone. My family—who knows? No one is saying if Perth was evacuated of abandoned. At least you have an answer. You have him close. Most of us never will. Assuming we even survive this." She turned and made her way back to the boat.

He cursed under his breath. He couldn't afford to put the sailors offside, especially not her. He took one last look at the beach, then made his way up the gangway. It was closed immediately, and the landing craft left the inlet.

No one slept. Everyone watched the shore or the sky, waiting for the second strike that would end them. At least it would be instant.

Xavier put his hand on Josh's thigh and lifted an eyebrow.

Josh shook his head. There was no privacy, and he had nothing to say. They were fucked. They wouldn't be able to make the trip. They were going to die of dehydration, of starvation. The hopelessness chewed at him.

He'd lost three men tonight.

It didn't matter what uniform they did or didn't wear. He was in charge, and it fell at his feet to keep everyone safe. And he'd failed. Again.

Chapter Six

BY THE TIME the boat pulled up to the beach in Georgetown, Josh had a thumping headache from too much sun and not enough water. His stomach had given up growling and was now a sullen ache. That, he could live with and had many times before.

Even as a kid, he'd learned not to complain if there wasn't anything for dinner. His stepbrother had often been out, leaving Josh to fend for himself after school and also for dinner, which had usually meant endless bowls of cereal as there was nothing else in the house to eat. By the time he was old enough to get a casual job, he'd spent most of what he'd earned on food.

The white sand of the beach stretched away in both directions. They were exposed. An ugly gray pimple on the pristine sand. Marsh was going to look at the other boats, to see if there was something faster, that offered better amenities. There must be an abandoned luxury yacht begging to be taken.

And if there were Geckos in town?

They'd soon find out.

From the beach, everything looked perfect. To the north and south of the beach were mangroves. In front of them, small red cliffs topped with more scrub. Stairs clung to the side of the cliff.

Marsh lowered the gangway. "This area can get big tides…" She glanced behind her to the ocean. "I have no idea what the tidal situation is at the moment."

"Guess we'll find out when you get the maps," Josh said. His tongue felt thick. The first thing he wanted to find was something to drink. "We move out together, get some tourist maps from the first hotel we find, raid their fridges for water, then we'll split up."

Xavier was going to slow them down, but he wasn't leaving anyone on the boat. The boat was too much of a target. And if the tide did a dramatic shift, the boat might be swept away. The medics would carry their kit and help Xavier.

With only two rifles between them, they were screwed if there were aliens waiting. They made their way across the beach, up the stairs, and to the road. There were what appeared to be several hotels along the beach front. He led the group toward the first one, hoping that the lobby was filled with tourist maps along with something more useful.

Despite the fear nipping at his heels, they made it into the lobby without incident. As he shoved open the door, he expected a blast of cool air, but if anything, it was just as hot and humid as outside with the added bonus of being stale. He was already behind the counter and rummaging through the staff only areas by the time Xavier and the medics made it inside.

Fallon started handing out warm water bottles. Josh cracked open the lid and took a long drink, knowing that it would be gone too soon but needing to dislodge the headache.

"Look at the queue. Can't you show these people to their room faster?" Xavier grinned.

Josh lifted one finger in a tiny salute as he finished his drink.

"I've got something about camel rides, boat tours, and crocodiles." Clarence held up some brightly colored brochures.

"If they don't have a map of the town on them, I don't care. Got it." He pulled out a pile of maps for walking tours. He opened one, spread it on the counter, and noted the important locations—not the tourist ones. Hospital, supermarket, petrol station, and chemist. There was no gun shop listed.

The crocodile farm would have guns, but it was farther than he wanted to travel.

"Right, grab your buddy and a map. You know what you need to take. If you need to borrow a car for transport, go for it." He looked at the sailor and civvie in charge of water. They were going to be heading out with the two on food duty. "Nothing that needs a fridge. The supermarket will stink of rotten food, and there may be wildlife. Try to take undamaged, shelf stable stock."

They had been given a list. Lentils, rice, pasta, tinned items such as tuna, fruit, and vegetables along with high calorie things like peanut butter and chocolate. They were taking one rifle. The other one was staying in his hands.

He watched them leave.

"Chemist or hospital?"

"Hospital is closer," Bird said. "They'll have everything I need."

Josh nodded. There'd be dead in the hospital. When the power had gone out, the generator would've kicked in. But it would've switched off by now. Would the aliens have taken the sick and dying or left them? He didn't want to think about it.

A tiny part of him had been hoping to find Georgetown forgotten and thriving. That there'd be someone in the hotel greeting them with a gun and a grin.

Xavier grabbed his hand as he was walking out. "I feel useless, waiting here for you all to come back."

Josh didn't like leaving him either. He'd be much happier if there was another rifle to leave with Xavier.

"Go through the kitchens and see what you can find."

Xavier dropped Josh's hand like it had stung him. "What did you think I was going to do, have a nap? I'm injured, not stupid."

"I know that, but..." He glanced at Xavier's leg. "I can't send you out into the field, and I can't give you my gun."

"I know. Doesn't mean I like it."

"Neither do I."

"You and your shit plans." Xavier shook his head and glanced away.

Josh drew in a breath. "You want to take a stab at running this show?"

For a moment, Josh thought Xavier was going to say yes. He shook his head. "I'll check us into some rooms. I'm sure everyone would like a wash and a good night's sleep."

Josh's body ached for comfort. He wanted to agree and say that it would be good for morale. But they weren't safe here. They weren't safe anywhere.

Still, if they were all going to die tomorrow, why not enjoy a little luxury? "Sure, I want a king-sized bed."

"Baby, we're getting the fanciest suite there is." Xavier grinned.

And hope swelled in Josh's chest that everything was going to be all right. Maybe it would be. "I'll be back soon."

For half a second, he was tempted to lean in and kiss Xavier, but there were too many people with nothing better to do than watch. That they'd overheard caused a squirm of discomfort in his belly.

Xavier looked at him and rocked back. He didn't shake his head or sigh, but Josh still saw the flicker of disappointment in his eyes. He wanted some of Xavier's don't give a fuck courage.

While no one said anything as they walked the empty streets, Josh knew they were looking at him, judging him. He was used to the looks and assumptions. He'd grown up with that after his parents were killed. All the teachers at school would watch and asked how he was every other day. How did they think he was?

What exactly were they expecting him to say?

At least with his brother, they didn't talk about the crash that had killed their parents. They hadn't talked about much at all. All they had to do was deal with the shitty circumstances that pushed them together as housemates.

As he'd gotten older, he'd became aware of other looks and snide comments and had done his best to make sure he was never on the receiving end of them. He'd buried that part of himself for years. All he'd wanted was to be ordinary. Invisible.

All he wanted was Xavier.

Why was that so hard to admit, out loud, when they could all be dead with in hours?

What if Marsh was right and their relationship was a distraction? But was it distracting because he was spending so much time trying to hide it?

He risked a glance at the others with him. They weren't staring at him or whispering. Maybe they didn't care as long as they got to live.

A snake rested in the middle of the road outside the primary school. When it heard them coming, it startled and slithered away. Even though Josh didn't like snakes, he liked that there was life here. There were birds in the trees and mosquitoes. No doubt, they were glad food had arrived. "You got insect repellant on your list?"

Bird nodded. "Yup."

The air was already hot and heavy, and scented with frangipani, even though it wasn't noon yet. As they walked, Josh scanned the empty cars. Some had been left with their door hanging open like the owner was coming back in a moment. It was like the town was waiting to inhale so life could begin again.

But if he looked closely, he saw the signs of death. There were scorch marks on buildings. Blistered asphalt. Old bloodstains on pale concrete footpaths.

It was the silence that was the worst. He'd been in places where there was no human life for miles, and they'd had the same feel— like he was an intruder. That he was interrupting the business of the animals.

The empty windows watched their progress. Their footsteps echoed. Even their breathing seemed loud.

The silence was deep and all-encompassing like it wanted to consume him next. No place he'd ever served had been as still as a photo. This was like moving through an image and didn't seem quite real. If not for the occasional whine of insects or rustle of leaves, it could have all been fake.

They stopped at the hospital. Josh went in first, pushing open the glass door, expecting the worst. He wasn't disappointed. The air was hot and stuffy and rank with decay.

He glanced at Bird. "Where will everything be kept? The drugs?"

"Give me a moment." Bird looked around as if waiting for someone to appear and point him in the right direction. Josh made his way deeper into the hospital. With no lights, the shadows thickened fast.

Something clicked. He wrinkled his nose. He knew that smell, but he couldn't place it. As much as he wanted to call out to see if anyone was alive, he kept his mouth shut. He paused to peer through the windows of closed doors but saw nothing. Behind him, the other three followed. Bird and Clarence, who was his helper, and Scott, the man who'd do the weapons run with Josh once they'd gotten Bird sorted.

Ahead, something moved. Josh froze.

Behind him, the others were talking in whispers that grated over his skin. That sound, like a fat drop of water, and something else, a discordant tapping. The smell was stronger back here. What was it?

And in the next heartbeat, he knew, as the memory of the farm filled his senses.

"Fall back." The thing on the floor was a larva. And where there was one, there were hundreds.

Clarence didn't need to be told twice; he was already halfway to the door.

"What?" Bird turned as though confused.

"We aren't shopping here." Josh grabbed him by the arm. "Everyone out."

"Why?"

Josh swallowed. He looked at the civvies, the ones who'd been captured. "Remember what they served us for breakfast?"

He used the rifle to point up the hallway. There were three of the larvae now, humping their way determinedly over the linoleum floor toward dinner.

"Out now."

This time, Bird and Scott listened.

He shut the hospital doors, slamming the sliding door shut. The little fuckers moved fast, and they'd brought all their friends. Their thick cream bodies hit the glass.

"What the hell are they? Are they giant maggots?" Bird stepped back, his face white.

"Gecko food. They seem to feed on the dead." Josh kept his eyes on the larvae as he stepped back from the door. His rifle was useless on them, but there were other ways. He wanted to blow this place up. The tapping intensified. "Does anyone else here that?"

Bird shrugged. "Insects?"

"Yeah," Scott said. "Like the clicky, crikety, chirping or something?"

It was the 'or something' that bothered Josh.

"If they are larvae, then there has to be an adult," Bird said slowly.

Josh nodded. "Maybe that's the clicking."

No one said anything, but their heads tilted and turned as they listened. Nothing moved. Whatever it was, and wherever it was, they couldn't see it.

Clarence shook his head. "The whole place needs to burn."

He wasn't wrong.

"What if there's someone alive in there?" Bird whispered.

Josh gave Bird a glare. "Really? After how many weeks without power and with those meaty fuckers crawling around, you think someone survived? You want to check? Be my guest, but nothing will convince me to step inside."

The larvae were piling up against the door as they stood there.

"Where's the nearest pharmacy from here?" Bird asked.

Did he not read the map and plan a route? Josh sighed. "There's a vet and then a pharmacy up past the police station."

"We could drive."

"Get us a ride then, Scott." Josh indicated for Scott to lead the way.

He found a four-wheel drive with the door open and the keys in the ignition. It started easily enough. The paint was blistered from heat on one side, and there was an empty baby seat in the back. Josh thanked whatever god still listening that it was empty.

They piled in, and Scott drove through the deserted streets while

Josh kept an eye out for something. If not aliens, then survivors. He didn't expect anyone, but that didn't stop him from hoping.

Josh said without turning to look at Bird, "Do you want to stop at the vet?"

"No. That's a last resort."

Josh kept his mouth closed. This was the last resort…maybe they'd checked in without even realizing.

In silence, they made their way up the block then down a few of the streets. It was the same everywhere. Small houses, lush green gardens, and absolutely deserted. There were a few signs of a fight —broken windows, blood, and burn marks—but no bodies.

Something wasn't right. There was no way all these dead could have been fed to the larvae in the farm. It was too many. Even though the aliens kept some men alive to fight, that didn't explain where the rest had gone. Where had the women and children gone? Had they all been tossed into the sea?

When he saw the police station, relief washed through him. Scott parked like it mattered where he stopped the car. Josh got out and walked up to the front door. He pushed, only to find it locked.

That was weird. While he could waste a bullet on the lock, he opted for the more civilized approach first and knocked.

"Are you shitting me?" Scott called from the footpath.

"There might be survivors." And he didn't want to piss them off.

Scott's eyes widened, and Josh glanced back at the doors. A man with a gun stood on the other side. His weapon was not held casually, and his finger was on the trigger. *Rude.*

Josh smiled and kept his rifle ready. "Sergeant Josh Rayne. Gathering up survivors, we've got a boat, and we're heading to Darwin."

More mouths to feed. And no doubt they had all the guns too. How many were in there? He didn't like the idea of an opposing force. It also meant the supplies they were after might have already been taken.

"We don't need your help."

"Okay." Josh took a step back. *We* meant more than one.

"You don't want to be out come dusk," the man said.

"Why?"

"You'll see." The man smiled, but it was cold.

"We should help each other," Josh said.

The man's smile faded. "Where was the army when we were invaded?"

"We were getting blown up for trying to stop them. Getting captured to check out their base. Losing our friends, the same as you."

"Why has no one come sooner?"

"I'm here now, and I'm all that's coming. This is no longer part of Australia."

"We don't have long until sunset," Scott murmured.

"I know." They needed radios. Some way to communicate with the other teams. "Do you want to come with us?" Josh asked the man.

"Why did you come here?"

"Thought there might be survivors in Georgetown."

"No, why the police station?"

Josh stared at the man. He could lie, but he couldn't come up with a decent one. "Weapons. Thought it would be the best place to get a hold of some ammo."

The man laughed.

Yeah, it was fucking hilarious.

"Okay, I'll leave you to it." Josh walked backward, refusing to give the man his back as target. It was always the insane cockroaches that survived.

What did that say about him?

Josh got into the car, pulled out the map, and read the list of places down the side, looking for ideas on where to find weapons.

In the back, Bird and Clarence sat, waiting to be dropped at the chemist.

"That was weird," Bird said.

Clarence laughed. "I wish that was the weirdest thing I've seen."

"There's no one here, no cops. We should hit up a bank. Go home rich."

Josh watched the bank roll by. "Money won't keep you safe or fed out here. Stop."

"Why?"

"Because I fucking said." The car jerked to a halt. "The chemist is down there. Let's go."

Scott turned the corner, and they rolled along the empty street. Blank windows stared at them. There was none of that dreadful clicking, but that didn't stop the dread from swelling in his gut like dough. Thick and sticky and heavy.

When they stopped, they all piled out. Josh led the way again, pushing open the door, expecting a waft of something foul. The air was hot, but there was nothing untoward.

Everything was on the shelves, just as it should be, but he swept each aisle before moving behind the counter. There was no one hiding there waiting for rescue. He didn't know when Georgetown had been attacked, and it didn't really matter. "All clear."

Bird and Clarence—who he'd put on meds because it would be easier than carrying food—came in to grab what they needed.

"Make sure you get multi vitamins, painkillers, you know everyday stuff."

The medic nodded. "I know what I need."

Josh cast his gaze around in case he was missing something. He grabbed himself a tube of sunscreen, a hat, and sunglasses. He ripped off the tags and left them on the floor before shoving on his new accessories.

Clarence waved a bottle of something at him. "You want to smell better?"

"Fuck yeah." Josh lifted his hands, ready to catch the deodorant. He needed a bath, and nothing was going to change that, but he still sprayed some on. "Get me a toothbrush and toothpaste too."

"I thought you said essentials," the medic said.

"I haven't brushed my teeth in over a week; I'd call that essential. Clarence, how long has it been for you?"

"A month. I'll grab everyone toothbrushes." He grinned.

"Good work. I'll leave you the car, and I'll see you back at the hotel." Where there was a bed and a wash waiting. He was looking forward to being clean, even if it only lasted a day.

He took a detour down the aisle where he'd spotted the

condoms and lube. He didn't care about the former, but the latter would make Xavier happy. Though there had been times when they'd skipped even that. They'd skipped a lot of things, probably for all the wrong reasons. Not tonight.

He wouldn't get into a dumb fight with him either. It was going to be perfect in case it was the last fuck they ever got.

He stepped through the door into the bright sunlight where Scott was waiting with the car like a getaway driver. He was glad he had sunglasses now.

"Grab yourself a hat and sunnies," he said to Scott.

Scott stepped into the chemist. Josh squirted out some sunscreen and rubbed it on his arms and face. While it couldn't undo the sunburn he already had from the morning on the boat, at least it would stop him getting burned worse. When the other guy came back out, Josh handed him the sunscreen.

The cop shop was out. And while they weren't going to hit up a bank, it had given him an idea. "Security guys have guns. You know where there's security? Airport."

"But the sun is—"

"And we need a new car. We're leaving this one with Bird."

Scott swore, but there were so many abandoned cars that it only took them a couple of minutes to find one with the keys inside.

"Better drive fast…" Josh peered out the window. The sun was still up. Sure it was arcing down, but he wouldn't have called it setting. His stomach rumbled, and his mouth was dry again.

"Did you want to stop for food?"

"Nah, we'll get something duty free."

The edge of the airport came into view, and then they were driving past the carpark full of empty cars that were never leaving. There wasn't a single plane on the runway. There wasn't even much of a runway; it had been fried. Even the dirt around the edges was blackened.

"This looks bleak."

"This whole town is bleak. What did you expect? Stranded tourists? Today, that's us. Pull up out the front."

"But the sign—"

Josh glared at him. "If we get a ticket, I'll pay."

Scott ignored what he'd said and parked in a bay.

"I said out the front. Drive up to the doors and don't lock it. Leave the key in the ignition."

"But—"

"Just do as you're told, and this will go a lot smoother."

Scott maneuvered the four wheel drive up to the front. For a man who'd just suggested robbing a bank, he was rather upset about parking in the wrong place. Josh shook his head. "Let's get some food and weapons."

The glass doors were stuck half open, so Josh slid through. Something was rotting in the building. The sweet stink of decay was heavy on the air. Maybe old food, maybe old bodies. If there were bodies, there would be larvae. He carried the rifle, ready to be used, but there were only ten bullets left. Barely enough to be useful.

Scott coughed. He followed but was looking around wildly like he expected something to jump out at him.

Josh didn't expect to find dead security guards, but they'd have an office. There'd be something he could use. There had to be. He walked over dark smears on the floor—blood streaks, the same as all the other places he'd seen. When he found the guard's office, it was locked. Blood had leaked from under the door and dried. There were scratches on the door like something had tried to find a way in and failed. He used the stock of the rifle to bust the lock.

And regretted it immediately.

He stepped back, gagging, glad he hadn't eaten. Someone had gotten away, but they'd been too badly injured to survive.

Scott vomited on the floor.

Along with the body, there were weapons and radios. Josh gritted his teeth and forced a smile, then stepped into the office. Insects of the Earth variety had found the body, and the wet heat hadn't been kind. Josh picked up the pistol. He made sure it was safe before shoving it into a pocket in his pants. Then he stepped around the body and the dried puddle, too aware that if he could smell it, he was breathing it in.

He moved through to the next room.

This is where the goodies were. He grabbed a belt which already had a pistol and ammo on it. Someone had brought a backpack into the office. He tipped it out and shoved all the extra ammo and radios in, then slung it over his shoulder. There was a safe, but he doubted there was anything in there that he could use, and he didn't want to waste the time breaking in.

"Ready to move on?" Josh said as he left the room.

"Didn't you get what you need?"

"Some. Let's go through security and see what we find." It was the first time he'd been through an airport without queues. No one checked his bag or asked him where he was going. This must be what it was like to be rich.

He went into rooms labelled 'staff only' but found nothing.

Finally, they stopped at the duty free. "Get a bag; you have sixty seconds."

Josh grabbed some chocolate, tossing it in his backpack, because everyone needed something nice after a day of foraging. He opened the till and took the cash—when they reached Australia, they'd need something, and if the power was still down, the ATMs wouldn't be working.

He stared at the perfume. Then the oversized bottles of alcohol. He grabbed a shopping bag and swept the little bottles off the shelf and into the bag, moving quickly. Then he added some of the cotton tourist T-shirts for good measure. Molotov cocktails for after dinner. All he needed was a lighter, and they'd be able to watch the hospital burn for entertainment. Aviation gas would be better, but he didn't want to spend the time finding where it was stored and then figuring out a way to transport it. He doubted it came in small bottles ready for making trouble.

"Times up." He grabbed two chocolate bars and put them in his shirt pocket for the drive back to the hotel.

Scott lugged two bulging shopping bags. He'd robbed the jewelry display

Josh shook his head. "You can't eat gold."

"You took perfume and liquor."

"Because I can set fire to it."

"What?"

Josh turned on his heel and they walked back the way they came. The shadows were longer, and the man's warning echoed in his ears. Maybe it was the ravings of a man who'd been locked in the cop shop too long. But Josh wouldn't bank on it.

He stopped at the magazine stand and went behind the counter. He found the lighters as expected and tipped them into the bag with the perfume and shirts.

Scott caught up, out of breath from carrying his stolen goods. "It's nearly dark."

"Yeah. Better hustle." Josh covered Scott as he put the bags in the back and got into the car. Then Josh put his bag on the back seat and climbed in next to it.

"What are you doing?"

"Drive." He made sure both pistols were fully loaded.

But the drive back to the hotel was uneventful. He was almost disappointed.

Chapter Seven

JOSH WAS the last one back to the hotel and the only one who seemed to have thought about barricading the front doors with the lobby furniture. "Where is everyone else?"

Xavier was sitting with a rifle behind the counter, bracketed by two big torches that were pointing up at the ceiling. "Eating."

Josh's jaw twitched. They'd left Xavier out the front. No, Xavier had probably volunteered.

He lifted one hand. "I told them to. Seeing the empty town kind of upset them. I thought a feed might cheer them up. You seem kind of paranoid…more so than usual."

"There're larvae in the hospital and the adult insects are out there. How secure is this place?"

"Completely indefensible from the Geckos, but it's structurally sound so theoretically it should keep the bugs out. Bird said there was at least one survivor in the cop shop?"

"Yeah. He's staying put."

Xavier nodded. "So no weapons."

"Took a spin out to the airport, got a couple of pistols and some radios." He opened the bag of perfume and liquor bottles. "Want to help me burn down a hospital?"

Xavier put his hand over his heart. "I thought you'd never ask. But can we eat first? I'd much rather commit arson on a full stomach."

Josh shrugged. "I was thinking of doing it as we left town anyway. No rush."

"Nice. Marsh found a boat with a bit more speed than the landing craft. And I did some research and found a shooting range. They might have some fun stuff on site." Xavier hobbled around the counter. "I also assigned everyone rooms."

A shooting range should have some ammo, and he was willing to bet there would be some rifles or pistols stored there too. They'd have to check it out tomorrow. It was too dark now. "Is there running water?"

He was hoping that maybe there was a generator or a water tank or something. Even an outdoor shower that was gravity fed would be grand.

"There's a green pool."

Josh wrinkled his nose.

"And a water tank for the gardens. I might have run a hose from the tank to our bath and filled it already." He put his finger to his lips.

Josh put his arm around him to help him walk to the restaurant. "You're the best."

"I know." He kissed Josh's cheek. "Between a bath and the toothbrushes, I might be able to die happy."

Josh pulled the lube out of his pocket. "Saw this and thought of you."

"Aww…I can't wait to destroy you." Xavier pocketed the lube with a grin. "After dinner."

"What is for dinner?"

"I have no idea, and I don't really care as long as it didn't once wriggle."

"We should secure the building."

"All the doors are closed. We'll be fine for a night."

They were not going to be fine, but he was too tired to argue about it. As Xavier had said, the building was watertight, so no bugs should get in unless they'd learned to pick locks.

The survivors were sitting around a table with another torch in the middle that was pointing up to the ceiling like a candle. There were tins of tuna and beans and mayo and packets of corn chips. He'd eaten worse, much worse.

Xavier dropped into a seat a little too gladly and propped the rifle up by his side.

Josh sat next to him and did the same. From his pocket, he pulled the pistol. From the bag, a radio and ammo. "Marsh, got you a present."

That left three radios. One each for him and Xavier and a spare that he'd hang onto it for the moment.

Scott had already put the chocolate on the table. So much for rationing it out for when things went to shit. Treats were a quick way to lift spirits.

Marsh picked up the pistol and inspected it. "Nice."

Josh reached for a water bottle, then he got stuck into eating what was close to the best meal he'd had in far too long. Maybe they could catch some fish and cook them up as they made their way north. He'd love a roast lamb with all the trimmings.

"I've got one more supply run to do in the morning. I'll take Xavier with me, and on our way back, we're going to take out the hospital."

Everyone looked at him.

Had no one mentioned it?

"It's full of…" He glanced at the faces of the survivors. "It needs to be gotten rid of."

"It's a farm," Scott whispered.

"An accidental one. We saw no sign of Geckos. Everyone can eat and sleep, and we'll head out in the morning. You lot can get the new boat loaded and ready, and Xavier and I will meet you there. Then we'll be on our way." He smiled like it was a perfect plan.

He could leave the hospital untouched, but he didn't want those larvae growing up into whatever it was that laid them.

The mood dropped. Before he'd sat, there'd been a measure of happiness and relief. Now there was only tension.

"What's a farm?" Tye asked.

Josh didn't want to be the one who answered. He shoveled food into his mouth without tasting it.

"It's where the aliens put the dead so the bug larvae can feast on them," Xavier said. "I had one in my leg."

"And they're here?" one of the sailors asked.

No, I'm making it all up. "That's why I'm going to blow up the hospital. So, they don't spread." Josh sighed and leaned back, his appetite gone. "I'm going to do a walk around, make sure everything is shut tight. Then we should all brush our teeth and turn in."

He stood.

Xavier lifted an eyebrow but didn't say anything.

Marsh got up to walk with him. It was only when they were back out in the lobby that she spoke. "How worried are you?"

"Enough to check. The larvae sensed life and marched down the hospital hallway after us. What did you find?"

"A nice boat. I filled the tank and stripped the nearby boats of supplies and jerry cans. I spent the day out there." She tapped her pocket. "I have the key. You expecting the man from the police station to give you any trouble?"

Josh checked the doors as they talked. Xavier had already done this but another set of eyes never hurt. Plus, everyone at that table wanted to feel like they were safe. He wanted to actually be safe. "No. He warned us not to be out after dark."

"That's not promising."

"No, it's not." He stopped. "Did you hear that?"

She opened her mouth.

But there it was again. A click and a thwack.

"It sounds like bugs hitting—"

"Windows," Josh finished. He turned and ran to the lobby. The big glass windows were covered with bugs the size of dogs. His gut clenched.

Marsh swore. "What are they?"

"I assume they are the parents of the larvae." And they'd already found them.

Chapter Eight

HOW MANY BUGS would it take to break the window?

Josh stared at the mass of bodies. They vibrated against it, scrabbling and clicking like oversized cockroaches. How much like cockroaches were they?

He walked over to the torches and flicked them both off.

"Rayne, we've got a problem," Xavier called out.

"I know, Fisher; I'm dealing with my own right now. Turn off the torch." So far, turning it off hadn't made a difference. Maybe they were attracted to body heat, or heartbeats, or something they had no control over. If that were the case, it was a bloody good thing no one was outside. A shudder rippled through him at the thought of being swamped by the alien insects. His stomach tightened at the thought of being turned into a farm while alive.

"Hotel bathrooms never have a view, right?"

"Sure," Marsh said.

"I think it would be wise if everyone went to their room and shut themselves in the bathroom for the night." Josh stepped back from the windows.

"We should stay together."

"If they are attracted to body heat, we'll be one big blob of deliciousness. I don't want to be delicious, do you?"

She shook her head. "I'll break the news."

"Where are the rest of our food supplies?" Because if they'd ripped into everything tonight, he was going to be pissed.

"There's two loaded up vehicles out the front."

"Good. Go and tell them."

Then he was alone in the dark lobby, watching the insects move over the glass. The noise made his teeth hurt.

"That is not conducive to a good time," Xavier said, running his hand along Josh's spine.

"That has never stopped you before." A stolen five minutes here and there. The only time they ever really had was when they were both home.

"Nor you."

"You know how you were filling the bath…"

"All shut up long before you got back. I'd been starting to worry that you weren't going to make it and that I'd wasted my time." Xavier's hand fell away as the others were herded out of the restaurant dining room.

They paused to look at the windows, then moved smartly past and down the corridor.

Xavier grimaced. "Worst case, we can all hide out in the stairwell."

"That's not how I want to spend the night," Josh said. He wanted one night of something good. He needed it after weeks of shit. *We need it.* "Will you be in trouble for doing too much and ripping your stitches?"

Xavier kissed the back of Josh's neck. "Be gentle with me."

Josh snorted. "You can lie back and enjoy."

That wasn't Xavier's style at all, which suited Josh just fine.

Moonlight broke through the insects' bodies. Then one by one, the bugs left.

Josh sighed, and his breathing eased as some of the tension released its grip. "It's the light, the same as any bug."

"Still couldn't pay me to go out there."

"Are we still getting paid, or do you think they've marked us as dead to save a few cents?" His brother would appreciate getting whatever was in the bank. His house in Perth wouldn't be worth shit now.

"Don't care. Follow your own orders and go to your room, Joshy." He took Josh's hand and led him to their room.

It was at the back of the hotel, and once upon a time, they could've opened the doors onto the balcony to sit at the table and chairs and drink champagne. The hose was coiled on the patio like a dead snake. Josh checked the door was locked and pulled the curtains closed. If there were bugs out there, he didn't want to know.

Xavier tugged at his shirt, and Josh let him pull it off. The paint on his chest glowed faintly. He wanted to scrub at it, pick it off even if it left his skin raw, until there was no reminder left of his imprisonment.

Beneath the paint was ingrained dirt from weeks in the scrub. He was filthy. They both were.

"Where's that bath?"

"Follow me. I think you'll like what I've done with the place."

The bath was huge, and on the edges of the tub were four tiny liquor bottles from the mini bar. On the vanity were clean clothes.

"Where did they come from? Did someone raid a clothing store?" He wanted to touch the clothes, but he didn't want to make them dirty.

"It was in the hotel. I went through some of the luggage. We have clean socks, jocks, and T-shirts. There are pants, but they are either jeans, dress pants, or shorts."

"You were busy."

Xavier grinned, his teeth bright in the ambient light. That they'd somehow managed to trip over each other and make something of the last three years was nothing short of a miracle. "We could go full feral...or we brush our teeth and pretend to be civilized."

"Maybe I'm getting old, but I'd really like to brush my teeth." It had been far too long.

"Same."

Having clean teeth was almost better than sex. His body was already hard from the minty freshness, the closeness to Xavier, and the promise of a bath and more. While Xavier finished, Josh undid his boots. He should've searched for new laces. No doubt there was a pair of shoes in the hotel that didn't need them. He binned his socks and undid his army issue pants. They were getting too loose.

He shucked his jocks and tossed them in the bin too. While the water was cold, he didn't care. He was pretty sure even his hard-on would survive. He stepped in and let the cold bite, then eased down, watching as Xavier stripped, leaving his clothes in a pile.

Josh grabbed the soap and started washing the sand and dirt out of places he definitely didn't want grit. Even though the water was icy compared to the ambient heat of the room, he groaned as he luxuriated in the soap's scent and the feeling of getting clean. It was a simple pleasure that never got old.

Xavier sat opposite him. "I've got shampoo if you want to turn around."

"Shouldn't you be keeping your leg dry?" But Josh turned around.

"Tye stuck a waterproof bandage on it because he doesn't trust me."

"I like him."

"Not too much, I hope." Xavier's fingers worked through his hair and massaged his scalp. It was an echo of the holiday they'd been on before the attack. He closed his eyes but couldn't pretend they were there. "Your hair's getting long."

"Don't get any ideas. I'm cutting it as soon as I can."

"I don't know; the wild man look suits you." Xavier pressed a kiss to the side of his neck. His hands smoothed over Josh's shoulders, then over his chest. Josh leaned back into the embrace. The cold of the water had nibbled through his skin and made a start on his bones.

"Turn around. I'll wash your hair." As they moved, Josh ducked under and rinsed. Already, he was feeling more human. He ran his fingers along the lines between the braids in Xavier's hair. It hadn't been braided when they'd left Perth. Like him, Xavier had a beard and was too thin.

There was a grim determination about tonight. They were taking it, no matter what—even if they were both tired and hurt because there may not be another chance. They had spent the last three years believing there would always be a tomorrow. They'd been wrong.

"You okay?" Xavier put his hand over Josh's.

"Just thinking."

"Don't. It only gets you in trouble." He reached out and opened two tiny bottles of scotch. "Cheers."

Josh knew he shouldn't, but it was only one drink. He downed it in a swallow and enjoyed the burn as it slid down his throat and bloomed in his belly. "You don't need to get me drunk."

"Do you remember…"

"Yeah…we were so shit-faced." They'd almost been caught. It had been hilarious at the time.

Josh let his pale hands drift over Xavier's thighs.

"This water is fucking cold," Xavier said after a few breaths.

"It's not the effect you were going for?"

"No." He moved, reaching over the edge to grab something. "I got you something else. To make good on a promise. He held out the face cloth.

"I'm not clean enough?"

"Open it, dumb ass."

Josh's heart thudded as he unfolded the face cloth. There inside was a ring.

"Will you marry me?" Xavier turned, so he was on one knee in the bath.

This was a shit time to ask, but when was going to be better? If they were married, then everyone would know about them, but who was left? He nodded. They'd wasted so much time sneaking around. "Of course I will."

"It should fit; it fitted me. There wasn't much to choose from in the hotel jewelry store."

"I can't believe you stole me a ring." The future wasn't something they had ever really discussed. It had been assumed things would go on as they had been until one of them pulled the pin. Too much had been assumed in their relationship. But the whole world had been thrown off balance, so maybe this was a needed change.

"I wanted to do it properly." Xavier stood, water streaming off his body and making his skin gleam. He held out his hand. "We skipped over so many things, or just avoided them."

Josh put on the ring, then accepted the offered hand. But he only made it as far as his knees. Xavier's cock was too tempting. He kissed the head. "I didn't want to ruin what we had."

It was easier not to talk.

He took Xavier in his mouth, running his tongue over the smooth head before taking him deeper. Xavier drew in a breath and his grip on Josh's hand tightened. The ring pinched his finger. He should've taken something nice for Xavier from the duty free, but it hadn't even crossed his mind.

Despite the cold water lapping around his thighs, his blood was hot and his dick hard. He drew back and teased the slit of Xavier's cock with his tongue.

Xavier shuddered and swore and pulled him up. "I want more than that."

Josh leaned into Xavier and took a kiss. His mouth was sweet like booze and minty from the toothpaste. Nothing had ever tasted so good. Xavier's hands were all over him, caressing, scratching.

He fisted Josh's cock. "I want to feel alive."

"We are." Though he could feel death stalking them. Or rather, aliens.

"Then like we have a reason to live. Something more than checking weapons and keeping others alive."

Josh gripped Xavier's face. His beard was rough against his palms, but it suited him. "We'll slither out of this, the same way we always do."

"Suck it up and push through."

"Yeah."

"This is different, Joshy…" There was a note of doubt in Xavier's voice that Josh didn't want to hear.

"Shut up and fuck me. We're going to survive because you owe me a wedding."

"Can you imagine when we announce it?" Xavier sounded almost wistful.

Josh smiled even though the idea caused his stomach to knot. No one knew was gay. His stepbrother didn't. It was another one of things they didn't talk about. His brother had once asked if Josh needed to know anything and had handed him a book, a packet of condoms, and told him not to get anyone pregnant—Josh had already known that wasn't going to be an issue—and that had been the end of the talk.

"It'll be fine." He stepped out of the bath, followed by Xavier.

For a few moments, they stood wrapped it the fluffy hotel towels. "I might steal a bathrobe."

"I doubt anyone will send you a bill." Josh looked at the ring in the moonlight spilling in through a gap in the curtains from the bedroom. It was a solid silver band with a dark pearl nestled in the center and a couple of diamonds thrown in for good measure. The kind of ring that neither of them could actually afford. It looked odd on his hand. He didn't wear jewelry...but he could get used to it.

"Do you like it?"

"Yes." But he'd have liked anything Xavier gave him. "Let me show you how much."

He dropped the towel and held his arm out for Xavier. Together, they walked to the bedroom. The door was still closed and locked with the privacy catch as the electronic swipe pad didn't work. He resisted the urge to check the glass doors again. They were alone.

And they were safe. Or at least there was the illusion of safety.

Josh flipped back the covers, and Xavier sat. He masked the wince, but Josh saw it. it was it tension of his shoulders and the tightening of his smile.

"Sit on me." Xavier opened the lube and slicked his dick.

Josh was more than happy to straddle his thighs and let Xavier finger his hole. If anyone walked in now, they'd get an eyeful off his ass being prepared. His heartbeat quickened as Xavier slid in one finger, then two.

It had been weeks, but he welcomed the stretch. He kissed Xavier. They were alive, and right now, that mattered more than anything else. He moaned against Xavier's lips, then pushed him onto his back. "Don't want you to rip your stitches."

"You just want it."

"Damn straight." He pressed against Xavier's cock, enjoying the pressure of the fat head on his hole, before he sank down. He drew in a breath and took his time easing onto Xavier's length.

Xavier put his hands on Josh's hips. He started slow, determined to drag it out, but his body had other needs. He quickened his movements, knowing he wouldn't last long. It was only a question of who got there first. Xavier's fingers pressed into Josh's skin, and he lifted his hips to fuck him harder.

Yes, that was what he needed. He moved slightly so every stroke hit just the right spot. He was so close, the need to come was tightening his balls.

"I want to suck you," Xavier ground out.

"Fuck." Josh lifted up. He drew in a couple of shaky breaths. "I'm so close."

"So get up here."

Pre-come slicked his dick as he leaned over and thrust into Xavier's waiting mouth. Oh God… He gave two thrusts then he unraveled, groaning as he spilled, and Xavier swallowed. For a moment, he could barely breathe as the climax rolled up his spine and gripped him in a wash of pure pleasure.

He pulled back, panting.

Xavier gripped the back of his neck, taking a kiss before giving him an order. "Get on your belly."

Josh did as he was told, the taste of his own come on his tongue from the kiss, and Xavier moved over him, spreading his thighs before sinking into him. Xavier thrust deep, and Josh lifted his hips for more. His dick wasn't sure if it should be waking up again.

Xavier didn't give him enough time to decide, thrusting hard a few times before he grunted and stilled as he came. His ass clenched, and Josh was sure he could feel the come slicking his channel.

Xavier lay on top of him, pressing him into the bed. Josh closed his eyes, enjoying the intimate embrace. He didn't let himself think about what their life could be like when this was over, because it could all be snatched away.

Chapter Nine

JOSH WORKED his lube-slicked hand over both their cocks. Xavier's leg was hooked over his hip. They should be sleeping. They had for a bit before waking up and teasing each other until they'd been too wound up to sleep. His breath caught as Xavier bucked his hips and came, spilling over his hand and stomach.

A car horn made him flinch.

Xavier wrapped his hand over Josh's. "Come for me."

The horn sounded again; it took him a moment to remember why it was out of place. This time, the person kept their hand on the horn. Something was wrong, and the sharp edge of climax vanished. "Fuck."

"Fuck," Xavier echoed, but they were already pulling apart.

Josh wiped his hand and stomach on the bedsheet. His dick was hard, flapping against his belly. "You owe me."

"Yep. I know."

They did that. A debtor's log in case they got interrupted. At first, it had been a joke, but it had become a thing. The one who missed out was the first one next time. He'd have Xavier on his knees.

He pulled on the clean jocks and his pants that felt crusty now he'd bathed. He was dressed and by the door, rifle in hand, in less than a minute. Xavier nodded, also ready in shorts and a black T-shirt. Without a word, Josh opened the door and stepped into the hallway. People were sticking their heads out and asking what was going on.

"Get into your rooms, lock the door," Josh barked.

A few stared at him, then obeyed.

"You need a hand?" Marsh asked. She looked rumpled, like she'd slept in her uniform.

"Keep this lot in their rooms." The fewer people he had to trip over, the better.

Xavier followed, his steps uneven, but Josh would rather have Xavier at his back than anyone else. "Good thing we were woken; I have to take my meds."

Josh nodded. "True."

The horn went silent.

That was worse. There was someone out there…were they still alive?

"What do you want to do?" Xavier asked.

Josh muttered a few curses that he'd picked up while posted overseas.

"That's not physically possible, and I don't think the donkey would like it," Xavier said. "I think we should have a look."

"I knew you were going to say that." He'd been thinking it, and he was already making his way to the lobby. The shadows were deeper, more malignant somehow.

"We can't leave them out there."

"It had better not be the crazy dude from the cop shop." But he'd deliberately said don't go out at night. Why would another survivor risk being out at night? They'd managed this long in the empty town, so they should know better.

The lobby was dark. Josh grabbed one of the big torches. It had enough weight to be a club if needed. "How much ammo you got?"

"Not enough for all the bugs that were on the windows."

There wasn't enough ammo in the world for all the bugs. The horn honked again, but it was muffled.

Josh's mind scrambled through options. He wasn't wasting ammo on the bugs. "Grab that shopping bag. Make me up a Molly or two."

"What are you going to do?"

"See if I can get eyes on the car."

"Don't go out until I'm ready."

"I'm in no rush." But it needed to be done if someone was out there. He peered through one of the windows but only saw their loaded vehicles, waiting for the valet to park them.

He moved on to the next window. Still nothing. Where was the car? He moved to the next window and risked turning on the torch. One quick flash. Maybe the person in the car could see him and would move closer. He heard the scuttle before he saw them. In the moonlight, he watched as the writhing mass of alien insects shifted enough for him to see a car beneath.

"Shit. Unknown in a car and the bugs are on it, crushing it." He glanced at the dark sky with no sign of dawn. Whoever was in there wasn't going to make it until morning.

The lobby filled with the scent of too many perfumes.

"I am going to smell like a whorehouse for a week," Xavier muttered.

"You can thank me later, just don't raise your prices."

"I need to start charging."

Josh grinned. "I'm going to open the door and lob a Molly at them."

"These are too tiny to do much damage."

Xavier was right but lugging back one-liter duty free bottles was a bit much. "Is there a bar with bigger bottles?"

"There's some booze in the restaurant."

They needed more than the two of them. "We'll go with what we have for the moment." Josh walked over to Xavier and grabbed two bottles. "I hope they don't like fire."

"You and me both."

"I'm going to have to step out. Cover me."

"This isn't even a plan, Joshy. It's just shit."

He paused and looked at the bottles that people valued so much;

they had aspirational names and fancy shapes, and he was using them as weapons. He'd use anything he had as a weapon. This is what his life had become. "I know. Got something better?"

"Where's the car?"

Josh showed Xavier; it was on the other side of the road like it had parked opposite and the person had planned to stroll over. But between the hotel and the car, there was now a river of bugs. Their shells glinted in the moonlight. "You think they've been out there all night?"

"Waiting for us to let them in?"

"Or are they everywhere at night?" Josh shuddered. "Why the hell didn't the person wait for morning?"

"No idea, but we don't have time to figure it out."

Josh unlocked the lobby door. He held the four bottles and waited for Xavier to light the cloth. Then he stepped out of the hotel. He didn't know if it was the heat or the light from the flame, but the road scuttled, and he was sure a hundred bug eyes were on him.

"Drive closer!" he yelled, then he tossed the first bottle as far as he could. He followed up with the other three before it had hit the ground.

Fire exploded, spreading wherever the perfume touched. Xavier was right; it wasn't enough. But it made the bugs move.

Xavier fired once, and a bug that had been sneaking up on his left edged back. Josh moved swiftly back into the lobby and shut the door.

The bugs chattered and clicked as though furious. They were drawn to the fire even as they were repelled by the heat. The car started and edged forward, pushing through the bugs. The bugs on the car moved and others jumped on as though trying to stop the prey from getting away.

"They need to turn off their headlights," Xavier said as he handed over another three bottles.

"They need to floor it. Light me up."

He opened the door and tossed a few more Mollies, aiming for in front of the car to clear the way. The car crept forward. Bugs crunched. It was sickening and thrilling. Like tires crunching over gravel.

But they weren't moving fast enough. They weren't going to make it. The car was too weighed down.

He stepped back and shut the door, then he picked up the torch.

Xavier put his hand on Josh's arm. "You are not going out there with the torch on. You'll be dead in seconds."

"I only need a second."

The horn honked again.

Xavier released him. "If you die, you'd better bloody haunt me."

"You'd better make sure I'm dead if I don't make it." He opened the lobby door for a third time. All he had to do was turn on the torch and toss it in the opposite direction. Easy.

His mouth dried.

He had to do it, no more thinking. He pressed the button and threw the torch as far as he could. It spun through the air and landed on the backs of the bugs on the road. The distraction was enough for the car to break free. The engine revved hard, then the car, freed of the bugs, accelerated toward him.

He scrambled inside, dragging Xavier away from the door with him. They hit the carpet as glass shattered and metal groaned. The rough scuttle of the bugs followed. Josh sprung up, hauling Xavier to his feet after knocking him down. Xavier fired in controlled single shots over Josh's shoulder as Josh moved them back.

"The bullets aren't stopping them. They're too protected."

Josh slammed the butt of his rifle into one that was getting too close. They were invading. "Turn off the lights. Turn off the fucking lights!"

The car engine stopped and the lights went out, but it was too little too late. The bugs were in, and they'd found the warm bodies.

Chapter Ten

THE GLASS DOOR was half open, wedged there by the car that looked like it had been in a major accident, rolled three times, then gone through a car wash made of wire scourers. More bugs were forcing their way in.

"We have to fall back," Xavier said, trying to keep the bugs away from him.

"I know." But he could see the driver. Her tear-streaked face was pressed against the glass. He pointed at her. "Get out."

He slammed the butt into a bug that was feeling out his leg. This is not how he was going to die. "The larvae didn't like piss. Maybe the adults are the same."

"Great," Xavier said. "I'll just wet myself." He backed up to the check-in counter.

Josh knew he was surrounded and more were pushing in, nudging the car.

Something thumped behind him, but he couldn't stop to look. "You alright?"

"Fine."

Josh climbed onto a chair with the bag of perfume bottles. The bugs put their feet on the chair like the universe's most hideous dog.

With their upturned faces and their feelers sweeping against his legs, Josh took aim and shot one point blank. It spattered.

"Found a weakness—their face."

"Found a fire extinguisher. You might want to take cover."

There was none. He wasn't getting on the floor with the bugs. He was trapped. "Do it."

Xavier stuck his head up and unleashed the contents of the fire extinguisher on the bugs. Powder sprayed over everything. Josh pulled his t-shirt up over his face. The bugs hissed and tried to scuttle away. Josh grabbed some of the perfume bottles and poured the contents on the shirts in the bag. Then he lit the cloth and tossed it on the bugs.

In the chaos, he was able to shoot a couple more in the face.

He kept his shirt up as a makeshift mask as he made for the car. Xavier sprayed anything that moved.

He yanked on the handle, but the door was stuck. He was going to have to break the glass. Something felt up his leg. "I've got a problem. "

"I see it. Don't move." The bug exploded, covering his leg in sticky guts.

He climbed onto the hood and used the muzzle of the rifle to make the first break. The windscreen shattered, and he used his feet to kick in the rest of the glass, then he reached in and half dragged the woman out. She knelt on the bonnet, sobbing. She was less of a woman and more of a teen, and she was clearly pregnant.

"Did the bugs hurt you?"

She shook her head.

"Great. Let's get out of here. Pull your shirt up." He yanked it up as he spoke. The air was thick with chemical powder from the fire extinguisher.

"Fisher, where are you?"

"Securing the dining-room door."

Xavier stepped back into the lobby. His skin was dusted with white. Fury blazed in his eyes, much like the first time Josh had seen him, *really seen him*. His team had been pinned. Josh's had gone into help. It had been rough, but they'd all gotten out. Somehow, after that, they'd been back at base cleaning up, and it had been on with a heat that burned them both and left them with nothing to say for the next three days. The next time had been more deliberate.

They'd gotten out of that, and they were going to get out of this too.

"Let's go." Xavier picked up the perfume bag.

Josh slid off the car and picked up the teen while Xavier covered their exit.

"Two o'clock," Josh said as something moved up the hallway.

Xavier fired, but the bullet deflected off the shell and into the wall. The girl flinched.

"I'm out."

Josh shrugged the rifle off his shoulder, Xavier took it.

Someone screamed. "I told Marsh to keep them all in their rooms."

"That wasn't the rooms. That's the gift shop," Xavier said. "Follow."

Josh did, hoping that there was nothing creeping up on his six. Light streamed out of the gift shop from a torch that lay forgotten on the floor. Four bugs were crawling over a man. One was digging in his gut, blood and intestines spilling on the white floor.

He writhed and screamed, trying to shove the bugs away. The one in his gut settled in. It seemed to stare at Josh, then its abdomen contracted as it emptied eggs or larvae or something into the man.

Josh's stomach twisted and hot bile raced up his throat. It was too late. "He's a farm."

Xavier lifted the rifle.

Josh turned away. Xavier fired, and the screaming stopped.

The girl cried, her face against his shirt.

Drawn by the light, the bugs crept through the corridor. Were they still forcing their way in through the broken lobby doors? This place would be overrun before morning.

"Josh. Joshy. Rayne."

"Yes." His gaze snapped to Xavier.

"We're going to move, nice and slow toward the rooms."

He nodded.

"You lead. I've got six, then we're all out."

"Keep three, just in case." He wasn't going to be used as a farm while alive.

They made it back to the lobby, but every time a bug brushed against his leg, he wanted to yelp and run. Moving slowly and carefully, they passed the bugs who were busy getting to the fresh body.

Don't think about it.

The dark corridor that led to the rooms seemed to be uninhabited. Only one door was open. Theirs. Fuck, how could they have been so stupid?

"We didn't close the door," Josh said.

There was at least one bug up here as he could hear it clicking, waiting. Probably in their room.

A door opened and someone peeked out. "Shut the fucking door unless told," Josh snapped. In a louder voice, he called, "The hotel has been breached. Keep your doors closed unless told by me or Fisher to open them."

"Scott's out there," came a muffled voice.

Josh sighed. He should've known it was Scott pilfering jewelry. He'd been thinking about ways to get rich since getting to town. "Scott's dead."

No amount of gold or pearls would bring him back.

"Marsh," Xavier called. "Open your door."

A door about halfway along opened an inch. Marsh only opened it fully when they got there. The room was lit only by moonlight. One bed had been slept in, the other was empty. Josh put the girl on the made bed.

"Is anyone hurt? Do you need a medic?" Marsh's gaze flicked between the three of them.

"Probably, but I think we can all wait until daylight," Xavier said. He dropped into the only chair, propped the rifle next to him, and stretched out his injured leg.

Josh leaned against the door like he could keep the bugs on the other side. He stared at the girl. "Want to tell us why you were out at night?"

The girl looked up. "It was the only time I could escape."

"What do you mean?"

"You came to the police station…the first people to come since the aliens took everyone. I knew if I didn't leave tonight, then I'd never be free. You have to take me with you." Her eyes widened. "You can't leave me here."

"I thought you only saw a man?" Xavier asked.

"I did. And he didn't want our help." And Josh knew why now. "Was he keeping you hostage?"

The girl's face contorted. "At first, he protected me."

"Let me guess. Then he wanted something for that protection," Marsh said, her face grim.

The girl nodded.

"Sick fuck," Josh muttered.

Marsh sat next to the girl. "How old are you?"

"Seventeen."

"What's your name?"

"Kayla."

Marsh smiled. "We'll look after you."

Josh glanced at Xavier. Of course they were going to take the girl, but the maniac in the cop shop was going to be pissed. "How did you escape?"

"I waited for him to fall asleep. Then I crept out. He knows I'm scared of the dark and the bugs. He threatened to throw me out if I didn't do what he said." Her body convulsed as she started crying again.

"Is that why you turned the headlights on? Because you don't like the dark?"

"They came on automatically." She sniffed. "Don't let him take me back."

"We won't." But they had six bullets, and he had the police armory. Josh tipped his head back against the door.

"Why don't you come with me to the bathroom? We'll clean you up and give you something to eat." Marsh got the girl moving and shut the door.

"This is a bad place to be stuck," Xavier whispered.

"I know. We need to leave now."

"The streets are crawling. We'll lose people, and I…I…can't." Xavier's voice cracked.

"It was a mercy."

Xavier nodded. "But I can't."

Could he? "What are we going to do with her captor? Save him?"

Xavier's lip curled. "We should. He's a survivor, and technically, he kept her safe."

"Did he? Really? He found himself a sex slave and made himself king of Georgetown." Josh wouldn't mind putting the light on him and leaving him to sort it out.

"What can we give her?"

"A chance to be free. She risked her life to get here. She's terrified of him."

"He's going to retaliate."

The bathroom door opened, and Kayla got into the nearest bed.

Marsh came over to them, water bottle in hand. She spoke softly, but Josh was sure Kayla heard everything. "The baby isn't his. She was working at the supermarket when it happened. She hid in one of the big fridges. He found her a few days later, promised to keep her safe. There were a few survivors, but now it's only them. She's pretty sure he'll come after her."

Josh accepted the water and took a drink before passing it to Xavier. "We're almost about out of ammo. We can't make a stand here."

He didn't want to make a stand at all.

Marsh checked her watch. "It's one in the morning."

They had hours and couldn't do anything until daylight. And he was too wired to sleep.

Chapter Eleven

JOSH SAT on the floor and unknotted the bits of laces holding his boots together. The last occupant of the room had left a selection of shoes, including a pair of hiking boots which Josh had stolen the laces from. He'd already changed T-shirt and tossed a clean one to Xavier. Xavier had used a little water to wipe the dust and muck from his skin.

Josh's pants were beyond ruined. Like Xavier, he needed to switch to something else. Not shorts though; this was not a golfing trip. He rummaged through the guy's wardrobe, hoping there'd be some sensible pants since there were hiking boots. He found what he was looking for and changed. They were a size too big, and that was before he'd lost weight on this mission. He belted them on. They'd do.

Xavier leaned against the headboard, hands behind his head. His eyes were closed, but Josh doubted he was asleep. The hotel echoed with clicks and scuttles.

Marsh and Kayla lay on the other bed.

It didn't matter how he ran the numbers, people died.

He expected cop shop guy to arrive heavily armed to take the girl back. People would die.

If they tried to leave early, the bugs would come after their warm bodies and lights. People would die.

The only thing keeping them safe were the pathetic doors that didn't even lock properly.

"I can hear you thinking," Xavier said, barely louder than the bugs outside the door.

"And I can hear you both, so shut up and go to sleep," Marsh muttered before turning over.

Josh scrubbed his hand over his face. He needed to sleep. Sitting up all night playing different ideas through his head wasn't going to change anything. He paced over to the bed and lay next to Xavier. Xavier slithered down into his arms and kissed the end of Josh's nose.

Neither of them spoke.

They didn't need to.

With Xavier held tight, Josh closed his eyes. When he opened them, the room was filled with pale gray pre-dawn light. For several heartbeats he lay there, listening to the roll of the ocean on the beach. If he closed his eyes again, maybe he could forget where he was.

He gave Xavier a nudge. His eyes flicked open. He glanced at Josh, then sighed.

Josh slid off the bed, then cracked open the door. The corridor was bug free. If they'd all gone to hide for the day, that meant the other guy would be on the move.

And if he'd stayed alive this long, he knew where they were. He must do resupply runs on a regular basis. There was only so much one man could carry, and Josh doubted he let Kayla out to help. He probably didn't let her out of the police station.

Xavier was right behind him. "You've got a plan."

"I wouldn't give it the dignity of calling it that." He shut the door. It was enough to wake Marsh and Kayla. Kayla was sleepy, but Marsh sat up ready to go even though her face suggested that she really needed a coffee or she was going to kill someone.

Josh was about ready to eat instant out of the jar. His mouth watered. Crunchy coffee granules sounded far too good. Perhaps he could find some in the restaurant.

"We need weapons, so we have to go to the shooting range—"

"He went there already," Kayla said.

"Fuck."

"So we hit up the cop shop," Xavier said. "While he's not there, meaning he'll be here."

Kayla paled.

"What did he take from the shooting range?" Josh asked, hoping that there'd be something left.

"Lots. Guns, crates of bullets…" She shrugged.

And he had the police armory too. Including bullet-proof vests and riot gear. Even a small town like this kept enough to equip a few cops.

"Why didn't he take a boat and leave?"

"He said that the rest of Australia was the same, that we needed to survive. He said when others came, we'd all band together. Then I heard him turning you away. I already knew he was an asshole… but that made me realize he's also a liar."

Josh glanced out the window. The sky was getting too light. They needed to move.

"Okay. Marsh, you're going to take Kayla and a couple of others down to the boat, load it up, and hole up there. If this all goes tits up, you're on your way to Darwin. Fisher and I are going to circle back to the cop shop and raid the building while he's out. Everyone else is going to stay put."

"Why not send everyone to the boat?" Marsh asked. "Why not flee now?"

"Because we need weapons," Xavier said. "A few pistols won't do much if the Geckos attack us."

"And he knows we're here. He expects there to be people, so we need to give him a welcoming committee. We'll also provide a distraction."

Marsh nodded but wasn't happy given the set of her lips.

"How are we getting to the cop shop?" Xavier asked, tapping his thigh. He wasn't up for making a quick run.

"Cars are too noisy. Bicycle? I saw some out the back yesterday. We can drive to the boat as it won't matter. Kayla, I need you to draw a map of the police station and where he keeps the weapons." Josh pulled the pen and paper off the desk and tossed it on the bed. "We have five minutes to get ready. I don't want to wait until sunrise."

They woke everyone up and told them they were about to be attacked by one man with lots of fire power but Fisher and he were going to head him off. A few muttered about helping Kayla and risking their own necks.

Xavier stepped forward, holding the one working rifle. "Our orders are to collect survivors and get them out of the infested area. That is what we are doing. If you don't like it, you are welcome to stay."

Dave crossed his arms and glared at Xavier. "I want to go to the boat."

"No. Marsh is taking Kayla, Clarence, and Bird. They will load up. Too many will be too obvious. He needs to think we are all here because if he sees us all running for the boat, what do you think he's going to do?"

"Sink the boat," Tye said, jaw locked and grim.

Young glanced around the lobby. "You're leaving us with the bugs."

"Yeah. They're everywhere, but they seem pretty quiet during the day. So let them get their beauty rest, and you'll be fine."

Dave's scowl deepened. "What happened to Scott?"

"He was out, despite being told to stay in the room, but you knew that. You're his room buddy," Josh said. It had been Dave who'd told them Scott was out last night. He knew Scott was dead. "You should've raised the alarm that he'd snuck out." He was sick of the questions. They were running out of time.

"What happened to him?" Dave pressed.

"The bugs got him." Xavier's voice was flat.

"You let them kill him." Dave pointed at Josh and Xavier. "You saved her though. Fancy a bit a pussy, do you?"

Josh laughed, startling himself. When was the last time he'd laughed? Then he swallowed the laughter, his heart beating fast like he was running for his life.

"I'm gay, mate." That shut the civvie up. And saying it out loud didn't kill him the way he expected it to. Instead, there was a loosening in his chest as though he could put that burden down for the moment. "Follow orders, don't fuck around, and we'll all get out of here. No one deserves to die like Scott, but we can't be everywhere."

"Is he your boyfriend?" Dave asked, nodding at Xavier.

"Fiancé, actually," Xavier said. "But what we do in our spare time doesn't affect this. Rayne is in charge. Marsh, you have your orders. Everyone else, you're to pack up. Take extra clothing. Fill vehicles. Prepare to leave. But do not leave. Do not draw this guy to the boat or we'll be stranded here, and no one wants that. If you see the man or anything else out-of-place, report it to Tye. He'll be in charge of the hotel. Consider the man armed and dangerous."

He was definitely unhinged, but who wasn't at this point of the invasion?

Xavier took a pain pill and his antibiotics with a mouthful of water. Fallon handed out sandwiches made of rice cakes and peanut butter. It stuck to the roof of Josh's mouth, but at least it was food.

He licked his fingers. "You ready to go?"

"Sure. Let's get this done."

They took the one working rifle and instructed the remaining sailors on how to use the perfume bottles. They left the last radio with Tye along with a pistol.

The bugs had retreated deeper into the hotel. The door to the dining area was still shut, but there was nothing they could do about the pile of insects in what had been the jewelry show room.

Josh waited until the vehicles with the supplies, Marsh, and the others were driving away. Then he waited to make sure they weren't being followed.

The streets were still.

He drew in a breath of warm salt air, then nodded at Xavier. They grabbed a couple of bikes, including one with a kiddie carriage at the back meant for tourists, and took off through the back streets.

They stopped at a few houses and borrowed the gas bottles attached to their barbeques, placing them in the carriage on the back of Josh's bike, before turning down the street where the hospital was. His legs were burning from the extra weight, but Xavier shouldn't have been riding. He'd be ripping his stitches open.

"You know, I have a bad feeling about this." Xavier stopped and stared at the building that must have been crawling with larvae growing into adults.

"Same. But it'll be a good distraction, and we really need to make sure the pests don't spread."

Xavier pressed his lips together and nodded. "There'll be oxygen and all kinds of gasses in there."

"I'm hoping so."

"The parents might get pissed."

"I love you," Josh said. "I just wanted you to know."

"No. You don't get to jinx a mission by pulling that shit. You take it back."

Josh leaned the bike against the wall of the building opposite. "I can't. All this time and we never——"

"For good reason."

"And now that reason has run out. We aren't going to live forever." Maybe not past this morning if this went badly. "I don't want you to think it meant nothing."

Why had they always been so casual? Pretending that it didn't matter, that they didn't matter to each other when his whole world spun around the times when they were both in the same place at the same time?

Xavier got off the bike and grabbed Josh by the scruff of his T-shirt. "I always knew. I always had a reason to come home so I could see your stupid face again. And I want to see it every morning for the rest of my life—and I don't want you shortening my life or yours because you've got another shit plan."

"I want to go to bed with you every night. Plus, you owe me one." Josh rested his forehead on Xavier's. Their noses touched, then Josh leaned in and took a kiss. "You're going to like this plan."

"I never do."

"I'm going into the hospital."

"I hate it already."

"And I'm going to put the bottles in a small room and turn on the gas."

"The larvae will be quick to find you."

"I'll be fast. We'll give it a few minutes then toss in a Molly. If I don't come out—"

"You will."

"If I don't, you need to do it. Don't leave me alive in there." He'd survived the farm once; he didn't know if his luck would hold a second time.

Xavier swore and glared at him. "You are such a prick."

"Just take up a position where you can keep watch and do the deed if needed."

"Where are you going in?"

"The back. The front is all emergency waiting rooms and foyer." Josh picked up both gas bottles, and they walked around the back. There was a staff only door that opened readily enough with a little encouragement from his boot.

The stink of death rolled out and made him gag.

"Hey, Joshy. Piss yourself."

"You just want to see my dick." But Xavier was right; it would buy him a bit more time. He took a moment, then wet his boots and new pants.

When he turned around, Xavier had walked away to crouch with the industrial bins. Josh picked up the bottles and made his way into the hospital. Without electric lights, the hospital was dim, but there were things moving in there. A squeak over lino as the larvae searched out new food.

Josh stepped into the first open door he found. It looked like a small staff room. Did he need to go deeper? Find something smaller that would fill up faster?

Out the window, the sky was already pink. He didn't have time for perfect. He never did. He opened the gas bottles, then shut the door. There were larvae in the corridor already. Overhead, something scuttled.

How many adult bugs were in here?

He didn't want to know.

That's when he noticed the ceiling was bowing. The larvae dropped through where it was coming away from the join. As he watched, the tear widened.

Chapter Twelve

JOSH DARTED across the hallway as the ceiling collapsed. Larvae and bugs hit the ground. He slammed the door shut and pressed his back against it. The scent of gas was already on the air.

"Fuck." He was running out of time, and his exit had been cut off.

The radio on his belt crackled. "What happened?"

"Ceiling came down under the weight...the weight of the larvae." He glanced up. How long would this bit hold?

"Get out of there."

"I'm trying." But his mind was static. Years of training and active duty had been erased, and he couldn't move.

"I'm coming to you."

"Stay where you are." He didn't want Xavier getting caught in this mess.

"Where are you?"

He glanced around the room. It was a bathroom with two showers and two toilet cubicles, each one with a high and narrow window that he wasn't even sure he'd fit through.

"See the small windows to your right of the doorway?" Something, a bug, scrabbled at the door. He couldn't go out there. And he couldn't fit through the window.

The scent of gas was getting stronger as it filtered out from the staff room and spread.

He couldn't light it from in here without blowing himself up or incinerating his lungs and giving himself burns that wouldn't be able to be treated. At least larvae could be plucked off. Bugs could be batted away. He was going to have to leave the bathroom via the door.

"Talk to me, Josh," Xavier's metallic voice ordered.

"Just thinking through a few things." He kicked open the locked cupboards. There were packets of paper towels, toilet paper, and cleaning products.

"Get your ass out here. I don't care if you have to swim through larvae and I'm pulling them off you for a week." Xavier swore. "I can hear a vehicle. We're out of time."

Yeah, he was. He'd pass out from a lack of oxygen soon.

He picked up a bottle labeled ammonia and cracked it open. There was ammonia in piss. It might work. "How clear is the exit?"

"It's not. It's full of rubble and bugs. You need another exit."

Josh nodded, wishing there were a good option. "Okay, here's the plan. I'm going to exit out of the big window on your left."

"Where the gas is."

"Yes."

Xavier was silent for a couple of seconds, no doubt having the same concerns as him. "I'm going to take the liberty of smashing one for you."

"Thanks. Be there in ten."

He pulled his shirt off and wrapped it around his face. Then he splashed ammonia on himself like it was holy water, wasting two seconds.

His heart pounded on his ribs, and his breathing quickened. He didn't know if that was because he wasn't getting enough oxygen or if it was stress. Maybe both.

"I'm not dying like this." He repeated the mantra as he cracked open the toilet door and threw some ammonia at the larvae and small pale bugs—teen bugs, he was guessing.

Like they had done with the piss, they backed away. But this time, they didn't stay away. Josh kept pouring the stuff, clearing a path as best he could, even though it was obvious the cleaning product wasn't working very well.

The ceiling was split, the way out completely blocked with rubble and equipment.

Glass shattered, and he really hoped it was Xavier.

He drew in a deep breath, then ran across the corridor, barreled into the staff room, and kept running, his lungs burning.

Xavier was using the butt of his rifle to clear the broken glass. He pulled off his shirt, tossed it over the frame, and stepped back. Josh vaulted through like aliens were after him. He hit the ground and rolled up to his knees, sucking in air that was still tainted.

"You right?"

Josh nodded. "Find some cover."

Xavier was half-way to the bins, jogging with a limp, before Josh pulled out the lighter and a little liquor bottle. His hand was bleeding, and he was pretty sure his leg was too as something was running down his calf. Josh took a few steps back, wanting to be close enough to get the Molly through the window but not close enough that he lit up.

He reckoned it was fifty-fifty. Not bad odds, but not great either.

There was gas out here now, wafting out of the broken window. He shoved the scrap of rag into the bottle, then sucked in a breath and flicked the lighter. When he didn't catch fire, he relaxed a little, but that didn't stop his hand from shaking as he held the lighter to the cloth. It caught, and he took a couple of steps forward and threw.

For half a second, he didn't think it was going to make it. Then it sailed over the windowsill.

He turned and ran. Xavier stood and yanked him to the gravel.

He hit the ground, air escaping his lungs. The gravel bit his bare skin, but before he could register the discomfort, the hospital blew up. Heat and noise surrounded him. Debris rained down.

But they were already getting up and running down the side street, pressing up against the wall. Josh glanced back at the now burning hospital, his chest heaving as he cleared his lungs of the gas.

"You good?" Xavier asked.

"Yeah. You?"

"Yeah. I think we're shouting."

Without saying anything else, they collected the bikes, Josh unhitched the bright kiddie carriage, and they rode to the police station. They parked around the back and watched the door for a moment.

"What are the odds there's a trap?" Josh whispered.

"That would imply that he knows this is our target."

Josh nodded. He might; one didn't survive by being stupid, and he knew Josh wanted weapons. He got up and pulled the pistol out. Like Xavier, he had a limited number of shots and no refills. He'd left the spare clip with the sailors, who were busy packing anything useful like they were going to drive away.

Keeping low, he approached the door. Locked. The glass would be bullet proof. He considered shooting the lock, but he didn't want to waste the bullets he had. He lifted his gaze to the roof. Or he could go in like he was an over fed larva. He shoved the pistol away, jumped up, and grabbed the gutter. His shoulder protested, but he ignored it and swung up onto the roof.

"We've got company," he called out as he slid over the ridge line and lay flat.

A cop car pulled into the carpark, lights flashing.

Xavier crouched between two cars, rifle ready.

Josh willed the man to leave. To see that nothing was amiss and fuck off.

He wriggled the pistol out. From this angle and distance he'd be lucky, and he was pretty sure that he'd used up all of his luck for the day, possibly the week.

If this guy were smart, he'd have crept up on them. Was he more worried about his supplies or the girl?

At least if he was here, everyone else was safe.

The car door opened, and the man put his hands up. "I know you're here. Don't shoot me."

Josh flicked the safety off and tracked the man through the pistol sights as he got out of the car.

He kept his hands up. He was fully kitted out in police riot gear, including the body armor and helmet. He didn't step away from the car, and Josh couldn't see what weapons he was carrying.

"I changed my mind; I want to go with you."

That was bullshit. He wanted the girl back. Josh sighed. That was uncharitable. Maybe he had changed his mind and wanted out. A sane person would want out.

He scanned the area, and his arms lowered a little as though wondering if he was wrong and talking to himself. "I saw what you did to the hospital. At least they were contained there. Now they'll be looking for a new place to breed."

Not if I burn everything first.

If they took out the Geckos food supply, would that make them leave?

Josh lowered his aim to the man's unprotected leg. It wouldn't kill him, but it would inconvenience him. It was also a much smaller target.

He lowered his hands. "Fine. I'll make you a trade. I'll give you some guns and ammo, and you give me Kayla." He turned around in a full circle. "I know you're here. Show yourself!"

Josh didn't move.

Where was Xavier?

Seconds ticked by. The tile roof was heating up, and sweat rolled along his spine. Blood dripped from his hand onto the roof and started its long journey downhill to the gutter.

The man muttered something and kicked at the gravel. He didn't look happy. He'd wanted someone to be here. For a heartbeat, Josh felt sorry for him. But only one heartbeat. The man could've welcomed them yesterday and let Kayla go. Not keeping a human hostage was always a good place to start if you wanted to be seen as reasonable.

Then the man lifted his gaze and looked straight at Josh.

He grinned. Then he dropped as blood sprayed out of his leg. He screamed like he'd never been shot before. It wasn't fun, and it stung like a bitch. But rolling around and crying about it didn't stop the pain or heal the wound.

Xavier scrambled up and approached the man, rifle ready.

The man's hand moved.

"Get back!" Josh called, but it was too late. The screaming had been a cover. The man fired.

Xavier dropped the rifle and lay twitching on the gravel of the carpark.

The man picked up the rifle, pointed it at Xavier's head, and grinned. "Get down here, or I shoot him."

Chapter Thirteen

JOSH CLOSED his eyes and rested his forehead on his arm. He had to think, but he wasn't sure he was capable anymore.

"I'm only going to count to three," the man said. "One."

Josh looked up. Xavier had stopped twitching and was lying perfectly still except for his right hand, the one the man couldn't see, which was tapping the ground with two fingers.

Josh waited, even though it was killing him.

"Two."

Josh swung over the ridge line of the roof and skidded down to the gutter.

"Throw me the gun." The man was watching Josh now, thinking Xavier was out of action. Josh flicked the safety on and ejected the magazine, then threw down the pistol.

Xavier moved, knocking the rifle out of the man's hands. Then he shoved his fingers into the bullet wound in the man's leg. The man howled like his soul was being ripped out.

Josh jumped down from the roof and scooped up the pistol. By the time he reached the car, Xavier had the man on his belly with his arms pinned.

Josh pulled the cuffs off the man's belt, and even though he struggled and fought, they got him cuffed and sitting propped up against the car. Xavier ripped off the man's helmet and body armor.

"Aren't you a piece of shit?" Xavier pressed the toe of his boot into the wound and twisted.

The man cried out. "You can't hurt me you—"

"I can and I am. Did Kayla beg you to stop?"

"She's a slut; everyone knows it."

Josh slapped him in the face. "You're worse than the aliens. You're human, but you were more than happy to hurt her and more than happy to kill us."

Xavier plucked the barbs from the Taser off his chest and dropped them on the ground. "Give me the key."

The man spat. "You aren't getting anything from me."

Xavier squatted. Only the slight tightening around his eyes indicated he was in pain. "Look mate, you have two choices. Give us the weapons and come with us to Darwin or stay here."

"What makes you think there's anything left?"

"What makes you think there isn't? What were you going to do when the food ran out? When the bugs decided to camp out front until you make a mistake?"

"Or they sit on the roof until it caves in?" Josh added. That was something he hadn't thought about last night. Now he'd never be able to forget.

The man glanced between them. "We were fine. We'd have been fine if you hadn't shown up."

"She'd have eventually stabbed you in the neck and left you for the bugs, and you know it." Xavier stood. "Give me one reason we shouldn't do the same?"

Josh got in the car and searched the front seat and center console for the keys. Then he looked at the bunch of keys hanging out of the ignition. Surely not... He pulled them out. "Fisher, I reckon one of these might do the job."

"Hey, you can't take that!"

"Why? Because you stole them first?" Josh glanced at Xavier. He nodded, and Josh went up to the door and tried a few keys until it unlocked. "Bring him."

Xavier hauled the man to his feet and half dragged him to the doorway. "Any traps?" When he didn't answer, they shoved him in first.

The man stumbled but walked through without setting off anything.

Xavier sat him in a chair and kept guard while Josh went through the station. He didn't have to go far. All the weapons were in a locked cell, opposite the one that had been set up as a bedroom. He opened it, and the first thing he did was put on a bullet-proof vest. He'd missed the friendly weight. Then he kitted up with everything he could lay his hands on. He stopped when he saw an unfamiliar piece of tech. It didn't look like a weapon, but he couldn't be sure.

He turned the hexagonal shaped device in his hand. It was like nothing he'd ever seen before. It was the same color as the metal the alien base was made of. Was it alien tech? He grabbed it and went back out to where Xavier waited.

He gave Xavier a nod, and then he went to arm himself.

The man watched wide eyed. "Who the hell are you people?"

"The rescue party. I told you that yesterday, but you didn't want our help." Josh sat on the edge of a desk and studied the guy. He must be mid-forties, and he looked soft. Like this was the first trouble he'd ever run into. "What's your name?"

"Andrew."

"What did you do before the invasion?"

He hesitated. "I ran a pharmacy."

"And how did you end up here? Where are the cops?"

"They went to help people when the aliens came."

"Tell me what happened." Josh put the alien device on the table next to him.

Andrew glanced at it and licked his lip. "It doesn't matter. You should know…where were you when it happened?"

Josh smiled. "I was on holiday. Got recalled real fast and dropped off in the desert, I've seen so many empty towns and stations. I want to know how it happens. And you're going to tell me." He glanced at the wound on Andrew's thigh. "If left untreated, that's going to fester."

"You blew up the hospital, but there's still three chemists. There's plenty of tinned and shelf stable food. I'd have been right for years without you."

"And if the baby was breech? What exactly were you hoping to do? Restart the human population?"

Andrew's cheeks darkened.

Oh, Christ… Josh shook his head. "What happened when the Geckos invaded?"

"They showed up—"

"On what? How did they arrive?"

"I don't know. They just showed up and started shooting people. I hid in the roof space of my pharmacy. I stayed there for two days. Then when I came out, everyone was dead or gone. I thought there might be cops still alive, so I came here. But they were gone. Then I went to find food, and I found Kayla. I took care of her, and she thanked me."

"Shut up." Did Andrew honestly believe that? That because he was helping, he was entitled to payment?

Xavier reappeared, dressed for action. He dropped a duffle bag on the ground. "A few extras. Found some flash bangs too."

"Nice." He gave Xavier a grin.

"Want to tell me what this is, Andrew?"

"Dunno. I found it."

"Found it where?"

Andrew shrugged and looked away. He was a liar and a rapist. They shouldn't even waste a bullet on him.

He grabbed Andrew by the arm and jerked him up right. Andrew went for a headbutt.

Josh deflected with his shoulder—which didn't appreciate the jarring. He slammed Andrew back into the chair and put his knee on the wound. "How about you stop trying to be a hero and do as you're fucking told?"

Andrew squirmed like a worm on a hook. "I was given it."

"By who?"

Blood dripped down Andrew's face from his smashed nose.

Xavier nudged Josh away. "Answer the questions, mate."

"I see what you're doing."

"No, you don't. You have no idea what we've seen and done." Xavier leaned in closer. "Now answer the damn question, or I'll walk out the door and let him cut out the answers."

"You'll be court martialed." Andrew panted for breath. "I'm a civilian."

"I really don't give a fuck," Josh said. And he realized it was the truth. There was nothing anyone could do to him that was worse than what he'd already survived.

Andrew stared at him, his eyes widening. "The aliens were rounding up people. I said I'd help."

"How?"

"They gave me this and told me to report if more people came here."

That was a punch to the gut that made Josh rock back. "You fucking traitor."

Xavier held him back so he couldn't lay into Andrew the way he wanted to. He was going to kill him and leave him for the bugs.

"Have you already told them we're here?"

"I don't want to die!" Andrew cried.

Shit. The aliens were on their way. "So you've condemned us?"

Josh stopped fighting Xavier and shrugged off his hold. "I don't want to take him. He's going to be nothing but trouble."

"He's a survivor; we have to." But Xavier's expression was grim.

There were only the two of them. No one else would know. But one look at Xavier, and Josh knew that killing Andrew was never going to fly. He blew out a breath.

Blood dripped on the floor.

Josh huffed out a breath. "You know he's going to try to shoot us the first chance he gets, right?"

"Probably," Xavier agreed.

"Then why?"

Xavier pinned him with a glance. "Because I don't want to be as bad as him. I'm still a soldier, and so are you."

Chapter Fourteen

XAVIER MARCHED ANDREW to the cop car and shoved him in the back.

Josh picked up the bag of weapons and the alien device and followed.

"We need to get the civvies out of here," Xavier said after he'd shut the car door.

"We all need to get out of here." Josh walked around and leaned on the roof; he'd rather talk there than in the car where Andrew was listening. "We'll call the others and tell them to head for the boat."

"The boat should go now. We can always take another."

"What about those at the hotel? They'll be ready to leave. We can be down there in five minutes."

Xavier shook his head. "If we run, we'll be hunted."

"If we stay, we'll be hunted." He was not going to be rounded up and sent back to the farm.

"I didn't say we should stay, just that we let the boat get away." Xavier held his gaze. "Make the call. Let Marsh know."

Josh looked away first. Someone had to make it home and make a report, and someone had to make sure they had a chance. "I hate it when you're right."

Xavier smiled. "I know."

Josh picked up the radio. "This is Rayne. Marsh come in."

"Marsh here."

"We've got a complication. The Geckos know we are here and are inbound. Get underway now."

"We can wait."

Josh closed his eyes and drew in a breath. "No. Leave now. We'll take another boat or drive across the peninsular and meet up with you. Leave before you don't have the chance. Tell the brass what we told you."

"Damn it…get your ass down here."

Xavier leaned over the car and took the radio out of Josh's hand. Josh didn't resist. "It's Fisher. Your orders are to leave and make haste to Darwin, understood?"

"Understood. But I don't like it."

"We'll hold them off. Have a safe trip." He handed the radio back to Josh, looking as sick as Josh felt.

It was the right thing to do, but it didn't make it easy. Josh took a moment before saying what felt like goodbye. "I'll see you around, Marsh. We'll send you an invitation to the wedding."

"Yeah. You do that. Marsh out."

Josh leaned on the roof and drew in a couple of breaths. "Guess we'd better prepare a welcome party."

Xavier reached out and took his hand. The ring on Josh's finger glinted in the morning sunlight. There was blood smeared over the silver and on his skin. He didn't know whose it was. Xavier gave it a rub with his thumb. "Want to pick a new hotel?"

"Sure, I fancied a few more days here. The sun, the beaches, all the free tinned food I can eat. It's almost a holiday."

"It's better because we can blow up things. It'll be like old times." Xavier forced a smile.

Except this time, there was no end date to their mission. There would be no flight home. He gripped Xavier's hand. It would be nothing like the old times. This time, they weren't hiding.

Revolt

Australia is split in half, humans on the east and aliens on the west, and Josh and Xavier are on the wrong side of the line. They need to make it from alien territory back home. But with aliens hunting them and survivors to protect, all their plans start to unravel.

To survive, they'll have to fight.

They have discovered the aliens are not invincible, and they have weaknesses. Armed with new knowledge, Josh and Xavier are determined to stop the aliens so no one else ends up imprisoned on the base. But going back to the base means risking their lives and the future they have promised each other.

Book Three in the Captured Earth trilogy. For readers who like action, explosions, and don't mind a little gore with their gay romance.

Chapter One

"SO ARE we going to run sneak attacks, set up an ambush and hope they walk into it, or confront them?" Xavier hefted the pack of water into the ute they'd commandeered. The owner was never going to look for it, so it wasn't really stolen.

Josh wanted to tie Andrew, the human who'd betrayed them to the aliens, to a stake in the middle of town and use him as bait. But he doubted he'd have any support from Xavier or the three sailors and one civilian, who'd remained behind and were none too happy about it. One boat of survivors was on its way to Darwin. Lucky bastards.

Josh didn't begrudge the sailors their ill feelings. He wanted to go home, too. But how long until the aliens decided they wanted to take over Sydney or Melbourne? Nowhere was safe while they were still breathing and using human bodies to feed to their bugs.

Josh leaned on the tray of the ute, sweat rolling down his spine. His clothes were damp, and his skin was slick. It was, once again, fucking hot. "What we need to do is get Andrew to tell us how the device works. I want to know what the aliens are doing."

Xavier shook his head. One dark braid slid out from beneath his hat and bounced over his sunglasses. "He's not saying a word. He knows as soon as he talks, he's got no value. I think we need to watch and wait."

Shits like Andrew had no value, anyway. They were the roaches that flipped and worked for the enemy as soon as they thought it was beneficial.

"Watching and waiting didn't work out so good last time." The three teams the army had sent out to observe and evacuate human survivors had all been picked up by the aliens. Josh and Xavier were the only survivors he knew of. "We don't have the numbers to spread out." If they set up sentries, they'd be too easily picked off by an invading force. They had no idea how many would turn up. "If we set it up right, we can get them to walk right in."

"How?"

"They are expecting to find more people for their bloody farm, so let's give them people." The pearl and silver engagement ring on his finger glinted in the sun. There was blood crusted in the setting, and it wasn't practical to keep wearing it. But he didn't want to take it off and risk losing it.

Xavier lifted one eyebrow. "Are you trying to create the shittiest plan ever?"

"I have to keep myself occupied somehow." Josh tossed him a grin. "We burn down the hotel, bugs inside."

"That part sounds reasonable." They walked back into the abandoned supermarket together. They were stripping it of whatever water and food they could carry. After running a couple of tests on the bugs in the hotel, they had determined that it was urea that killed the bugs. Another team of two had been sent to gather as much as they could from the hardware store.

They'd left one sailor and the one remaining civilian to watch over Andrew, who was tied to a chair in the bug filled hotel.

They had enough food and water and weapons for a sustained fight.

But the fight wouldn't last more than a day. Either they'd be dead or the aliens would be. If they survived, they'd hop on one of those nice boats in the pens and hightail it to Darwin; Marsh said

she'd left a sign on the one they should take. If they didn't survive…
well, all the supplies would go to waste.

Josh didn't like wasting supplies. And he didn't want to die
fighting the tall, oversized, see through skinned, lizard-like invaders
either.

He was sure scientists would say they weren't lizards, but they
had a tail and ate bugs. And they looked a lot like the tiny, pale
skinned geckos that scampered up walls. Which was why everyone
had taken to calling them Geckos.

"It's not too late to run, Joshy."

They'd been having this argument on and off for the last few
hours, ever since Andrew's betrayal had been revealed and the boat
had left without them. It was too late to run. He was sick of running
and looking over his shoulder. They had to make a stand. "They'll
hunt us if they find no one here. They'll take out the boat."

"They might have done that all ready."

"I know." He just tried not to think about it. He liked the idea of
the other's getting away and telling the people in charge what they
knew. What the base was like. They'd both given Marsh a report.

"Maybe I like the idea of running away with you and never
having to worry about fighting off aliens again," Xavier said
without a smile. He was serious.

For a moment, Josh let himself indulge in that pleasant dream,
but they were living in a nightmare, and it didn't matter what he
did, he couldn't wake up. It didn't matter where they went; the
aliens were everywhere. Except for the colder places, but that news
was over a month old. Still, he wanted to believe that it was true. "I
heard Scandinavia is nice this time of year."

"Bit far away given there's no plane travel." Xavier led the way
along the aisle.

Josh followed, tossing things into the trolley. They were packing
as if they were going to survive. He wasn't sure they would. They
already had enough food and water to make it to Darwin. This was
just time wasting, but he wasn't ready for it to end. "We could sail
south to Tasmania."

Neither of them had ever sailed anywhere. He knew nothing

about sails or ropes, and while he could read a map, he wasn't sure that was the same as reading a nautical chart. He hoped the sailors would know what to do.

"That's more like it. It's meant to be pretty there."

"If it's Gecko free, that's pretty enough for me." Josh picked up another crate of water, leaving the lighter stuff for Xavier as his leg was still healing. And while most of the time he was getting around with only a small limp, by the end of the day, it was clearly giving him trouble. The antibiotics had cleared up the infection, which was a relief.

Josh couldn't do this on his own. He needed Xavier.

They put the last lot of supplies in the ute and got in. Xavier shut his door and glanced over. "So, do you actually have a plan?"

"Do you?" He was tired of thinking of solutions to problems that shouldn't exist. Nothing in his training had prepared him for fighting aliens or the bugs they'd brought with them as a food source.

Xavier nodded. "We burn down the hotel."

"That was my plan."

"It was a good start. Then we turn on the lights in a different one and set up nearby to pick them off one by one."

"That's what I'd been thinking. But Andrew or that device will give us away."

"He's going to be in the building with the lights."

"I don't want to lose the device. If we can figure out how it works…" No one was ready to start chopping off Andrew's toes until he spoke except him. He didn't like what that said about him. That he was desperate, pessimistic, and ready to break?

Xavier hadn't said a thing; he hadn't needed to. The look in his eyes had been enough.

In the afternoon sun, that spat had been forgotten, and they were pretending that everything would be fine, the way it had been so many times when it was clear nothing was ever going on be fine. It was exactly the same way they'd avoided talking about their relationship for three years.

"We'll figure out how to get it working, and if we don't, someone in Sydney will."

We aren't going to make it to Sydney. Josh wasn't even sure they'd make it to nightfall.

Josh started the ute. The air-con blasted him with the promise of arctic winter. He lifted his arms so the breeze could hit him in the pits for a few seconds. He closed his eyes and let himself imagine living somewhere cold and alien free.

Cold.

"What?" Xavier asked, as he slammed the door.

Josh cracked open an eye. "Nothing."

"You had an idea."

"It's not an idea." It wasn't even half an idea. "The Geckos don't like the cold."

"And?" Xavier turned the vents on him and paused. "You want to chauffeur them around town?"

"No…maybe. What if we could find a refrigerated truck?"

"Ice cream truck?"

"Supermarket delivery truck."

"And then what?"

Josh shook his head. "I told you it wasn't really an idea."

He doubted they could force a bunch of heat loving aliens to walk into a nicely chilled truck to die. And once they were in there? Then what? Would the cold kill them? Put them to sleep? Or just piss them off?

"What about liquid nitrogen?" Xavier said.

"What's that got to do with a truck?"

"Nothing, but I bet there's some in the doctor's clinic. It's not the kind of thing people would think to steal as it's only good for freezing off warts."

"Except you." Josh smiled at his lover. "We'll stop off and grab it."

Xavier shrugged. "Don't know what we'll do with it."

"Doesn't matter at the moment. Better to have it and not need it." Josh drove them around to the clinic. The building had a broken window. No doubt it had been raided by survivors early on. Those survivors had either died or moved on. Maybe they'd fled along the coast, hoping to eventually make it to civilization again.

They both got out, leaving the keys in the ignition. There was no one left to steal the car.

Josh shoved open the door. Xavier had his pistol drawn, ready to fire if needed. The building was empty except for a few critters that startled and fled deeper into the shadows. He'd never realized how dark buildings could be without lights. "Where's it kept?"

"No idea." Xavier walked through the reception area toward the treatment room. It was all set up, ready for the next patient. The bed was covered with a sheet. A drip stand lurked in the corner. He poked around a few cupboards, then opened the fridge and shut it just as fast. "Ugh."

Josh grabbed the packages of bandages and suture kits—that shit was always useful—and shoved them into his pockets. He followed Xavier through the rest of the clinic, opening doors and peering in cupboards.

Everything was waiting for the humans to return. Even though he should be used to it, Josh still found it eerie. There was a sense of the building holding its breath. He was waiting for someone to step through a door and ask what they were doing. He'd felt the same in every town and homestead. He always hoped that there'd be someone.

Andrew counted as someone. One survivor, and he was a traitorous asshole.

Xavier rattled the handle of a locked room. He didn't hesitate, just broke the lock and forced his way in. Josh winced. But no one was going to complain about the damage.

"Jackpot." Xavier shone a torch over the shelves. He picked up a small silver flask. "Liquid nitrogen."

Josh took the canister. "You think it's still good?"

"No idea. But now we have some. So let's make a plan to mess up some Geckos."

Chapter Two

JOSH WAS RELIEVED to find Andrew still tied to the chair when he returned to the hotel. He'd been worried that Young and Dave would take pity on him and let him go.

"Where's Fisher?" Young asked.

"I dropped him at our new base with the supplies." Xavier was setting himself to give them early warning of the aliens approach.

This hotel had been a safe base. He closed his eyes for a few seconds, wanting to hold on to the happy memory before Andrew's captive had made a break for it and driven through the front doors, bringing a herd of alien bugs with her. Was it too much to ask for even one night of peace? "How has our guest been?"

In his absence, Andrew had been gagged.

"He wouldn't shut up," Young said. "Begging and bribing and promising to put in a good word with the aliens if I let him go. This hasn't lit up or made a sound." He handed over the alien device.

It looked like metal, but it was too light. It was the same greeny yellow color as the alien base. And like the base, this was hexagonal. It was a bit bigger than human palm sized, and there were some grooves on the outside, but nothing that made him think it was a comms device like Andrew claimed.

But then what did Josh know about alien tech? Nothing except that getting shot hurt. His shoulder wasn't great. While it ached from the dislocation, the wound also hurt. And not in the way he was used to wounds hurting.

"Great."

He tipped the chair that Andrew was sitting on back. Andrew startled and freaked out, his eyes widening. As much as he wanted to give Andrew more than a couple of ways to remember him, Josh knew he wouldn't be able to look Xavier in the eyes if he did.

"How were you going to put in a good word? You speak Gecko? Does this translate? What exactly did you tell them?"

Andrew laughed behind the gag.

Josh shoved the chair upright and ripped the gag down. "Answer me."

"Or what? They own us now. The sooner you get used to it the better."

He'd never accept that Earth had been taken over, and he sure as hell wasn't going to roll over for the aliens.

"Fuck off." He pulled the gag back into place, then turned to Young. "We're relocating, and he's coming with us." *Unfortunately.* Josh would've been happy to leave Andrew and let the bugs feast on him when they woke up at dusk.

He put the device in his pocket. If they didn't know how to use it, it was just fancy junk, but it was the kind of thing that was best handed over to people who were paid to study those kinds of things. He wished they'd been able to send it with Marsh and the other civilians. They'd have been able to take it to Darwin and maybe farther. But there was the risk that the device was a locater. That if they had sent it with Marsh and the others then it might have led the aliens right to them.

He didn't feel good having it in his pocket.

"You ready to go, Dave?"

"I was ready this morning." He picked up a bag loaded with who knew what. The grudge that he'd been made to stay behind soured his expression.

Josh didn't feed it. There was no changing what had happened.

After learning about Andrew's betrayal, he and Xavier had made the call to send Marsh and the others on their way, leaving the rest of them stranded.

A last line of defense.

It might be funny in a few months if they made it.

Between him and Young, they wrestled the office chair with Andrew attached out of the hotel and into the road. The chair wasn't made for rolling along the main street. It spun and bounced over the rough surface. The next hotel wasn't far up the strip, but Josh's shoulder was throbbing, and he was sweating by the time they got there. Dave didn't offer to help.

Josh opened the door, and they wheeled Andrew into the lobby. This was a really fancy joint. The kind used for weddings and honeymoons or by rich people who planned on staying by the pool and never leaving the resort.

He could've never afforded to stay there, not for more than a night anyway. For a few seconds, he was tempted to search the rooms, but there was no point. He didn't care if there were corpses and bugs hiding out in the honeymoon suite.

Only Andrew would be here come nightfall.

And Josh didn't care if he got eaten alive.

"Your new home until after your friends have finished visiting." Josh carefully turned on a couple of high-powered torches that they'd picked up. They'd last for six hours. They only had to last for two. Then it would be dark. "I'll leave the door open for them."

Andrew kicked his legs and struggled against his bonds.

Yeah, that's right, fucker, you know what that means.

The lights would draw the bugs even if the Geckos didn't arrive tonight. And the bugs would make short work of Andrew.

Young looked at Josh like he'd gone mad. "You can't leave him."

Maybe he had. Maybe weeks in the outback thinking his lover was dead and being captured by aliens had knocked a few things loose. He thought he was holding it all together pretty well, but maybe he was one bad day away from snapping.

Unless he'd already snapped?

Would he know if he had?

"Yeah, I can. And I am," Josh said. "So who's going to arrive here first, the bugs or your buddies?"

Andrew spoke, but it was so muffled, Josh couldn't understand him.

"Let him speak. Maybe he has some words of wisdom to impart." Josh crossed his arms and waited.

Young untied the gag. He was far too gentle.

"Don't leave me for the bugs. Kill me if you have to."

"I'm not allowed to. You're a civilian." Josh smiled, lobbing Andrew's words when they'd captured him back at him.

"You can't leave me to be eaten."

Josh shrugged. "That I can do. Accidents happen."

"It's not an accident. It's murder. Turn the lights off."

"No, the area needs to be lit for safety."

"But it won't be safe."

"Yeah, it will. For the rest of us." Josh turned away. "Put the gag back on. I don't want to hear him screaming." He already had more than enough nightmare fodder to last for the rest of his life. He suppressed a shudder, knowing what the bugs would do, but unwilling to save the man who'd damned them all.

"Wait!" Andrew shouted.

Josh kept walking.

"The device is a translator."

He stopped. When he'd been imprisoned, he'd suspected that someone had been reporting to the aliens. The promise of extra rations could turn a man against his own even if it was only a temporary benefit. He turned ninety degrees. "Translates how?"

"Give it to me, and I'll show you."

"Do you think I'm fucking stupid?" The moment Andrew got it, he'd probably send some kind of distress signal.

Andrew shook his head. "You have to slide your thumbs along the grooves to activate it."

"And then what?" Josh pressed.

"And then you talk. And they talk."

"That's it?"

"That's it. I don't want to die like the others. Please."

"Neither do we. Gag him," Josh ordered Young.

"But I helped you."

Josh stalked over. He pointed at Andrew, who had the decency to shrink back as Josh leaned over him. "You fucked us over. You reported us to those clear skinned, maggot eating freaks. You were happy to watch us die so you could keep your hostage and be the King of Georgetown." Josh stepped back and gave a mock bow. "Enjoy your reign."

He walked out, the alien device cool in his hand. His fingers brushed the grooves and he pulled them back, not wanting to accidentally activate it. He didn't trust Andrew not to have lied. But at some point, either he or Xavier was going to have to give it a go. It would be a luxury to be able to listen in on Gecko communications.

And they were smart enough it probably wouldn't happen. Aliens didn't fly through space and knock out all of Earth's satellites only to handover tech that would let the humans gain the upper hand. He turned the device over, this time tempted to run his thumbs up the grooves to see what would happen. Would an alien answer?

What would he say?

What would they say?

He put it back in his pocket before his resolve weakened.

Dave stared at him as he walked past. "Who's next?"

"What do you mean?"

"Who are you going to feed to the bugs next? Why are you the judge and jury, the king of Georgetown?"

Josh clenched his jaw. He didn't have time for this, and for a few seconds, he regretted not sending all the civilians to help Marsh load the boat. Then Dave wouldn't be here whining about how prisoners were treated. "He's a traitor. He's working for the aliens."

"He's human."

Josh was about to argue that but chose another argument. "I can't protect you if I'm watching and waiting for him to knife me in the back. Do you trust him?"

"No…but…what I mean is…how do I know I'm not next?"

"Have you been helping the aliens?"

Dave shook his head. "I've done everything you've asked."

"Then what's the problem?"

Young jogged over and caught up with them. "You aren't actually going to leave him to die are you?"

Josh scratched at the stubble on his jaw. He could lie, but he couldn't be bothered. "I don't want him anywhere near us, and I sure as hell don't want to be dragging his ungrateful ass to Darwin." He glanced at both men. "He held Kayla hostage and raped her repeatedly while reporting to the aliens."

"So he's a shitty person. That doesn't mean he should die," Young said.

Dave nodded.

Josh bit back on a few curses. As far as Josh was concerned, Andrew had proven himself to be a shit of the first order more than once.

Dave licked his lip. "He deserves a fair trial."

Josh laughed. "Jesus fucking wept. Take a look around. The only law around at the moment is survival. If the Geckos capture you, you'll be fighting other humans until they feed you to the bugs. If we don't get our weapons and plan sorted ASAP, they'll catch us with our pants around our ankles, and I can tell you straight up, sunshine, that I am not going to be their captive again. What about you, Dave? You want to go back to that?"

Dave shook his head.

"Andrew is a traitor and can't be trusted. If you want to hold his hand and keep him company to make sure he doesn't escape and make things worse, be my guest. But then we have one less person fighting for our survival, and I don't have the resources or manpower to devote to his safety."

"We should've gotten on the boat. You made us stay," Young snapped.

"One tiny boat has a chance to make it to safety. We are the distraction." His voice broke. "I hope they make it. I hope we make it. We would've all made it together if not for Andrew reporting our arrival. Think about that as you defend him."

Young lifted his chin and considered Josh. Josh held his gaze.

Young would be the first one to cry if taken by the Geckos. He'd scream the loudest when the bugs filled him full of eggs and the larvae ate him from the inside out.

Young looked away first.

Josh started walking. "I'm trying to keep us all alive. You can help me or you can help Andrew, who was happy to see you dead. Your call."

He had no confidence that Dave or Young would make the right one.

He walked up the block and stepped into the shade of the church. This was their new base; it was on high ground and the belltower gave them a few more meters. In the belltower, he saw a flash of sunlight on Xavier's rifle.

The building was old and whitewashed. As churches went, it wasn't that fancy. It was much smaller than the one where his parent's funeral had been held. But this place had some history judging from the numerous plaques around. It also had clear lines of sight to where Andrew was. It was the perfect place to watch and wait. He had debated trying to find somewhere more defensible, but nothing was safe when it came to the aliens, so surprise and the best vantage point were worth more.

For a moment, he considered the idea that making a run for it might be the smart move, but then they'd be covering their tails, and they lacked the weapons to do that on the move. He doubted very much that they could hide. One person might be able to, for a short amount of time…

He shook his head. He was tired of running and fighting, and even if he got away, he didn't know how he could live a quiet life knowing that aliens were claiming land and killing everything in sight.

What was going to happen when they'd stripped this land bare?

He already knew the answer. They'd move on to the cities on the east coast.

The door to the church hung open, and he stepped into the gloom. It was a welcome relief after the sharp, bright sunlight.

Someone had set up some water bottles on a pew along with

some food. He helped himself to a slightly soft chocolate bar, knowing that it wasn't real food and he should be eating properly but wanting it all the same. If he died today, he wanted some damn chocolate, and if he survived, then he'd pop a few of the vitamin tablets that would hopefully stop their teeth from falling out since there was no fresh fruit or vegetables.

Dave followed him in. "Where are the others?"

"Probably still looking for urea."

Once they had it, they had to figure out how to use it as a weapon. He hoped it worked on the aliens the same way it worked on the bugs. If nothing else, at least it would keep the bugs and larvae away, and that was enough of a win to be worth the effort.

Had Dave been hoping to gossip and cast doubts on Josh's decisions? How many were disgruntled? He exhaled slowly. Did they want to die? Did they not understand that war wasn't pretty and neat and organized? Sometimes shit had to be done, and sometimes it was nothing but bad choices and a prayer.

"Isn't that dangerous? The aliens will be here soon. The bugs will be coming out." Dave's eyes were wide, and he kept fiddling with the strap of the bag he held. He was scared.

Was there anything Josh could say that was reassuring?

Josh considered him for a moment then gave a one-shouldered shrug. "Everything is dangerous. They might be safe while we die."

"Doesn't that bother you? Do you want to die?"

Josh sighed. "No, I don't. I'm just a realist. This is not the first time I've thought I wasn't going to make it home." Of course, this time he didn't have a home to return to. At some point his luck would run out. It happened. "We're in the shit. We might make it out if we work together, but if people start to pull in different directions, then we'll all go down."

Read between the lines, Dave.

"Rayne, get up here," Xavier called from the bell tower.

"Coming." He gave Dave another glance. He was going to be the one to fuck everything up. He was one step away from breaking and running. Holding the church and killing a team of aliens would be much harder with a smaller team. And if Dave fled, he might take others with him. Young had seemed keen to run. "Pull up a pew, have a bite to eat, and try to have a nap. We don't know what's going to happen later."

Dave licked his lip like he was about to say something. Then he looked at the food and nodded.

Josh left him to it.

At the back of the church was a staircase, though that was being generous. It was more of a ladder with illusions of grandeur. He made his way up, aware of every creak. When the world was silent, every noise was too loud.

"Took the best spot for yourself, I see," Josh said with a grin.

"Always. Take a look." He eased back, and Josh peered through the scope on the rifle.

It wasn't set up for doing any serious long-range shooting. For a few seconds, he saw nothing of note. The fire from the hospital was still burning, but it wasn't life threatening nor was it moving fast enough for him to be worried. It would be nice if their biggest problem was a fire.

"What am I supposed to be looking at?

"Exactly. There's nothing out there. Where are the aliens that Andrew promised us?"

Josh stepped back and leaned on the windowsill. The air smelled like smoke, but he was so used to it that it didn't matter. "Do you think we caused them more grief than we thought when we blew up the farm?"

"That had to hurt. And now we've taken out the hospital. If we keep taking out their supplies, it's not like there's more around the corner."

Josh glanced up at the sky. They didn't have long until sunset. They'd spent the day preparing for attack. The adrenaline rush was long gone. All he could do now was push through.

He'd been saying that for what felt like forever. At some point he'd stop and wouldn't be able to get going again.

Was getting rid of the aliens as easy as taking out their food source? Cutting off supplies was an old, but effective tactic.

"What if they are all dead?" That was a bit too much wishful thinking, but it didn't stop him from hoping.

"Nah. I think they don't care about a handful of survivors as much as Andrew wants us to think they do."

"You think he lied? Why?"

Xavier held out his hand, and Josh gave him what was left of the chocolate bar. It had turned to glue in his mouth anyway.

"'Cause he's a germ," Xavier said with a mouthful of chocolate.

Josh smiled. "Yeah, but it didn't win him any favors. What did he think it would achieve?"

"That we'd get scared and piss off and leave him to it. All he wanted was the girl."

Josh's lip curled. He crossed the floor and stared out over the ocean. The waves rolled onto the perfectly white sand. But instead of the beach being full of holiday makers, it was deserted. As his gaze skimmed over the white caps on the water, there was only more nothing. No little boats, no swimmers, no big boats, or ships. The breeze whispered through the open windows of the belltower.

Xavier didn't move from his spot, holding up the wall. "How's the leg?"

"If I was lying down and resting, it would heal up faster. Tye's concerned about the lack of new skin."

Josh frowned. "Are you?"

"The infection's gone; I feel better."

"But?"

"But something isn't right. How's your shoulder?"

"A mess." It ached, and he wanted to rest up too. "Someone else could've kept watch."

"No. I don't trust them to do a good job, and you don't trust them at all."

Josh turned. He kept his voice low. "Young and Dave think we should coddle Andrew because he's human."

He saw the argument form on Xavier's lips before he shrugged it off.

They didn't have time to fight; they both knew that. But there was still tension. Everyone was frayed and tired. Tired people made bad calls.

"Should we have run?" Had he made the wrong decision?

"No. If they are looking for people, we are a distraction. We discussed it; we did the right thing with what we knew at the time."

It was too late to switch course now. Sometimes it didn't feel like there was ever a right choice, only a slightly less wrong or painful one.

"How long do we wait?"

Xavier drew in a breath and sighed. "I don't know."

"How long can I keep Andrew tied up for before there's a mutiny?" Not nearly long enough to make Josh happy.

"Tomorrow morning is probably a safe bet. After that, people will grumble. We can't lose support."

They were outnumbered, but it wasn't only that. If they didn't work together, they were an easy target, and if Andrew wormed his way into their ears, they might think he was talking sense.

Josh pulled the comms device out of his pocket. "He told me how to work this. It's some kind of translator."

Xavier grimaced and gave him a look that said more than any words.

"Fuck, mate, I didn't hurt him. Young was standing right there." That Xavier thought he had stung. He might have, though…

Xavier jerked his chin at the device. "How?"

Josh mimed running his thumbs along the grooves. "That simple unless it was more bullshit."

Xavier raked his teeth over his lower lip as he studied the cube in Josh's hand. "What do you think?"

"I don't know." It might explode. Or it might work… He wasn't sure which was worse at this point. "Last time, they bombed us and then sent in two to clean up. I think we need to expect the same."

"That didn't work though, so maybe they'll try something different."

Josh kept glancing at the sky, but it was clear. There was absolutely no sign that they were about to be under attack. "Do you think we took the advice of a madman?"

Xavier shrugged. "Even if we did, we have the supplies to roll out. We'll cut across the peninsula and meet the boat on the other side. That way, we can check the mining camp for survivors on the way."

"And if the boat doesn't arrive?" He was assuming Marsh would make it.

"We can always drive the rest of the way."

"So if we aren't attacked overnight, we move out by vehicle not boat?" Josh preferred driving to sailing, but any method out worked.

Xavier nodded. "I'd like to be far away from this place this time tomorrow." He put his hand out, and Josh handed over the cube. "I'll do it; you go downstairs."

"Like hell." He wanted to see if it worked and how it worked, and he wasn't leaving Xavier alone.

"Joshy…"

"Nah." He crossed his arms. "I'm not going."

If Xavier died, he didn't want to fight on. What would he be fighting for?

"You're a stupid fuck. Come here."

Josh stood shoulder to shoulder with Xavier.

Xavier turned the device over in his hands until the grooved side was facing up. He glanced at Josh. "I love you."

"I love you too." He leaned in and kissed him. Their lips met, and for a few seconds, nothing else mattered. Their foreheads touched, and Josh drew in a couple of breaths. "Let's see what they have to say. Get an ETA."

Xavier placed his thumbs in the grooves. While it was a bit too big for a human palm, it seemed to have been made for human hands. The alien's hands were bigger and would've dwarfed the cube. That realization was a little disconcerting.

How long had they been watching and learning before landing?

Xavier glanced up at him with a look Josh had seen a few times before. *Last chance to change your mind.*

Josh gave him a small, single nod.

Xavier ran his thumbs up the grooves.

Chapter Three

JOSH HELD HIS BREATH. For several seconds, absolutely nothing happened. The cube didn't light up, and it didn't crackle with static. But he didn't dare speak in case someone was listening. He hadn't asked how to turn it off.

Xavier ran his thumbs along the grooves again, and this time he kept them there. He lifted his eyebrows and spoke. "Hello?"

Josh shrugged and shook his head.

"Report." The voice sounded human, female, and right beside them. Had the aliens decided humans prefer female AI voices and copied?

Xavier nearly dropped the cube. He put his thumbs back in place. "When are you getting here? They're preparing to leave. Loading up cars with food and water."

He grimaced at Josh as though he didn't know what else to say.

"Noted."

"And?" Xavier pressed.

"The situation will be attended."

"Ow." Xavier let go of the cube, and Josh caught it. "It zapped me."

"Conversation over." A good way to make sure the humans

didn't stay on the line for too long. "Do you think it only has a few set phrases?"

"Attended doesn't mean turn up."

"Nor does noted." Josh leaned against the wall and let the tension trickle away. For the first time today, he could breathe. "You think Andrew misunderstood?"

"I don't know what to think." He gave the device a shake, like he expected it to rattle. "I don't know enough about anything."

"Maybe we should grab some rest."

"I might stay up here, just in case," Xavier said.

Josh wanted to stay and keep him company, but he should go back down and keep an eye on the others. In the time he'd been up here, Young could have freed Andrew. If Josh knew Andrew, he'd then make straight for the police station to grab any remaining firearms. They'd taken what they could realistically carry, but there was still quite an armory left. Josh peered out the window. There was no movement on the street. From his vantage point, there was no movement in the town at all.

His heart tightened as though threatening to stop. They could be the only people left in the whole world and they wouldn't know because there was no communication.

He closed his eyes. No. There were others. There had to be.

For a start, anywhere cold, where there were no aliens, people would be thriving. They'd be planning ways to help the countries that had been invaded. He was sure that talks were happening, orders were being made, and people like him were preparing to fight.

"You okay?" Xavier placed a hand on Josh's lower back.

He drew in a breath. He was so far from okay he didn't remember what it looked like anymore. But he couldn't say that, because if he broke, then he was damning everyone. They needed him to be okay. He nodded because he couldn't lie out loud.

Xavier moved closer and put an arm around him, and then rested his head on Josh's shoulder. If he kept his eyes closed and concentrated on the way Xavier's body was pressed against his, he could pretend that they were a million miles away. Somewhere aliens didn't exist, and they were safe. Even if that meant going back to keeping their relationship secret.

Josh turned and put his arms around Xavier. They leaned into each other as though drawing support. It felt like Josh had spent his entire life trying to survive. He knew that wasn't true, as before his parent's death his childhood had been normal, but he couldn't remember much of it. With Xavier, he'd found someone to call home even if they weren't in the same country, even if they didn't speak for weeks. Everything was always as they left it, waiting for them to return. It was safe, and it was secret, and it was theirs.

With the ring on his finger, he felt exposed.

The old fear of wondering what everyone would say lurked beneath the more immediate danger of the aliens. Part of him didn't want to hide, but the rest of him was terrified. He was a soldier, they both were, and he could only imagine what the people in charge would think even if they didn't say it.

Xavier kissed the side of Josh's neck. "We'll get out of this. We always do."

Josh huffed out a breath. He wanted to laugh but couldn't. He was beginning to think they weren't going to get out of this no matter what they did. And it wouldn't matter in the end as the Geckos would kill them. They'd take over the whole world.

Xavier drew back and cupped Josh's jaw.

Josh opened his eyes and stared up at Xavier, wishing it was as simple as believing. "This is a little different to outrunning insurgents."

"Not really. They all want us dead or captured. The only difference is these guys have better armor and weapons."

Josh opened his mouth to say something, but Xavier cut him off with a kiss. His lips were hard and demanding against Josh's. He surrendered, not wanting to fight, needing to forget. His hands slid under Xavier's shirt, and the kiss deepened. Xavier's tongue teased, and he ground against Josh.

"Do you think we can steal a few minutes?"

They were alone with only the breeze to whisper about what

was going on. But at least one person was in the church below, so they needed to be very quiet.

Josh nodded. Xavier's fingers quickly undid Josh's pants. He went from half hard to stiff and aching for Xavier's touch before his fly was fully down. His cock sprung forward as soon as it was released from his jocks.

Xavier grinned and dropped to his knees. He ran his tongue along the underside of Josh's dick, then teased the slit before taking him in his mouth. Josh's fingers pressed against Xavier's head, and he rocked his hips.

He knew he should keep watch, one of them should, but all he wanted to do was watch Xavier suck his dick. Xavier took him deeper, and Josh fucked his mouth for what felt like only a few seconds before Xavier pulled back so he could torment the head of Josh's cock with his tongue.

Josh tipped his head back against the wall as Xavier worked him over. Xavier cupped Josh's balls and gave them a gentle squeeze. Josh bit his lip to stop himself from groaning. The way Xavier's mouth was sliding over the head of his dick, he wasn't going to last long at all—not that they had the time to draw things out. The tension knotted in his belly, and his breathing shortened until he wasn't sure if he was holding his breath to stay silent or to hold back from coming.

Xavier released a small moan that vibrated through Josh's cock. Josh glanced down to watch him tongue the slit, lapping up the beads of pre-cum.

His grip on Xavier's head tightened. "I'm…"

He didn't need to say anything else. Didn't have time. The climax spilled from him into Xavier's mouth. Xavier swallowed, looking up at Josh with a hungry gaze. He was ready to turn around and give Xavier what he wanted. Usually if they met like this, there was rarely time for both of them to get their way. Their tally had begun as a joke, then as a way to make sure one wasn't always getting the good time in their few stolen minutes. Sometimes a mutual hand job with a kiss to silence every noise was all they could manage for months.

But those old rules that had kept them safe no longer mattered.

Xavier gave Josh's dick a final lick. Josh turned and shoved his pants the rest of the way down.

Xavier gave a low laugh. "Good thing I grabbed the lube."

Josh didn't really care.

Then Xavier's slick fingers probed Josh's ass, pressing deep and stroking in just the right place. Josh tilted his hips and rocked back, ignoring the stretch and sting. Xavier took the hint. He guided his dick to Josh's hole and pushed until he was sinking in. One hand on Josh's hip, the other wrapped around his chest.

He grunted softly in Josh's ear. "I want to fuck you every chance we get."

"Yeah." That seemed like a good plan. The best one either of them had come up with.

Xavier's teeth raked against his neck, and Josh tilted his head as Xavier bit down. He fucked hard, his balls slapping against Josh's ass. Josh closed his eyes as pleasure rolled through him. He wasn't in control, and for those few seconds, he would do whatever Xavier wanted of him. This wasn't the first time Xavier had left teeth marks on him. Xavier grunted and stilled, breathing hard as he came deep in Josh's ass.

The ground seemed to shake, and it took him a moment to realize it wasn't from pleasure. The building trembled, and Josh grabbed the windowsill as parts of the town erupted. Brilliant streaks filled the sunset bruised sky. Where the light landed, fire flashed, and the ground shook.

"Fuck." Xavier pulled away and grabbed the rifle, his pants around his knees as he peered through the scope. "Where are the fuckers?"

The hotel they had used as a base exploded, sending frag into the air. He pulled Xavier to the floor. Metal and bricks flew through the open bell tower, striking the bell and drowning out all other sounds. Josh lay on the floor, wriggling back into his pants and shoving his dick away. He glanced at Xavier, who was doing much the same.

It might have been funny if someone else were telling the tale…

His head rang, but the floor was no longer vibrating. The building was still standing. Did that mean this part of the attack was over?

Josh gave Xavier a thumbs up. Xavier did the same, then pointed up.

Josh nodded. They got up cautiously and peered out the open window. Half of Georgetown was on fire. The hotel that had been their old base was gone, along with the bugs that had taken it over. The hotel next door, where he'd put Andrew, had fared no better.

Andrew was gone.

He stared at the rubble. He shouldn't have left him there…but he couldn't be trusted to be with them. Had Young stayed or was he downstairs?

He squeezed his eyes shut, knowing that he'd receive an earful, and he'd have to take it. Had it been a bad call or the right one given the situation?

Xavier tapped his hand, getting his attention. He held up all five fingers, then pointed.

The aliens were following the same pattern, bomb first then send in a team. They'd gotten smarter this time and sent in a bigger team.

Where were the two sailors who were gathering the urea?

He shouldn't have sent them; he should've gone himself. Hopefully, they'd stay hidden. Though he didn't know if hiding made a difference. The aliens were very efficient at finding anything with a heartbeat.

"They aren't close enough for me to take a shot, and the moment I do—"

"Yeah, I know." They'd give away their position. The device lay in the rubble. He stared at it. Despite the devastation around them, they were untouched. He picked up the device. "They already have our position. That's why this building is standing."

"Right. So we should prepare for visitors?"

"Yeah. I'll have Dave make some tea and put out some cookies," Josh said.

"Sounds good. Wouldn't mind a cuppa." Xavier smiled. "You

want me to take a shot when I can, or do you want to wait and let them think we're cool?"

"The minute they see me, or you, the game is up." Their skin was streaked with the paint from the prison. It didn't seem to scrub off or pick off—he'd tried both. All he could do was hope that he lived long enough for it to wear off.

"How close do you want them to get?"

"Young and I will take positions up the street. When we start, you start. Face shots and tail shots." He turned away to go downstairs.

Xavier grabbed his arm and yanked him back, kissing him hard on the lips. "That was amazing, by the way. Fireworks." He winked and released him.

"Maybe fewer fireworks next time." He offered the device to Xavier. "You want this?"

"Sure." He held out his hand, and Josh tossed it to him. Then Xavier shoved it into his pocket.

Josh made his way down the steep, narrow stairs. "Anyone alive?"

For several long seconds, no one answered.

Young crawled out from behind the altar. "Me."

Yay. "I wasn't sure you'd made it back."

"I locked up the hotel and turned out the lights. He might be a traitor, but he doesn't deserve to be eaten by bugs."

The bugs don't eat people, their larvae do. But he kept his mouth shut. Let Young think he'd done that right thing for a few moments.

"I'm alive," Dave said from under a pew.

"Great. Dave, I want you to stay here and pack this shit up in case we have to move out fast with only what we can carry." He turned to Young, not caring if Dave was still under the pew or getting up. "Have you ever been in combat before?"

Young shook his head. "I passed the shooting course."

Josh pasted on a smile. "You're going to need it. We're heading up the street. We have five coming in, and they are looking for us. Their armor is better than anything we have. If they catch you, it will be bad, so don't get caught."

"Can't I stay here with Dave?" Young pointed to Dave, who hadn't moved from under the pew.

"No, we need to take out some of them. Xavier…" *Damn it.* "Fisher will take the rest, but I need him up there. He's the best shot we have."

"What about the others?"

"I have no idea where they are. Let's hope they are taking cover somewhere." Fallon and Tye were smart. He hoped they were survivors and wouldn't think twice about killing an alien.

"Why don't we do that and wait until the aliens are gone?" Young had turned pale and was more than a little sweaty.

They were fucked. Josh put a hand on the young man's shoulder. He'd been like this once. Getting shot at had been life changing. Actually, getting shot had been unpleasant at the time. Now it seemed like a fun summer holiday memory. He'd happily go back to the Middle East and take a bullet and some frag for a few days rest in hospital. Hell, he'd push to the front of the line. "Because they seem to look for heat signatures. They will find us. We have to shoot first."

Young nodded. "We need to get Andrew. They'll find him, and you left him tied to a chair."

Josh grimaced. "The hotel is gone. There's not many buildings left standing."

"What?"

"Their weapons are better than ours." Shit, he needed to say something reassuring. "We have the element of surprise, and if you shoot them in the face plate, they die. That's all you have to do. Pick one and shoot him in the face."

They'd only have time for one shot. Then it would all be over. But he didn't say that.

He grabbed a rifle and a full magazine. Then he saw the flash bangs, so he took a couple of them too. He looked at the police armor. It might reduce the sting if they had their weapons on low, but he doubted it would stop them. Still, if it made Young feel better, it was worth it. "Get kitted up like you're facing a riot. Grab a rifle and be ready in a minute."

He picked up a radio and turned it to the frequency they were using. "Do not respond. Base is expecting guests. Out."

Two raps came from above. He shook his head. Their minute of prep was up. He checked his pocket, making sure he had his backup plan. "We need to move out. Ready?"

"Why aren't you wearing a helmet?" Young at least looked like he was ready to face the enemy, though Josh wasn't sure if he'd break and run at the first sign of trouble.

"I always grab it on the way out." He didn't like the idea of spilling his brains for the seagulls to squabble over. The large, clear shield would slow him down, but he grabbed it anyway. They didn't have far to go, and for all he knew, it might deflect the alien weapons. That, or it would melt.

Loaded up, he moved toward the door and checked outside. "Follow me and don't say anything unless you see an alien and it's seen you."

He stepped out into the humidity and dusk. Overhead, the bats had already started their nightly fly over, and the mosquitos were out in force.

Yeah, he was ready to kill aliens, but like Young, all he wanted to do was hide in the church and pray.

Chapter Four

AFTER GETTING INTO POSITION, all he could do was wait for the aliens to get within range. He'd prepped his experimental weapon and was now sweating and being eaten by mozzies as he lay on the roof of the house. The tin was hot against his belly and thighs. From Josh's vantage point, he could follow the tall aliens as they made their way up the street. Three at the front and another two much farther behind. The front three were in an arrow formation, with one taking point, and they were all armed like they expected trouble. Josh was more than happy to hand deliver them some.

The two behind the point man swept each side of the street. Yeah, they were looking for heat signatures. But they weren't looking up, which was very sloppy. If they were his men and this were a training exercise, Josh would be tearing them a new asshole afterwards.

He let the arrow formation move past him.

He knew Xavier was watching him, so he very deliberately pulled the pin on the grenade then held it up for three seconds—which felt like something closer to hours as the mosquitos buzzed in his ears—before he let it fall in the street midway between the two waves of Geckos.

Josh ducked and protected his eyes and ears as best he could. He felt it go off, then picked up his rifle and hoped that Young was doing the same. Ideally, he'd have stuck Young on the building opposite, but he wasn't sure that Young wouldn't accidentally shoot him in a panic. Instead, Young was one building over, both of them firing from the same side.

Josh wiggled up to make his shot. Three aliens were stumbling around, clutching their guns. One was on the ground. The one from the point was searching for trouble. Josh willed him to turn enough that he could make a head shot. His heartbeat marked time. Then the alien turned a few more degrees. Josh took aim and fired three quick shots. The alien dropped.

Two others fell.

He wasn't sure where the bullets had come from and didn't have time to think as the remaining two had figured out they were under attack.

The aliens blasted the roof line on both sides. Josh lay flat as heat scored over him. He was sure he smelled charred meat, but the adrenaline kept the pain at bay for the moment and would be good for a bit. Their guns were clearly dialed up to not-fucking-around, which was always good to know.

His heart thumped against the roof. How no one was hearing it, he didn't know.

What the fuck was Xavier doing? Why wasn't he taking some shots?

Had he been hurt?

While he'd be able to see the belltower if he looked over, he was too far to see anything inside. He had to act on trust. Young, on the other hand…

He tilted his head just enough to glance over. Young was cowering against a brick chimney. The house would have been considered cute and historic once. Now it was the center of a street battle. He'd done this before. It was no different, if he pretended they weren't aliens below.

He blew out a breath. Before he could move, bullets peppered the road.

Josh took that as his cue to join in. The aliens were past him now, giving him a clear shot of their pearly see-through tails. They held their tails rigid and off the ground, but he knew they made effective, and painful, whips if one was unfortunate enough to get close.

He sighted on one and fired. Blood burst from the creature, but the shot was more of an inconvenience than incapacitating. It spun and saw him.

"Fuck."

Josh scrambled back, wishing he had a chimney. Instead, he slithered over the ridgeline and down the other side. Young was being absolutely bloody useless—no worse than useless, as now Josh had a body to worry about.

A horn sounded, echoing off the building. His ears rung. Whoever was driving was leaning on the horn. Curiosity got the better of him, and he hauled himself back up in time to see a truck barreling along the street and taking heavy fire from the two remaining Geckos.

Fallon and Tye had made it back to join the fight; Josh hoped that was a good thing for everyone.

With the aliens distracted, Josh resumed shooting at them. They couldn't take on everyone, even with their better weapons. But their armor protected them well, meaning he had to be accurate—very accurate—or he might as well empty their limited rounds onto the street.

Or he could attempt something more unconventional.

Josh pulled two carefully prepared condoms out of the bag lying next to him. The rubbers were filled with piss, and now seemed as good a time as any to deploy what he guessed could be classified as chemical warfare.

He took one in each hand then lobbed them at the alien giving the truck the most grief. It caught him on the back and exploded beautifully. For a second, nothing happened. Then the alien started screaming as it soaked through his armor.

The other alien, the one he'd shot in the tail, glanced around, then dropped his weapon and put his hands in the air.

The truck rolled to a stop. Using the door for cover, someone got out and slotted a shot through the screaming Gecko's face plate.

The other alien knelt as if he knew it was all over.

Josh didn't trust the fucker.

He slung his bag over his good shoulder, grabbed his rifle, and got down on the street. Had they actually caught one of the bastards?

He kicked the alien's gun away. With the sailor from the truck covering him, he pushed the alien face down on the road and cuffed him. Josh's hands shook. That was too easy.

"Good work." He didn't need to share his doubts. Instead, he smiled. "Nice ride."

Fallon grinned. "Thanks. We needed something to put the urea in. And while we're a bit short on armored vehicles, I thought a refrigerated truck might do the trick."

Josh nodded. "Does it get cold in there?"

"Yeah, but it smells like a sewer from the rotten food even though we scraped it out."

Josh glanced at the alien lying on the asphalt, then back at the truck. "I have a theory that they don't like the cold."

"That's why they've only taken over the deserts." She looked at the truck. "Just another point in this beast's favor."

"Shall we test it?"

With Tye standing watch on the read and Xavier watching from the belltower, Fallon and Josh pulled off the alien's helmet. The flat, pale face and wide, dark eyes would forever haunt his nightmares. But it was the tiny, pointed teeth that really got to him.

He checked the alien for weapons. Then they hauled him up and shoved him in the back of the truck with the bags of urea. It was so nice and cold in there, Josh was almost tempted to join him despite the smell.

With the alien locked up, Josh picked up the helmet. The displays still made no sense, but this time, he wasn't tossing away anything that might be useful. "Take their armor and weapons. Young, get your ass down here and help strip the aliens."

While the others were working. He checked on the one he'd

showered with piss. He was definitely dead. Blood seeped out the faceplate of the helmet, but when Josh tried to remove the armor, it was stuck. He pulled harder and skin tore away.

His stomach bucked, and he dropped the armor, needing to turn away to catch his breath. The piss had melted the alien's skin or something. Whatever had happened had been effective and had made the armor useless.

The air rippled.

Josh glanced up, even though it was already too late, and ran for the doorway of the nearest building. "Take cover!"

But the blast wasn't close to him and the dead aliens. The pretty wooden church went up, sending shards of wood and metal and glass everywhere. Josh stared, unable to breathe or move.

Xavier.

Chapter Five

AROUND JOSH, the world continued to erupt in fire and fragments. Something cut his cheek. Dust stung his eyes. He screamed, his voice that of a wounded wild animal. The sound was lost in the noise and confusion.

Xavier couldn't be gone. He had the comms device; it was supposed to protect him and make the aliens think he was friendly.

One of the aliens must have made a report before dying. Josh would've done the same thing. He'd have wanted the comms destroyed if it had fallen into enemy hands, too. As much as he hated them, he understood them.

When the air was still, he stood. He stumbled out of the doorway. The buildings around him were missing chunks and burning. Embers drifted along the street and lit up the dusk. At the end of the road where the church should've been, there was only the gold coin of a sun sinking below the dark waves.

"No!" He should check on the men in the street and the others who'd been with him, but he had to reach the church. Xavier couldn't be dead. Not like this. Not now.

The asphalt was tacky beneath his boots from the heat. He'd lost his rifle somewhere. Maybe he'd left it in the doorway. He didn't care. He half-jogged and half-tripped his way up the street.

Behind him, someone called out. He ignored them.

"Xavier?" Was he shouting? He couldn't tell. "Fisher!"

A few pieces of the church were standing, burning but upright. Where did he start? There was no upstairs. Had Xavier fallen? There was too much rubble to sort through.

"Xavier." He stepped into the ruins and past pews that were no longer upright. He coughed. He needed to find Xavier; he couldn't leave him to burn to death.

Then Josh remembered he had a torch. He pulled it out of his pocket. It was tiny, but he started scanning all the dark corners with the narrow beam of light. He made it to the front of the church and stood in front of the broken alter. Above him was only sky where there had once been the ceiling. Where was the bell?

"Xavier?" Had he missed him? Was he underneath everything? He turned, ready to lift every piece of wood if he had to.

"Here," a voice croaked.

Josh spun. His light landed on a crumpled figure at the base of the stairs. "Shit."

He ran over and dropped to his knees at Xavier's side. Relief that he was alive warred with the knowledge that he was hurt and… and he didn't want to think what that might mean. There was no medivac here.

He pressed his forehead to Xavier's. "What did you break this time?"

Xavier pulled him close. "Nothing I don't think."

Josh didn't fight the awkward embrace. He breathed in the sweat and smoke and held tight, not wanting to ever let go. He sniffed, knowing that it wasn't because of the smoke in his lungs and eyes. "We need to get out of here."

"I know. I just need a moment. I don't remember getting all the way down the stairs."

Concussion. "I'll check your head out." He drew back and looked at Xavier, his lips turning up in a small smile. "But let's face it, your skull is so thick, you'll be fine."

"Yeah, I know. But I like it when you play doctor and kiss me better."

Josh obliged, brushing a light kiss over Xavier's lips. "You sure you're okay to move?"

"Even if I'm not, I don't want to roast in here, so help me up."

Josh stood, then helped Xavier up. Blood streaked the side of his face, but it would have to be dealt with when they left the church. "Come on."

"What did you see, Joshy?"

"Bit of blood. I'll have a look outside." Head and facial wounds bled; it was probably just a scratch. He hoped that's all it was. They made it out of the church, and Xavier sat on the pine log fence that formed the boundary between church and cemetery.

"Close your eyes. Only one of us needs to be night blind." They couldn't stay here. The bugs would be out soon, searching for fresh meat, and he was not going to be dinner for their hungry babies.

When Xavier closed his eyes, Josh inspected the wound. There was a flap of skin, almost in the hairline. They'd be able to clean it and glue it closed, and it would be fine. Then he checked the rest of Xavier's head for lumps. There was one on the back of his head.

"Ow."

Josh ignored him and continued checking. "The skin doesn't seem to be broken."

"So I'll live?" He opened his eyes and tipped his face up to Josh.

Josh leaned down and kissed him. "Yeah. I thought…"

Xavier put his hand on Josh's cheek. "So did I. I saw it come in and figured it was for me, so I tossed the device, hoping it was honing in on that, then I slid down those stairs like the devil was after me."

"He was." He pulled Xavier close, not wanting to let him go.

Xavier's arm went around his legs and they stood there, locked together. They couldn't keep doing this. *He* couldn't keep doing this. Every time he thought Xavier was dead, a part of him died. How many times could his heart be resurrected? Did he have nine lives like a cat?

"I didn't think it was true." Young's voice broke Josh out of his reverie.

He glanced over, but it was too late to pull away as the three sailors and one civilian were all staring.

"Are you two f—"

"Fucking? Yes," Josh said. There were four of them against him and Xavier, and Xavier was injured. He wasn't up to fighting. Josh's fingers curled even though the humans had to stand together. The pearl ring bit into his fingers.

"No." Xavier stood. He kept one arm around Josh as though he were protecting him, not using him for support. Had he ripped his stitches and made his leg worse? "We're engaged. If you don't like that, you can piss off. I've spent too bloody long hiding from people like you instead of living." He kissed Josh's temple.

Josh could barely breathe; he was trying to be calm, but the attack and the fear that he'd lost Xavier was running wild through his body.

Xavier pulled his hand away. There was blood on his palm. "Are you hurt?"

"I'm good." Wasn't he? It was just adrenaline.

The world shrunk to a pinpoint of light, and his ears buzzed. Then everything tilted.

Chapter Six

IT TOOK Josh several goes to open his eyes. When he did get them open, it was daylight. For several heartbeats, he lay there, unable to remember how he ended up in bed. Or even whose bed he was in. He ran his hand over his bare stomach, then lower. He had briefs on. That was probably a good thing.

He was alone in the room, so he pushed himself upright. Pain streaked across his ribs and made him gasp. That was when he saw the bandages wrapped around his chest. He frowned as confusion took hold. This wasn't a hospital room. This was someone's bedroom.

Not his.

Not Xavier's.

He drew in a slow breath. What was the last thing he remembered?

Kissing Xavier in the twilight. He smiled, but something was wrong with the memory. Xavier was bleeding. The world was burning. Memories of fighting aliens filled his head in a sickening rush.

He hunched forward as though absorbing the blow. He wished he'd remained oblivious. With every breath, his back and ribs burned. Not a break—he was familiar with how broken ribs felt.

With grim determination to find out what was going on, he gritted his teeth and gave himself to the count of five to get his shit together. On four, the door opened. Josh's head snapped up and tension filled his body.

Xavier grinned. "I was checking to see if you were up."

Josh stared at him. There was a bandage around his head, and he walked with the now familiar limp, but otherwise he seemed fine. "Yeah."

"What's the last thing you remember?" Xavier said even though it was him with the bandage on his forehead.

Josh didn't have the right answer. Something had happened after they'd kissed.

Xavier sat on the edge of the bed. "It doesn't matter."

"We both know it does." If he knew that, what had he forgotten? "I know we're in Georgetown and that there's fucking Geckos everywhere. That should be enough." He flipped back the sheet but really wanted to lie down and pull it over his head. "I'm going to need some pants."

"They're over there." Xavier inclined his head at a pile of clothes slung over a chair.

"How's your head?"

"Glued back together. Your head seemed fine. Your right side is a mess. Looks like you caught a blast from their weapon."

He shook his head. "I have no idea when. I remember running to the church."

"That's gone."

"Right." He knew that. Or at least he knew he should. "Where are the others?"

"They realized we're boyfriends and ditched us."

Josh blinked. "What?"

"Of course they didn't, you dumb fuck. They were freaking out that you were dead. I don't think they care what we do as long as they get home." He glanced away, hiding something. "Most of Georgetown is gone. This place is a bit out of town. There's a water tank, so you can have a wash, but you have to do it outside as there's no electricity to run the pump. We voted against wasting time to find a generator."

"This our new base?" It sure as hell couldn't be home. They had to keep moving.

Xavier pressed his lips together. "For the moment…" He sighed and stared at the wall. "The urea worked really well. We might have a chance to eradicate—"

Josh shook his head, knowing what Xavier was about to say. "No."

"It's the right thing."

"It's the dumb thing. We'll be killed."

"We might be killed anyway. What do you think the odds of us retiring and living quietly somewhere cold are? Seriously?"

None. The army would pull in the reservists and anyone who'd left in the last ten years. They'd be signing up recruits and anyone who could hold a gun. But they could disappear if they never made it to Darwin.

He held onto that thought for a few breaths, knowing that he couldn't voice it. It was unrealistic. The aliens would eventually find them, and he couldn't sit back and watch as the world was taken over. Though it was nice to imagine that he could.

"So what's the plan? We drive back to the base and squirt them like some bad kitties?"

Xavier grinned. The kind that got fixed to his face when he expected the worst. "Pretty much."

"And you think I have the shit plans." He put his hand over Xavier's.

"Someone had to lead while you were taking a nap."

Josh forced a smile.

If they didn't go back, then all the men still imprisoned would die, and the aliens would keep their toehold. If it worked, they could spread the word and tell everyone that urea killed the aliens. "What happened to observe and not engage?"

"To be fair, they attacked first."

Did the rules of engagement apply to aliens? No one had told them. No one had known what to do. They'd been stuck out here for so long everything might have changed. They might be fighting for a world that no longer existed.

He wanted to tell Xavier that he was wrong and that they should take a boat and get out of there. That they were too injured to fight on. The men they were with were too inexperienced. They were outclassed by an enemy they knew very little about.

But as he looked at Xavier, he couldn't form the words.

If he'd taken his team and run for the coast instead of approaching the base, he'd have never found Xavier. Xavier would have been trapped on the base, fighting until he succumbed to the infection in his leg. He'd have been leaving his lover, his fiancé, to die. And he would've never known.

If he had known, he wouldn't have been able to live with himself. But by following orders, his team had been killed. Who was he to decide who lived and who died?

"Our orders were to get eyes on the base and report back," Josh said carefully. He didn't want to sound like he was too afraid to do anything more than run. He didn't want Xavier to call him a coward or look at him with disgust the way he had when Josh hadn't wanted to follow the order to return to base while they were on holiday.

It was smart to know when they were beat. Retreat and fight another day. "We have intel that could help defeat them worldwide, and it will be lost if we are killed."

Xavier's jaw clenched. He'd spent longer as a captive than Josh had. They hadn't talked about what had happened. "Marsh will give a good account and tell them about the piss. Some scientist will figure out the rest."

"You're assuming they even make it."

"You're assuming they don't. Clarence can tell them all about the base. We both gave reports."

"And if they don't make it, what then? We need to report back."

Xavier pulled his hand away. "I have to go back to the base. I can't sleep at night knowing that we are leaving human beings there. They'll be sent to the farm." Xavier glanced at him. "Can you live with that?"

Josh wanted to live. Maybe he'd hate himself in time, but at least he'd have that chance.

He closed his eyes, unable to take the intensity of Xavier's stare.

He knew what it was like to be imprisoned by the aliens and be sent to the farm where they fed the bodies of the wounded to the larvae. He knew that there were survivors who stood no chance if he walked away. Xavier had too much bloody honor to do anything but the right thing even if it meant risking his neck.

"We can return with back up."

Xavier's eyes narrowed. "You know that's not going to happen."

"And you don't know that it's not. For all we know, they think us dead. They might have formed an agreement with the aliens that we'll muck up if we go in there and start killing them." He got out of bed and stood, immediately regretting the movement as his head spun, and the world hazed to gray and hummed like he was out of synch.

Xavier pushed him back onto the bed. "Is this you done, then? When did you decide you'd had enough?"

"Straight after I signed on again." It had been a mistake, but he'd thought it the only way to keep Xavier. If he hadn't signed back up, he'd have been a free man when the aliens arrived. He'd have put on his boots and disappeared, never to be seen again. And Xavier would be gone.

"It doesn't matter. I made the choice, and I'll live with it. If you're making this call, you need to be ready to live with the consequences. You have to be ready to have the deaths of your men, your team, on your hands."

He wasn't willing to wear this one.

"What are you saying?"

Josh drew in a breath, knowing it was the right call. "I'm not leading."

Should he? He had the experience that Xavier lacked. Could he? Or was he too fucked up and not just physically?

"You're standing down now? What the fuck, Josh?"

"I'm not standing down. I'm stepping aside because our orders were to——"

"I know what our fucking orders were. You think anyone over east gives a shit? We don't even know if they still exist. They sure as hell don't give a shit about us or they'd have done something after the ship was taken out. I'm pretty sure someone must have noticed it was missing by now. It also means that those see-through fuckheads can take out any ship they view as a threat. That means all human movement has effectively been halted. We are prisoners on our own planet, and they'll come a long and scoop us up and feed us to their bugs." Xavier raked his fingers through his braids as he stood. Fury radiated off him. He took two paces away and turned. "Fuck."

"I know we're fucked." Not only them, but humanity as a whole. They were two people in the middle of nowhere with no backup. What they did wouldn't change anything. For the first time, he didn't believe that he could make a difference. All the fighting was pointless.

"Yeah. So why don't you want to do anything?"

Because I am a coward, just like you said. I'm scared and hurt. "I don't want to lose you again."

Xavier dropped to his knees, his frustration reducing to a simmer. "I don't want to lose you either, but I can't do this without you." He lifted Josh's hand and kissed the stolen ring he place on his finger. "Joshy…"

"We are both barely standing. The odds of getting out again…" Josh shook his head. It was a suicide run. And for what? To test out a few theories about how best to kill the invaders and save a few humans who'd die trying to make it to Darwin?

"We know more this time."

"And so do they." With every contact, both sides learned something.

"Would you have left me there? If you'd known we'd been captured, what would you have done?"

"Did you not like my rescue mission?"

Xavier pressed his lips together and stared up at him.

Why did Josh end up feeling like the asshole? He was following orders. Xavier wanted to mount a full rescue for any human being held captive. "You can't save everyone, Xavier."

"I know. That didn't stop you from trying with the girl."

Josh drew in a breath that made his side burn. When the drugs wore off fully, he was going to hurt. "Have you even told the others?"

Xavier's silence was the only answer he needed. He hadn't said shit to anyone. The others would never back this plan, and they couldn't do it with just the two of them.

"Why do you want to do this?"

Xavier rocked back on his heals with a wince. "It's not a want. I need to. I dream I'm back there. Sometimes you're there, sometimes you aren't. I hear the men screaming and dying."

"They may already be dead." They had no idea how fast the aliens churned through fighters or how hungry the larvae were.

Xavier swallowed and nodded. "I know."

"Look, if this is an elaborate way to call off the engagement…"

Xavier laughed. "I want to marry you. I want to skive off to somewhere cold and alien free after this. I want to hang up my kit and have a home. I want all the things we talked about."

It had always just been pillow talk. The things lovers said in the small hours as they basked in the afterglow. The kind of things that might happen if the stars aligned. If they ever got the courage up to admit they were seeing each other. To date in public. Truthfully, he'd have said there was a better chance aliens would land, yet here they were, engaged.

"You want to tempt death one more time," Josh said.

"I want to know I did everything I could."

Josh studied Xavier's face. He looked as rough as Josh felt. But there was only earnest, honest need in his eyes. This wasn't about being a hero and taking glory. "Are you prepared to be court martialed?"

Xavier lifted one eyebrow. "For marrying you?"

"No, for fucking with the aliens when we were told not to. I don't care what they think about us." He doubted they would care beyond the fact that they worked together. He realized now the fear had been an easy excuse they could hide behind.

"I think we crossed that line a while ago. We didn't exactly break out stealthily. You dropped an IED in their farm."

"That's probably justifiable. Going back and making a mess is going to be much harder to explain." He didn't even know how that briefing would go, only that he'd stand there and wear the responsibility with Xavier because it would be the right thing to do. If it ended his career, he was fine with that.

"We have the opportunity to erase those fuckers and reclaim Western Australia. We can show the world how it's done."

Since no one had showed up to wipe out the aliens, Josh was assuming no one else had been successful. Or perhaps someone had been, but they couldn't get word out.

He looked at his lover kneeling on the floor. He understood the need for vengeance. To strike while they had a chance, while the aliens were expecting them to run. But while Xavier was fueled with the need to act, Josh was filled with the need to flee. He had a gap in his memory, a busted shoulder, and now his side was medium-rare.

He needed proper medical care. But he'd blown up the nearest hospital because it was full of bugs and larvae feeding on the dead. He wasn't going to be treated until they reached human civilization.

"How bad is it?"

"A bit raw."

Josh lifted his eyebrows. He needed more than that. "Blisters, third degree? How much skin is missing?"

He lifted his arm, glad the damage was all on the same side. It hurt, but it seemed functional. He studied the bandage covering the wound. Would peeling it back and having a look do more than confirm he was in a bad way?

"It's a mess. Tye removed the melted riot armor and the damaged skin. He cleaned it and bandaged it. We gave you some morphine to help you sleep."

They'd knocked him out to treat it. No wonder he had no memory. "Antiseptic?"

Xavier handed him the bottle of antibiotics. "I guess we're both taking these until we get somewhere."

Josh nodded, then shook his head. "This is insane. We need

serious medical treatment. Our team comprises three sailors who might be able to hit the side of a barn at twenty paces and one reluctant civvie."

"Ten paces. But one of them knows how to fight fires."

"And?" They didn't need a fire crew.

"And if we fill up some of the tenders from the fire station with liquid urea fluid, we can do more than squirt the aliens. We can hose them down."

That wasn't a plan, not even by his standards. Which, as Xavier often told him, was shit. They might be, but they worked because they weren't complex. "It won't be as simple as rocking up and turning on the hoses."

"So you're in?"

Their job was done. They should walk away. They should've gotten on the boat with Marsh and the civilians. They'd be on their way to Darwin and the tissue thin illusion of safety that offered.

As much as he wanted this to be over, while the aliens were setting up camp and calling the desert home, there was no such thing and no such place.

"Yeah. Why not? What else am I going to do? Lie around and heal up?" Risk dying of infection while waiting for the aliens to find him? No, he'd bring the party to their door.

He doubted he'd be alive to face the consequences.

Chapter Seven

JOSH ATE another spoonful of peanut butter. It was smooth, unfortunately, but he wasn't going to be fussy. The people who'd lived in this house didn't have much in their pantry that made good eating. Mice had already gotten into the cereal and rice, and the fridge was swollen with rotting food. The tins were still good, so they'd added them to their supplies and had a good cook up of tinned beef soup with added lentils and rice from their existing supplies. The peanut butter was dessert.

His shoulder and ribs hurt worse than having a larva digging in and eating him from the inside out. That he couldn't see the wound on his shoulder and was relying on others to tell him how it was faring was annoying. He'd tried to have a look in the bathroom mirror, but it was too neatly bandaged, and he knew it was best to leave it alone as every peek would let in bacteria. But he knew from the feel of it that something wasn't right.

He popped a painkiller and antibiotic with his next mouthful of water.

Xavier hadn't raised his plan with the others.

Josh sure as hell wasn't going to. He'd meant it. This was on Xavier. He was running this mission. A part of Josh already wanted to take control. If he were in control, it would be safer. But he breathed out and pretended he didn't notice the shake of his hand as he did up the water bottle.

They had enough water and food to get to the base and back. Enough to reach to Darwin with survivors from the base? Probably not. It would be reduced rations for everyone, and that was assuming they got that far into the plan.

The alien in the refrigerated truck was dead. From the smell or the cold or the proximity to the urea, Josh couldn't be sure. The one that he'd launched the piss bomb on had suffered what appeared to be severe chemical burns and died.

Did that count as chemical warfare?

He was sure lines were being crossed with every move they made, but they were stuck out there with the enemy. They weren't sitting in nice offices, in clean uniforms, calling the shots. Not that anyone was calling anymore.

The fire crackled, and if he closed his eyes, he could pretend they were camping. That they'd have a few drinks and then slink off to share a sleeping bag.

He still couldn't remember anything that happened between fighting the aliens in the street and standing with Xavier in the cemetery. In a few days, memory gaps were going to be the least of his problems. The injury might kill him before the aliens did.

Xavier cleared his throat. "Now that Josh is up, we need to debrief."

"We need to fuck off," said Dave. "Before your boyfriend gets us all killed."

Josh frowned. He'd missed something if they all knew.

"Fiancé," Xavier corrected. "And he didn't get anyone killed. It was Andrew who called up the aliens and told them to come over."

"He left Andrew to die."

He'd left him in a hotel because he hadn't wanted Andrew to interfere.

Xavier shook his head. "If you hadn't noticed, we're at war, and he was consorting with the enemy. You need to get your head on and concentrate on the people who aren't selling you out." Xavier paused and took a moment to look at everyone as though weighing who the next traitor was. "For the first time, we took on those assholes, and we had a decisive win."

Josh wouldn't have called it that. They had lost no one—aside from Andrew, but that wasn't really a loss—and they had killed all the aliens, but the aliens had levelled the town. Did that mean they were assumed dead again?

"We can kill them. Their high-tech armor doesn't save them if they're splashed with urea. We can free the men they are holding in the prison, ready to be fed to their bugs."

"You want to go back to the base?" Young leaned forward and stared at Xavier like he was insane. Josh knew the feeling.

"Yeah." Xavier leaned back, legs stretched out like he was discussing the football results.

"You want to clean up the Gecko infestation?" Fallon said with a smile on her lips.

Xavier nodded. "Exactly."

Josh bit back a grin.

"We can wipe them off the face of the Earth," Fallon continued.

Josh stifled a laugh.

Xavier frowned.

"You want us to go out there armed only with fertilizer?" Young asked.

"Of course not. We have weapons. We have their armor. The little four-wheel-drive fire trucks? We can fill their tanks with urea and spray them. Josh made a mess when we escaped, so they'll be rebuilding. We hit them hard and fast, and they'll be melting in the sun before they realize what's happened. We get hailed as heroes for figuring out how to solve the alien problem." Xavier smiled like he had it all figured out.

Josh had no idea how far the hoses threw water or if urea would gum up the system, but the way Xavier was talking, it sounded easy.

Xavier had always been like that. At first, Josh had thought him full of bullshit, all talk and bluster, but with no follow through. That hadn't stopped him from hooking up for convenient liaisons. He wasn't sure when it had gone from convenient fuck to something more. Maybe around the same time he'd realized Xavier wasn't full of shit. He talked a good game and backed it up.

Josh ran his thumb over the engagement ring.

Xavier had suggested stepping into the open once before, but Josh hadn't been ready. He still wasn't ready.

He remembered his stepbrother having a rant about *those types of guys*. It was one of the few things he remembered his brother getting riled up about, like it was somehow an affront to him.

Josh had known by then, but he'd tried very hard to date girls, only quitting when he'd joined the Army. He'd given himself the excuse that it was because he was too busy. In truth, he didn't want to fake it anymore. But he hadn't been brave enough to hang out with the other gay soldiers even though he knew who they were. He'd done everything to avoid them in case people made the correct assumptions. Then with Xavier, he'd worried what the higher ups would say. *Soldiers shouldn't date each other. It might affect the mission.*

Tye looked at Josh. "You on board with this?"

Josh glanced at Xavier. These guys didn't care about their original orders. The sailors' orders had been erased the moment their ship had gone down. So he nodded. "There's people being held there. We should make every effort to free them. Fucking up the aliens is a bonus."

"Or are you agreeing because you're fucking him?" Dave asked. "We need to go home."

Now the glances started.

Josh's cheeks heated. He'd rather be in the farm than have this conversation, but he was in it now, so he had to press on. "We've been together for three years, been in more shit than you can imagine. You want to go home and tell everyone that you left people to rot?"

Sparks flew up into the air, drifting higher on the breeze until they winked out. Overhead, the sky was clear and blue. Earth would go on even if humans were wiped out.

He took another drink of water already pulling together ideas that might become a plan. If they could free the people, they'd have more fighters.

But in his gut, something wasn't right. It had been bugging him for a while. Every settlement and town had been cleared out. That added up to more people than he'd seen on the base. He hadn't seen a single woman or child on the base either.

"No," Tye said. "No one should be left in their care."

The other two sailors stared at their feet. Josh knew exactly how they felt. Torn between running and helping. Were they doing the equivalent of taping up an arterial wound to buy someone a few more seconds as they gasped their last breath? Or could they make a change?

"There's only six of us," Fallon said.

And if they were all trained, that wouldn't have been a problem. Josh glanced at Xavier. This was madness; he almost wanted everyone to vote against Xavier. Xavier wouldn't go off on his own, but he'd be pissed.

And he'd feel responsible for leaving them behind.

That was never a good feeling even though it was impossible to help everyone.

"That's all we need," Xavier said. "The plan is simple. Get in and get out. Maximum impact."

There was no plan beyond spraying aliens, but Xavier spoke like there was definitely a plan.

"Josh, can you draw up the base?"

He lifted an eyebrow. "Sure. Got pencil and paper?"

Xavier smiled and pulled a notepad out of his pocket. "I found us some stationary while you were sleeping."

Josh flicked up his finger in response, then accepted the paper. "The base is laid out like honeycomb, all hexagonal buildings. There was a central, larger structure which the other captives called the farm." No one needed more details. He closed his eyes for a moment, orientating his view from the roof with what he'd seen on the ground. Then he added more information. "There's a main gate, but there's no visible fence; it's made of electricity or lasers or something. Don't cross it. You can see it with their helmets on." He added the prison area. "The cells are here."

He added a north arrow and some rough measurements to finish the mud map, then passed it around.

Young studied the plan. "How long did you spend there?"

"A few days. I was uninjured and wanted to stay that way," Josh said. "They make you fight until you break down."

"How do we get in?" Young handed the plan on.

"We don't," Xavier said. "We get close, and they will come out. It will probably be a two-alien team—that's what we've seen so far until yesterday when they had five—and they'll bring a sled for bodies."

"You want to drive to the gate or have two men walk up?" Josh asked. Both had their advantages and disadvantages.

"I want two walk-ins, just like we did when we were captured. Don't want to spook them. Then before things go to hell, I want our fire trucks to open up and douse them. No need to go wild though—only takes a squirt."

Dave shook his head. "We're fighting aliens with water balloons filled with piss and fire trucks filled with fertilizer."

"Yeah. If that's what works, that's what we do," Josh said.

"We have to be all in. This doesn't work with fewer people and leaving men behind isn't an option." Xavier appeared to be open to defeat, but Josh could tell from the set of his jaw and the tension in the way he sat that he wasn't. This wasn't about saving people but about Xavier killing his demons.

And maybe all of them in the process.

"Are we going to hit up the mine sites on the way there or on the way out?" Tye asked.

Xavier frowned.

"Our job is to evacuate survivors." Young gave Xavier a cool smile. "That was our mission. That's why we were sitting out there waiting for you. That's why we lost our ship and our friends."

"Where are the mine sites?" Xavier asked.

Young pulled a map out of his pocket. "You aren't the only one keeping track of everything." He laid it out. "The main ones are here, north of the base." They were on the coast, forming the third corner of a triangle.

"Marsh will wait for us here." Josh jabbed a finger at the map, pointing at the other side of the peninsula. It was only a few hundred klicks, not that far given that there were roads. Or had been. The first thing he'd have done, as an invader, is take out the roads.

"After makes more sense," Xavier said. And he was right.

"And if we die attacking the base? Who's going to get those people out?" Young pressed.

"You're assuming there are people at the mine sites. We went through settlements and farms and all kinds and found no one alive," Xavier said. "Just like Georgetown, everything is empty."

"Not even a body," Josh added.

"Then where are they? You can't make ten thousand people vanish," Fallon said. She shook her head.

"This isn't right. We need new orders," Young said.

Xavier crossed his arms. "And how are we going to get them? They all think we're dead. They aren't looking for us. They aren't sending help."

"We have to go to Darwin to get new orders." Young crossed his arms like he'd made the winning point.

Josh couldn't fault him. It would be nice to rest and let his wounds heal. Eventually, he'd be reassigned. They all would be. He glanced at the sailors. If they'd been on the ship when it was attacked, they'd be dead. While this wasn't much better, at least they had a chance, and Xavier was doing his best to reduce it to something close to zero.

But they knew the aliens' weakness. They knew how they fought, what their weapons were, and how their base was laid out. It was a small edge, and he didn't want to spend the rest of his life thinking about the men he'd left to die at the base.

Josh forced out a breath. "To do this, we need to leave at dawn. We hit them at dusk with the sun at our backs. That means we need to prep today."

"That fast?" Fallon asked, looking concerned for the first time.

Xavier nodded. "Yeah. Sitting around isn't going to change anything."

Twenty-four hours wasn't going to fix his wound. If anything, it would get worse. And they didn't have a week to recoup fully—assuming it was that kind of wound. Given the way his shoulder was feeling after taking a blast, he was pretty sure that without a hospital, he wasn't getting better.

Fallon bit her lip.

Young stared at the dirt.

Tye folded the map and gave a single nod.

"I want to go home," Dave said. "I don't want to go back to the base."

They couldn't force him, but he was going to be a weak link.

"We all do," Xavier said. "Every man locked up on the base wants to. But while the aliens are camping in the desert, we don't even have a home."

Chapter Eight

"HOW ARE YOU HOLDING UP?" Xavier dropped onto the bed next to him, jostling Josh's shoulder.

Josh opened one eye. He'd been trying to have a nap while sleeping on his stomach because his back and side hurt too much. "Great."

"You think I'm being a dumb fuck."

"Yep." Josh rolled over onto his good side so he could face Xavier. It didn't matter how he lay. Everything hurt all the time now. "But I get it. And if we had a proper team, I'd back you without a doubt." They'd go storming in, stage a rescue, and wipe out the enemy.

Xavier pressed his lips together. "We can make a difference."

"I've already agreed. You don't need to convince me."

"Did you agree because you don't want me to be killed or because you believe in what we're doing?"

Josh considered his lover. He reached out and put his hand over his. "Does it matter?"

"Yeah, it does."

His hand slid away. "I need medical treatment. Two days spent fucking around in the desert is going to work against me. I'm not operating at one hundred percent…not even seventy-five." And if they got captured again, he was farm food. "Are you thinking of medals or me?"

This job had been everything. He'd been so proud. Had loved the training, the missions, no matter how tough they were. There'd always been a sense of doing something useful even if he didn't see the big picture. For the last year, he'd been showing up and putting in the effort, but it had stopped being his life.

Xavier was still living it and determined to push through even though he was injured.

"I'm going to help Fallon and get the little trucks filled up." Xavier got off the bed.

"It doesn't matter how many you kill; it won't stop the nightmares."

Xavier paused by the door. "I know, but we have something that works, and I can't sit back and do nothing."

Then he was gone. A few minutes later, an engine started up.

Josh rolled on to his stomach and rested his forehead on his hands. The pearl dug into his forehead. Why couldn't they stay in the place where they weren't constantly bristling and preparing for a fight? He should've just said he believed in the plan.

He moved his hand so he wouldn't have a dent in his forehead.

He'd always thought things would be better between them if they were open, but at the same time, he'd known that would never happen. Now it had, and nothing had changed. They kissed and fucked and then pulled away to fight. But neither of them was able to let go.

Someone knocked on the door.

"I'm not asleep." He forced himself to sit up and bite back on the wince. He had to at least appear up to the job.

Young stood in the doorway looking like he had something to say but unable to spit it out.

"How old are you, kid?" Josh was feeling about one hundred.

"Nineteen."

"Why did you get a spot on the boat to pick us up?"

"I don't know. Luck?"

Josh almost shrugged but stopped himself. Moving hurt. "Sometimes that's the only difference between living and dying. You're here, and your crew mates are at the bottom of the ocean." Or more likely incinerated on impact.

"I don't want to join them. I don't want to end up with bugs eating me. I didn't sign up for this."

"None of us did. I joined up at eighteen because my brother couldn't wait to get rid of me. My parents died when I was twelve, and he was only your age. Can you imagine raising a kid? He didn't sign up for that. We have to deal with what gets thrown at us. Sometimes it's good, and you hold on to it no matter what. Sometimes you have to dig your way out."

"Why does Fisher want to go looking for it? We can flee."

Josh nodded. "So we run away…and then what? We make it to Darwin, and how long until the aliens come hunting up there? How long until they spread over east?"

"Then someone else can spray them."

"As Fisher said, we have the solution. We are in position."

Damn it, he'd convinced himself that they should go in. If he wasn't feeling like roadkill, he'd have been all in from the start.

"How did you get out?"

"I watched and planned and got my cell mates in on the plan."

"How many of them survived?"

Smart kid; he knew what to ask. "You met Clarence. Frank was killed and ended up in the farm with me." He held Young's gaze. "The others were recaptured."

"What makes you think this will be any different?"

"Because we know their weakness now." He had to believe that along with the layout of the camp, it would be enough.

Young stared at him like he'd lost too many brain cells. Maybe he had. He'd lost a chunk of a day, and he'd agreed to return to the alien base.

Josh got up. He ran his hand over his beard knowing he looked like shit. "I'm going to have a bite to eat and wash. Then I'm going to start laying out weapons and armor and getting everything sorted. If you want to learn something, you can help. Or you can keep griping about how unfair it is that you're alive and killing aliens while your crew mates are dead."

———

JOSH WORKED with his shirt off, wearing only a pair of borrowed shorts and his hair tied back with a hot pink elastic band that had been abandoned in the bathroom, laying out all the weapons and armor on the floor of the lounge room. Tye and Young had moved the furniture and fetched and carried everything for him. Dave sat on the sofa and watched. They had all been mercifully silent.

He didn't care that they were sitting and watching instead of helping him strip the alien guns of their power source. Whatever signal the weapons used to be active, Josh expected them to be useless now, but the power source could be rigged to explode.

He separated everything into piles.

They had flashbangs, pistols, and rifles from the police station.

Riot gear and Gecko armor.

Enough condoms to keep a platoon happy for a month of R&R.

"What exactly are you doing?" Dave finally said.

"Inventory."

A truck pulled up outside, followed by another. Xavier and Fallon were back.

Xavier walked in, grinning. "Fueled up and ready to roll." His gaze flicked from Josh to the floor. "You've been busy."

"Thought I'd make a start."

With one look, Xavier did exactly what Josh had done. He watched the thoughts scroll over Xavier's face. Was it enough, too much, or too little? What could they leave and what should they take? Who would carry what? Josh tracked Xavier as his gaze skimmed over everyone in the room.

Josh and Xavier would be on the ground to lure the Geckos out. Since Josh couldn't drive and Dave was a liability but could, he'd pair them up. That left Young and Fallon to take control of the other truck. He'd keep Tye away from the action as much as possible because if anyone needed medical care, he was it.

It would be better if Xavier was in a truck, as his leg was still on the mend. But they didn't have those kinds of luxuries, and it had to be one of them acting as bait.

Should it be him? At least he was able to run. He could go on his own.

Josh started redoing the teams, then stopped. It was Xavier's problem, not his. All he had to do was show up and do as he was told.

Xavier's gaze landed on Josh, and he nodded. "Thanks. Looks good."

He wasn't talking about the weapons, but he was also lying. Josh had lost weight and felt like a starving street cat one fight away from getting the green dream at the vet.

Josh ran a hand over the paint that marked his skin. He'd given it another scrub out by the water tank. Nothing had come off. But he was clean and had a stomach full of chocolate and tinned pineapple—if they were going to do something dumb, he was going to fill up on his favorite foods first—and for the moment, that was good enough.

"We picked up some extra weapons while we were out." He opened up a bag and dumped out some large, heavy-duty water pistols…rifles. "Thought they'd be better than the squirty bottles."

They would be, but that didn't stop the unease that they were going to be fighting a war armed with water pistols and baby fire trucks. They almost deserved to die—or to be given medals and early retirement for ingenuity.

"Let's sort out everyone's kit, have some dinner, and grab some sleep." Xavier gave the order, and no one argued.

Between the two of them, they gave everyone weapons and armor. Then it was all set out so in the morning, it could be put on.

Josh put on flip-flops that were a size too big but had been left by the door and went outside as Xavier and Fallon filled the water tanks on the trucks with urea and added water. He wanted to help, but knew as soon as he lifted anything, he was going to do more damage. The painkillers weren't doing much more than dulling the edge.

What he wanted was another shot of morphine, but he didn't want to be incapacitated, so he was saving it for after the fight when he'd really need it. He'd like a beer, but they were all warm, and it would probably clash with what he was taking. So he sat on the step and watched them work. The air was soon thick with the smell.

When it was done, Xavier came and sat next to him. Fallon gave them a grim nod and went inside.

For several minutes, neither of them spoke. They sat and watched the sky darken. Xavier leaned his head on Josh's good shoulder. "Odds?"

"It doesn't really matter, does it?" They were preparing to go in. He licked his lip. "I need to know that you're going to fall back if it looks like it's going to fail. That you won't press on if we're taking casualties. The people we have with us come first. One of us needs to make it back to report." They could gather all the intel they wanted, but if it never made it back, it was useless.

"I keep running through what we could've done differently when we escaped."

"So have I. At the time, we did what we could with what we had. It was up to everyone else to take the chance or not. Some of them would've stayed put out of fear."

Xavier nodded. "Do you dream of the farm?"

"Yeah. And the hospital. Why couldn't I lose those memories?"

Xavier gave a short laugh. "Still nothing?"

"Nope. I have no idea how I got from the roof to the cemetery." He must have walked or ran. "You were in the church, weren't you?"

"I thought I was done. When I came to at the bottom of the stairs, I thought I'd broken something serious. Then you appeared through the smoke to haul my ass out."

"Again."

"Again," Xavier conceded. "I know this is tempting fate, but I want to take them down. They're trespassing."

Josh blew out a breath. "We pull back and run if we have to."

Xavier nodded, yet his jaw was set, and he was staring out across the yard.

"I mean it. We front up, we assess, and we decide. The same as any other job."

"I know, but it doesn't sit right leaving them there. Leaving the other men when we know what will happen to them."

"You're more use alive than dead."

Xavier elbowed him. "You're so sweet."

They sat for a few more minutes until all the light had gone from the sky and the mosquitoes came hunting for blood. Josh stood. "You coming to bed?"

"In a few."

Josh left him sitting there. He couldn't carry any of the burden Xavier had taken on. All he could do was make sure he didn't drag the rest of them down.

Chapter Nine

THEY DID MOST of the drive to the base on roads that were little more than hardened dirt tracks. There was no point in waiting for nightfall and hoping to creep up on the base as the aliens had the tech to see, and they didn't. They didn't try to be stealthy either. Josh worked on the assumption that any movement was going to be noted by the alien's surveillance teams. He hoped the aliens were spitting out their morning coffee—or whatever they drank—and scratching their hairless heads, wondering how the humans had survived the bombing of Georgetown.

The red dirt stretched on as far as the eye could see. Xavier was in the lead vehicle with Young and Fallon. Dave was driving the second little fire truck in a resigned and reckless manner. Every bounce rattled through Josh, making his pain flare. He was surprised his arm functioned, but every movement tore at the wound on his ribs, and the bandage had been soaked through this morning. His shoulder joint ached in a bad way, too. Had the larva left behind an infection that was now in his bone?

The antibiotics that he was taking might have been the wrong kind. Did they even have the right kind if they were alien germs?

The vehicle jolted over a pothole, and Josh bit back the curse. He couldn't hide the wince, though.

They reached the designated rendezvous point far too quickly. Xavier's team had left their vehicle there before being captured. They all piled out of the trucks to see what had been left behind. It appeared to be untouched as it was still under the net and still loaded up with goodies including a rather unhappy snake that had decided the stolen four-wheel drive was a good place to call home.

Xavier got onto the roof racks and scanned the horizon for the base.

Josh finished kitting up with others. They drank and ate in silence, waiting to be told when to go. This was always the worst bit. Being alert and ready but not too ready as the wait could be awhile.

"Joshy, take a look." Xavier handed over the binoculars.

Josh stared out across the hard landscape. The need to run flared as he sighted the base.

While it was there, it seemed different somehow. Because they'd blown up bits? Or because he was coming from a different angle? Or because something was wrong? "What do you see that's different?"

"There's no movement for a start."

Josh checked again. Xavier was right, but that alone wasn't suspicious. "I didn't see any on my original approach until they attacked."

"It's smaller."

Was it? Possibly. "What do you want to do?"

If they got closer, they were committing to an attack. Why was no one coming to greet them? Were the aliens waiting for them to get closer? "You don't suppose they're all dead?"

Xavier shook his head. "No. Nor do I think they've gone home."

"So where the fuck are they?" He'd much rather they all be at the base, prepping for the pathetic human attack. "Are they setting their own trap?"

The aliens had the time and weapons…

"We need to move closer."

Josh closed his eyes. He'd known that's what Xavier was going to say. "How close? You want to drive through the gate and knock on every door?"

"Only the prison block."

He glanced up at Xavier, lying on the roof of the four-wheel drive. This wasn't his job to call off. Something wasn't right, but was it right in their favor?

Xavier looked at him. "We're still good to go."

Josh pressed his lips together and turned away. He addressed the team. "We are rolling in as planned. Fire one, be ready to open your hose. Remember you only have four minutes' worth of liquid in your tank. Do not waste it. Cover Fisher as he tries not to get captured."

They couldn't drench the entire base. They couldn't enter the base because of the security fence. All they could do was draw them out and kill them. The aliens would wise up pretty fast, though.

"Fire two, which is me," he reminded them, "is going to lob some flash bangs and IEDs into the base." With the confusion, hopefully the humans would get an edge. "We will not turn our hoses on but use the water balloons if approached."

With only a few grumbles, everyone got into the vehicles. Xavier clung onto the outside of the truck as they made their way closer to the base.

Two hundred meters away, which felt like standing on the alien's doorstep, there was no welcoming party. They hadn't gotten this close last time. This close, it was clear that there were buildings missing from the base. It was gappy whereas before, it had been a tightly packed honeycomb.

Xavier called a stop. He stepped down and shoved one of the alien helmets on. Fully dressed in the Gecko armor, it was enough to make Josh shudder.

"There's no perimeter fence," Xavier said.

"Is the helmet still active?"

"Yeah."

"Or they're feeding you fake intel." Josh wouldn't put it past the aliens.

"I don't think there's anyone home."

Josh swallowed, his mouth thick with dust. They should pull back and head for Darwin instead of wasting more time.

"I want to take a closer look." Xavier started walking, favoring his injured leg more than he had been.

"Xavier." He walked away, ignoring Josh. "Fisher."

That made him stop. He turned, but Josh couldn't see his face behind the face plate of the helmet.

"This is not the mission."

"It is. There might be people in there."

Josh muttered a litany of curses in several languages as Xavier turned away again and resumed his march to the base. As planned, the other truck followed Xavier.

"What are we doing?" Dave asked.

"I'm not going to blow up the base while Fisher is exploring. We wait." He'd kick Xavier's ass later.

The minutes ticked by.

Xavier made it to the entrance and threw a piece of clothing through the gate. Good, Josh smiled. At least he wasn't trusting what the helmet was showing him. When nothing happened, Xavier stepped through the gate and into the base.

Josh's heartbeat quickened, even though he was on the outside.

"Get closer." If it all went pear shaped now, it would become a rescue mission.

Dave swore under his breath. "I just want to go home."

"You will. Shut up and pay attention." His heartbeat was loud enough that it should have been be heard outside of the truck. He was breathing too fast. He tried to slow it as he scanned the base for any movement.

There was nothing. No trap sprung closed.

"Fisher. Base appears to be deserted," Xavier said over the radio. "I'm going to the prison. Fire One, stay with me. Fire Two, remain outside."

"Fire Two remaining outside the perimeter," Josh confirmed.

The engine idled. He had the oversized water pistol in his lap, a pistol on his chest, and several alien guns waiting to become explosives behind the driver's seat.

"I don't like this," Tye said from the back seat.

"You don't have to."

He knew Xavier would move carefully through the base and to the prison. What they should be doing was going through the buildings that were left looking for other intel. Maps, orders, tech, anything that might give the humans an edge.

Josh picked up the radio. "Fire One, status?"

"At the prison. No signs of life."

Fuck. He didn't know if he should be glad or not. The other men were probably dead, or they'd been taken to wherever the aliens had gone.

"I'm going to set some charges in the prison, then look in some of the other buildings."

"Roger that." Josh looked at Dave. "You can turn the truck off. The base is deserted."

Dave sagged with relief. With no engine, there was no air-con, and the vehicle heated up even with the windows down. Josh was sweating his ass off in the armor. It brought back too many happy memories of waiting around for something to happen.

Forty minutes later, Fire One rolled out of the base. Xavier was riding on the outside, with no helmet on. They retreated to the rendezvous point, then piled out to strip off armor and discuss.

Xavier wiped the sweat from his face. "Not a single body, just like every other town. The farm was destroyed, well and truly." He flicked Josh a grin. "Half the buildings are gone. Don't know how or where. I picked up what I could; it's in a bag on the back of the truck. I don't know what I grabbed but I don't think their operation room was left there. I didn't see a hospital either. There was definitely a gym. I took photos." He handed the camera to Josh to review.

"You think they they've left Australia?"

Xavier shook his head and shrugged as if he couldn't make up his mind. "They launched an attack on Georgetown; they can't be that far."

Usually Josh would agree, but with the aliens, he didn't know if that held true. But it was better to be cautious and assume they were still there. Somewhere. "We've checked the base; the mission is over."

Xavier stared at the sand, shoulders lifted like he was preparing to argue. If they did that now in front of the others, the tenuous agreement they had was going to fall apart. Josh put a hand on his arm. "I know you were hoping to find the others."

Xavier shrugged him off.

"Does this mean we can go home now?" Dave asked.

Josh didn't wait for Xavier to agree. "Yeah. Let's have a bite to eat and map a route."

He wasn't really hungry, but he had to eat something. He forced himself to chew through a muesli bar and eat a small tub of peaches in jelly. Given the things he'd eaten in the past, that was fancy rations.

Xavier sat on the back of the truck, eating tinned tuna and crackers.

While Josh wanted to move as little as possible, leaving Xavier to stew in his own turmoil wouldn't help everyone else. "What's bugging you?"

"We fucked around for so long that they were gone."

"That fucking around was called surviving, prepping, and fighting."

Xavier grimaced. "Just give me some space."

"Fine." Josh stepped back. "You happy for me to run us into Darwin?"

"Sure. Whatever. It's what you wanted anyway." He slid off the back of the truck, lips pressed tight, scowl in place.

"Pull your head in. We checked the base. You searched for survivors. Now we follow orders and take these people and the intel to where they need to be."

Xavier gave him a mock salute. "Ready to obey, Rayne."

Josh gritted his teeth. He should let it slide, but he couldn't. "Even if we knew where they'd gone, we can't go chasing them all over the outback. We don't have the supplies."

"I understand that. But that doesn't stop me from feeling like a failure."

"You were half dead the last time you were here." And Josh was on his way to getting there this time. "Be glad you're alive."

"Yeah…" Xavier walked away.

Chapter Ten

ON JOSH'S ORDERS, they drove to the nearest road and headed north. The route would take them past a couple of mine sites. Josh stared out the window with a smile on his face. They were heading home. The aliens had retreated, and while he was feeling like warmed up shit, the hope that this was almost over had taken hold.

Hope didn't stop him from scanning the sky and the horizon for anything that didn't belong, though. He remembered to take the painkillers and antibiotics, but he wasn't sure they were doing much. Every breath hurt, and he really wanted to pass out and wake up in a hospital bed somewhere—he wasn't fussed where. Eventually the pain and exhaustion claimed him, and he slept, only waking up only when his head smacked into the window or snapped back against the headrest.

At dusk, they stopped and made camp without fire. The trucks smelled. He hoped the urea wasn't eating through anything essential. Hopefully, they could switch out the vehicles at one of the mine sites. There was sure to be a nice four-wheel drive they'd be able to borrow.

Fallon and Young handed out rations. The food was cold, but he wasn't even hungry, even though he should eat. He made himself take a few bites and drank, but he was in bad shape. "Everyone okay?"

There were mumbles and nods as they ate, but no one was in a mood to talk.

They arranged the watches with Josh going last. He wasn't up to going first, and he was sure everyone was noticing the way he was coming undone. Xavier volunteered to stay up and seethe.

Josh couldn't be bothered trying to talk to him. He'd sort himself out. Usually they'd just spend some time apart.

He lay in the sleeping bag and ran his finger over the ring. He shouldn't be wearing it; it was a hinderance. It might get caught on something. But he couldn't bring himself to take it off, either.

He didn't know how fast he went to sleep, only that someone woke him too soon.

"You got to take your meds," Xavier urged.

"I was sleep." His knew words were slurred.

Xavier pressed the tablets into Josh's palm and held out the water bottle. He accepted them and the drink without argument and then lay back down, but he couldn't get comfortable. His whole back hurt, his fingers tingled in a bad way, and he couldn't decide if he was hot or cold. It was probably because of the burn. Burns had a way of fucking someone up.

The next time he was woken, it was for his watch. He got up, sweaty and nauseous. If he died when they were so close to safety, he was going to be furious. If they hadn't wasted a day checking out the base, they'd almost be there…

He swallowed down on the annoyance. If he wasn't feeling so shit, the stop would've been fine.

The air was cool on his skin. He took a leak, had a drink, and did a lap around their camp. There was nothing to see and there'd been nothing all night according to the others. That didn't mean they weren't being watched.

If he were an alien, and some jumped up mammals had taken out part of his base and the team send to eradicate them, he'd be watching them. He'd be wanting to take them out to make sure they didn't become a bigger problem.

The aliens were out there. He just didn't know where, and that bothered him. He much preferred knowing where the enemy was lurking.

He'd like to forget they even existed. If they hadn't arrived, he'd have finished his holiday with Xavier. They'd have gone back to work and been friends but nothing more when others were around.

At what point would one of them have gotten tired of it and wanted more?

He twisted the ring on his finger. Would Xavier have needed more first?

And when Josh backed off, too scared to admit the truth, would Xavier have walked away?

He wiped the sweat off his forehead and resisted the urge to doze off. He'd been wounded and pressed on before. They were maybe two days of solid driving out of Darwin depending on the roads and what they found along the way.

By the time they got there, he wasn't going to be upright.

Movement behind him made him turn, but it was only Xavier moving through their camp, getting some food and water. He was up too early. He should've slept a little longer. But the sunrise was pretty, and it would be nice to share it.

Xavier sat and offered the packet of chocolate chip biscuits.

Josh shook his head as his stomach turned.

"How are you?" Xavier murmured after he'd eaten two biscuits.

"Rat shit."

"I'll ask Tye to change the dressing."

"Yeah." Like that would make a difference.

They clearly weren't talking about yesterday.

After several more minutes spent studying the sky and the scrub, Xavier spoke. "You aren't supposed to die on me."

Josh glanced at his fiancé. Were they actually, or had it been a heat of the moment thing? Josh had meant what he said. He wanted all that life would give him and everything he could take. He wanted to be able to put his arm around Xavier and kiss him without worrying about what everyone might say.

"I'm not dead yet. I spent weeks thinking you were dead."

"I'm still surprised that I'm not." He patted his leg. "It's not healing at all. Tye said something about the tissue being dead. That's not a good thing apparently as it needs to be cut away."

Josh closed his eyes. His side and his shoulder…

"I don't know what their weapons do, but it's not good."

"They're not just heat the way we thought." He wasn't burned. He was dying.

Xavier shook his head. "It's not rotting, but it's like the skin's forgotten how to grow or something. He seemed to know what he was talking about."

Josh took a sip of water, thinking about the artificial limbs and the metal plates that covered alien injuries. "That actually explains a lot. Did you notice the metal legs and such?"

"Yeah, real clever."

"They attach to raw tissue and only come off when the body is dead. Danny took a gut shot. I'd taken a plate like a piece of armadillo off a scout a week earlier, and I stuck it on him to cover the wound; it was all I could do." He still didn't know if it had been the right thing. "It molded to him. Stopped the bleeding and stopped the pain. Their tech also has living parts. I saw them in the console in the farm."

"Thanks for the additional nightmare material; I didn't have enough already." Xavier smiled, but it was tight.

"What I'm saying is, if they made weapons to injure and prevent healing, they also found a solution."

"The metal parts."

Josh nodded.

Xavier glanced at the truck. "And they work on humans?"

"I only tried once. Danny didn't live long enough for me to know if his insides worked." It might have fixed up the outside, but sepsis would have set in if his guts were ripped open on the inside.

"Tye said the docs in Darwin will do skin grafts and it will be fine."

"I can't wait." He was going to end up with his ass on his ribs.

"You'd rather a metal part?"

Josh pressed his lips together as he debated what to tell Xavier.

After a few heartbeats, he decided on the truth. It was easier. "By the time we reach Darwin, you're going to be carrying me out of the truck."

Xavier stared at him, realization sinking in. "Why didn't you say you're so sick? We've wasted a whole day."

"Because you needed to do this, and I was fine until I wasn't."

"Does it hurt?"

"Yeah. I'm too hot, can't eat. I think my body might be having some kind of trouble because of the fluids leaking out of the wound." Too much of his skin had been blitzed by the alien weapon. "You better today?"

Xavier shook his head and grimaced. "You're dying."

"I'm not there yet so don't plan my funeral."

"I want to plan our wedding."

Josh smiled, unable to imagine it. He didn't know anyone who'd come.

Xavier stared at the rising sun. "Everyone who came with us is dead. It was a shit job. Destined to fail from the first."

"It had to be done. Someone had to take a look at the base. We did that—and more closely than they expected. We need to try the radio. See who we can raise." Maybe they someone would meet them.

"The range on these things is shit."

"Then we stop at a mine site and borrow something with more grunt. We can't do this alone."

Xavier shook his head. "That will take us off course and waste more time."

"You wanted to look for survivors."

"You don't have the time."

"They might send someone to us."

"Send another boat?" Xavier laughed. "They won't collect us. We need to get back over the Simpson line before they'll even acknowledge we're alive."

The Simpson line jagged around Darwin. The city was a valuable link with Asia that the people in power hadn't wanted to lose. Southeast Asia, last time he'd heard the news, was alien free.

"Okay then. Where's the nearest crossing?"

Xavier pulled a map out of his pocket. It was meant for tourists taking road trips and marked exciting things to see on the way. He'd drawn in the line they had to cross. "I hope they stuck to that and didn't change it without telling us."

"We're working on the assumption that Darwin stands, that there is someone running the country and the military." The last he'd heard had been over a week ago. A lot could change in a few days. What if they reached Darwin and there was nothing there? His fight was over if that were the case.

"You got word about it. What did they say?"

"Just that it had been enacted."

"We're 600 klicks from the border. A thousand from Darwin. If we take turns driving…"

"I know. I've already thought it through."

"Okay. So we get everyone up, and we start driving."

It sounded so easy. So doable. He wanted to live. Not because he wanted to fuck up more aliens but because he'd tasted what was possible. He wasn't sure he could go back, but he wasn't sure how to go forward either. "Do you want to keep doing this when we get back?"

"What do you mean?"

"Us."

"What?" Xavier frowned. "I know I can be a shithead, but…"

"No…yes, you are, but this." He held up the hand with the ring.

"I meant it. I had a lot of time to think in prison. I don't want to go back to how things were. I want better. I need better. It's all or nothing."

Josh nodded, his throat dry. "I do too."

All the jibes and slurs he'd heard over the years rolled through his head. All he'd wanted to do was fit in, but was it fitting in when he was cutting part of himself off?

He wasn't sure he knew how to be himself unless he was with Xavier. He couldn't imagine a life without him.

He hoped Xavier would be planning a wedding, not a funeral.

―――――

JOSH WAS no use with the driving, so every time they stopped, Dave and Tye switched. He wasn't used to being useless. Xavier had taken control of the drive to Darwin without Josh asking.

He woke up as the truck stopped again.

Xavier jogged over. "Kit up. We have contact at ten."

Josh glanced past the other vehicle, hoping Xavier was wrong. There was dust on the horizon. Something was out there. Josh prayed it was humans even as he struggled to put the armor on and get his weapons ready. They'd gotten complacent after finding the empty base.

"Where are we?" Josh asked as Xavier peered through the binoculars.

"About one hundred from the border. There's an abandoned mine not far from here. I bet that's where the fuckers are coming from."

"What's at the mine site they might want?"

"I don't know. Buildings? People?"

If the internet still existed, he'd have looked up what was out there, checked out some aerial footage, and they would've had a clue about what they were facing.

"If they've seen us, they are ignoring us," Xavier said.

"Or they're calling for backup. I'm getting on the radio." He didn't expect much, but he tried anyway. No one responded. He went to wipe his forehead out of habit, but there was no sweat. That was definitely not good. "What do you want to do?"

Xavier glanced at him, then back at the aliens.

Josh saw the wheels turning. Once they crossed the border, they would hopefully get military backup. Maybe. There was no guarantee that the military was holding the Simpson Line. However, they had four hundred kilometers to drive before reaching Darwin. It wasn't that far, not really. But at the moment, it was like asking him to swim to America.

They ran, or they stayed and they fought and hoped someone lived.

"We need to deliver the intel," he said even though that made him a coward for not wanting to fight. He'd written down what he'd told Marsh. A plan of the base and what he knew about the weapons and armor. Then he'd added what had happened after she'd left. A detailed report with the others filling in the missing part of his memory. That's what needed to be delivered.

Xavier nodded. "Go. I'll cover you. Take two drivers and don't die before you deliver it."

Josh shook his head. They didn't have enough people to split the team. Those left behind would die. "No, we all go, or we all stay."

Xavier shook his head right back. "You know I'm right."

"Fuck you."

"I'll drive," Fallon said. "It's only one hundred across the border. I can do it. If there's no one there, then I'll drive straight through to Darwin."

No one was going to cross the line to recover five men who were presumed dead. No one would want to tangle with the aliens when they could avoid them. And he didn't want to be leading the aliens into human held territory.

Xavier shook his head. "You'd be alone, an easy target."

"We should all be running for the line," Dave said.

Josh drew in a breath that felt like blades were being shoved between his ribs. "They'll be on us before we reach it." He glanced at Xavier. "We send Fallon and Dave, and the rest of us will make sure they get away."

"You should go; you can't fight."

"Dave's a civvie. I can shoot, but I can't drive." He owed Dave the chance to get away after he'd been forced to stay behind.

Xavier pulled him into a hug that jarred in all the wrong places. "You need to go."

"You can't ask me to listen to you die over the radio again." Josh closed his eyes, knowing it would be for real this time. If they stayed behind, they weren't getting out of this. No wedding, no funeral.

Xavier pressed a kiss to his cheek. "I want you gone. I want you to tell everyone how to fight the fuckers."

"I don't need to do that. I need to be with you." He gave Xavier a shake and drew back. "We do it together."

Xavier's eyes were glassy, and he blinked rapidly. "It wasn't meant to be like this."

"I know. We fucked it up when we had the chance to be better." Too scared of what ifs.

Xavier cupped his jaw and kissed him again. "We should have gone AWOL."

Josh laughed. "You're too good for that."

"You're too good for me."

Fallon coughed.

Xavier pulled away and studied the horizon as he pulled himself together.

Josh pulled the notebook out of his pocket. "Deliver this." He thrust it at Fallon. "Don't stop until it's in the hands of someone with stars and the authority to do something."

Fallon stood there. "Are you sure you won't come?"

"Are you sure you can do this?"

She nodded. "I'll make sure they know. That they help you."

Josh smiled like he believed her.

"Get the weapons out of the vehicle," Xavier ordered.

Young and Tye did as they were told. Then Fallon and Dave got into the little fire truck and drove away.

Josh watched them go, knowing that he'd signed his own death certificate by staying but unable to leave Xavier to fight alone.

Chapter Eleven

XAVIER AND YOUNG hung onto the outside of the truck as they turned down the track that led to the abandoned mine site. Xavier was on Josh's side of the truck. Even though Josh wanted to be a million miles away from here, he'd never have been able to live with himself if he survived and Xavier died.

He didn't really want Xavier living and him dying either.

Right now, the chances were good that they'd both die. Maybe that was acceptable.

The scent of the outback changed to the overripe stink of death. He leaned out the window. "You smell that?"

"Yeah. Death," Xavier confirmed.

"That's a bit more than one kangaroo."

Xavier nodded.

Josh picked up the binoculars. With the truck bouncing over the corrugated surface, it made focusing hard. "There's some kind of cloud." But it was too low to the ground. "That's not a cloud; it's insects."

Tye took his eyes off the road. "Their insects or ours?"

"I don't know." Josh did not want to fly into a cloud of alien bugs that would use his body to hatch their eggs.

Xavier tapped on the roof, and the truck stopped. He jumped down, and Josh handed him the binoculars. They were sitting in the middle of the track, exposed. He almost laughed. He was still thinking like this was human on human conflict. The aliens knew where they were, even if they hid behind trees and rocks. They couldn't sneak up on them, so they might as well drive right up.

Xavier handed the binoculars back. "I think it's flies. I've never seen their bugs fly."

That was true. And the first piece of good news for today.

"And aliens?"

"Nope."

Josh doubted that. There had to be a couple of scouts keeping an eye on the perimeter. But as long as they weren't chasing Fallon, he didn't care. "What do you want to do?"

They could pull back and hightail it across the border. But if this was where the aliens had moved to, it was too close to human civilization, and that would only end badly for the humans.

"I think we should check it out. Put your helmet on and keep on the radio. Hopefully we'll get in range and someone will be listening."

"Fast or slow?"

"If they're here, they know were coming. If they aren't and we're in the wrong place, then it doesn't matter."

"That doesn't answer the question.

Xavier looked at him. "What would you do?"

Josh's face reflected in the alien visor. "Proceed until we have contact. There's no point in wasting energy walking and trying to be sneaky if they can read our heat signatures."

Xavier nodded.

Tye tapped his hand against the steering wheel. "If they can read heat signatures, why don't we start a fire?"

Josh stared at him.

"What? They won't be able to see us coming. It might give us an edge."

That was true, but they also risked cooking themselves, and their baby fire truck wasn't loaded with water.

Xavier picked up a handful of dirt and watched how the wind caught it. Sideways. If they were careful…

"The only way out will be through the camp and to the coast," Josh said. All they had to do was clear any aliens between them and the coast. That was incentive if nothing else.

Tye pulled out the map. "There's a river we can follow. We can ask Marsh to pick us up."

Assuming they managed to raise her on the radio. Josh nodded. "Good plan."

Xavier pulled a lighter out of a pocket. "Are we sure about this?"

Josh drew in a few breaths. "Yeah. If it spreads, we can't get done for burning national parks because we aren't in Australia."

"Nice technicality. If the aliens are here, they're going to be pissed."

"That will save us the trouble of trying to find them." If the aliens were here, they weren't going after Fallon and Dave. "We need to be a big distraction."

"That I can do." Xavier walked away from the truck.

Josh closed his eyes and drew in a few breaths. "You'd better be able to outrun this, Tye."

"I'll do my best."

"You'll do better than that."

Josh smelled the smoke before he saw the flames. They licked across the dry grass and tasted every scrubby bush. Xavier set the fire in more than one location, giving it a chance to get going. All they had to do was stay in front of it and pray the wind didn't change.

The engine idled as they waited for Xavier to return. "Let's go, nice and easy. I don't want to get too far in front."

Josh got on the radio, letting anyone who was listening know where they were and what they were doing.

The truck started moving again. He ignored the hot tearing in his back and the rolling nausea in his gut. He didn't know if there was anything the human doctors could do for him anyway. No one had treated the burns caused by the alien weapons. What if his skin never grew back and just kept dying? They couldn't cover all of in a skin graft. He'd run out of skin.

At least this was useful. A few less aliens on their doorstep. And if no one was here?

Then it would be easy.

A nice drive to the coast. People paid a lot of money to holiday in the far away beauty of the outback, and he was doing it for free.

Along the track there were warning signs about trespassing and the dangers of old mine sites. There was no fence or gate, though. If there ever had been, it was long gone.

Smoke coiled around the truck and slid in through the open windows. Behind them, the flames had taken hold. The crackle filled his ears. He was too hot; it would be nice to be sweating. He took a sip of water, more because he knew he should than because he was thirsty.

After another half hour of creeping forward with the fire at their backs, he was almost itching for something to happen.

The cloud of insects didn't like the fire. It rose and spread out.

Between the noise of the fire and his own breathing, it was hard to hear anything and just as hard to see. Tye kept on going, never speeding up and never slowing enough to let the fire catch them.

The first building of the abandoned mine site came into view.

Josh sat up straight and scanned the building, searching for movement that didn't belong.

A flash of blue in front of the truck kicked up dirt. Xavier tapped the roof, but Tye had already stopped the truck so Xavier and Young could get off. Josh closed his eyes, knowing what was coming next. His eyelids still lit up as the flashbang went off.

"Are we going to hose them?" Tye asked.

"There's no one to hose yet. Follow the track." Xavier would do the same on foot.

Josh got on the radio again to give an update, even though he doubted anyone was listening. He gave coordinates and hoped for the best.

The radio crackled to life. "Fallon, twenty to the border."

Josh smiled. "Good job. Keep going."

"Good luck, Rayne."

Blue light cut through the smoke. Something screamed.

Young scuttled back to the truck, bent over like he was trying to hide in the smoke.

Xavier stepped out of the smoke, water gun in one hand, thumbs up with the other as he ran for the cover of the truck. Xavier and Young put the truck between them and building. A minute later the building exploded, sending debris up into the air. Josh flinched.

No one was surviving that.

Xavier handed Josh the empty water gun, and Josh switched it out for a fully loaded one. They'd been filling them with piss the whole drive.

They crept through the site. Every time they came across a building, Xavier blew it up with one of the alien's own guns rigged to explode.

It wasn't subtle, but Josh hoped Xavier felt better.

He added destruction of property to the list of things they shouldn't have done on this job.

Behind them, the fire was creeping closer.

Blue slashed out of the smoke and hit the truck. Tye jerked, and the truck stopped.

"Fuck!" Josh didn't need to check for a pulse; the door and half of Tye were missing. The aliens weren't dicking around. They didn't want captives, they wanted them dead.

Figures moved through the smoke.

Josh flicked the controls, hoping that the pump still ran. He couldn't see Xavier or Young. He was going to have to kick Tye out and do his best to drive. He glanced at where the door had been, knowing that he'd be putting himself in the line of fire as soon as he moved.

Another blast hit the car, slicing across the hood.

Then the aliens were screaming; they ran out of the smoke clawing it themselves. Xavier took them down with neat shots through the face plate. He wasn't wasting ammo. But Josh couldn't see him, and he didn't want to drive in case Young or Xavier were under the truck.

It took only seconds, and then they were alone again.

Josh's pulse hammered in his ears. He leaned over, too aware that something was tearing and burning in a bad way. He undid Tye's seatbelt and pushed him out with a murmured sorry. Without the medic, he wouldn't be alive, and now Tye was dead.

Before he could slide over, a figure stepped up, holding three alien guns. Josh reached for his pistol, but he was given the thumbs up. Xavier.

He got in, sitting in Tye's gore, checked that Young was holding on, then eased the truck along the track. "What have we got left?"

"Three piss pistols, three working alien guns, two flash bangs. Assorted other guns and pistols." Josh was keeping a careful count. "How many have you killed?"

"Confirmed, six between us."

They moved faster now. The aliens knew they were there, and the fire was gaining strength, and they were now down a man.

Josh glanced in the wing mirror. There was no way they could turn around. They had to press on. He squinted into the smoke. His eyes stinging. "There's something ahead."

"Flashbang."

Josh tossed it out of the truck. It bounced up the track. Even though he expected it, the blast ricocheted through him.

"I'm not sure that worked," Xavier said, as he stopped the truck. "We have an official welcoming party."

Josh glanced at the toggles in the truck one last time, then at the aliens with their guns pointed at them. "Young, hose at will."

Maybe they'd take out half if they were lucky.

Several heartbeats passed and nothing happened. Then the truck hummed and liquid urea jetted across the track and into the aliens. Some of them fell over. Some fired. Josh and Xavier scrunched down as far as possible.

Xavier clasped his hand, and Josh gave it a squeeze. The old arguments didn't matter out here; they were in it together, no matter what, the same as always.

The truck hissed and smoked with each shot from the alien's weapons. The windscreen cracked but held.

Then, aside from the inhuman screaming and the fire, everything went still.

Xavier motioned that he was getting out. Armed with a piss pistol and a rifle, he eased out the door. Josh grabbed a rifle and prepared to exit. The truck was fucked and not going any further.

He drew in a couple of breaths, then sat up slowly. Aliens lay on the track, twitching as they died.

He opened the car door and used it as cover as he found his balance. It took longer than it should have. He was as fucked as the truck. Xavier gave each alien a bullet through the faceplate to make sure they didn't get up.

Josh scanned the smoke for any others. But this time there was nothing moving.

"Young?"

No answer. Josh turned and made his way to the back of the truck.

Urea leaked out of the ruptured tank and splashed on the track. What was left of Young was slumped over the tank, hose still in hand.

Bile rose up his throat, and he turned away. The fire they'd started was gaining.

"We have to move," Josh called out.

From the truck, he grabbed two supply bags. There was water and food and a med kit in each. He had no idea where they were fucking going, only that they wouldn't get far.

He put out a final radio call. "Alien camp has been cleared out. Two casualties. Fire approaching. Requesting immediate assistance." He paused and tried again. "This is Sergeant Josh Rayne, Australian Army, requesting immediate assistance." He gave the coordinates, knowing they were too far from the Simpson line for it to matter. "I'm confirming that urea is highly effective on the aliens." He closed his eyes and jumped when Xavier put a hand on his shoulder. "If anyone can hear me, please acknowledge."

"Let's go," Xavier said.

"Go where?"

"The coast."

The radio sparked to life. "Marsh here. I'm north of your position. If you can make it to the lake, you might be able to pick up a boat and meet me at the coast. I will hold for twenty-four hours."

There was no way they were going to make it. Xavier pulled the map out anyway. Everywhere was too far on foot. They were in the middle of nowhere without a vehicle.

There was only desert and bush in every direction. If they weren't injured, it would've been an easy hike out. They'd have made it with hours to spare.

Xavier pointed at the creek that lead to the lake which turned into a river and kissed the coast where Marsh was waiting. They'd done this shit before.

Josh nodded like he thought it was doable. He wasn't going to make it. Xavier might.

"Rayne here. Glad you're alive. Hold for twenty-four." There was no need for her to wait any longer. They'd either be there or have died trying.

"I'll keep the beer cold and pass on your message about the urea."

"I'm looking forward to that beer. Out." Josh put the radio down. They couldn't take it with them. He was half tempted to try starting the truck, but the front end was a smoking mess.

Xavier took both packs off him. "Are you hurt?"

Josh shook his head. "You?"

"No." Xavier grabbed a couple of magazines.

Josh made sure that he had weapons and a piss pistol. He might be able to refill it later.

Together, they crept past the dead aliens, scanning the smoke for movement. Despite the smoke, the flies were thick, and he was glad of the helmet keeping them off his face. His breathing was fast and loud as they kept on the track. Xavier motioned a stop. He pointed to his left. It took Josh several seconds to realize what he was looking at.

It wasn't a temperature-controlled farm like they'd had at the base. But he'd found where all the people and animals had gone.

What had been an open cut mine now seethed with alien bugs. His stomach rolled, and he turned away before he was sick. They hadn't brought enough urea to take care of that.

Would the fire?

He hoped every alien critter crackled and burned.

Xavier pulled him on.

Weighed down by armor and weapons, Josh was exhausted already even though he knew he shouldn't be. This should have been easy. He followed Xavier, knowing that they couldn't stop, not with the fire and the bugs so close. The bugs would flee, which meant they'd be following them. That thought was enough for him to find a new burst of energy.

There were hexagonal alien buildings to the right. Xavier led them that way as though looking for more to kill.

"What are you doing?"

"Hoping they have one of their hover sleds and one of us can figure out how to use it, so we can get the fuck out of here."

"That sounds better than walking."

"Yeah, well, you aren't going to make it far on your two legs and neither am I."

They crept around the buildings, expecting to see an alien every time they rounded a corner. Josh was breathing hard. His muscles were screaming, and even though he wasn't carrying a pack, he was still ready to drop. He slid into the mind games of one more building to clear. One more corner. One more step.

And he kept going.

No sleds.

They needed another plan. Could he make it to the creek, which would give them some protection from the fire, and find a boat? Even if it was a five-foot tinny with a sewing machine for a motor. Thinking through options kept him ticking over. And if they couldn't find a boat, they could make a raft.

"Jackpot," Xavier said.

Relief swept through him as he followed Xavier through the smoke and drifting ash.

The sled sat on the ground, an oblong of greeny-yellow metal. There was some kind of control panel at one end. Josh turned to cover Xavier's rear while he fiddled with the controls.

The fire was eating some of the alien buildings now. And things moved along the ground. "Bugs."

Xavier tossed the piss pistol over so Josh had both. There wasn't nearly enough, and worse, he had to wait until they were close. Unless. He squirted out a perimeter and watched as they scuttled closer.

They hesitated at the line. Those that got too close he shot with a regular bullet. The deaths seemed to agitate the living ones. He knew how that felt. He'd watched two men die today for no good reason.

"How's it going?"

"A bit shit. Want to trade?"

"Sure." Josh backed up a few paces, and Xavier took the weapons from him. He made his way to the control panel and stripped off his gloves. It was smooth except for a few grooves and buttons. "Maybe it's flat."

"It had better not be, because I'm fucked, and my leg feels like it's ripped open." If Xavier was whining, it was bad.

Josh didn't look over his shoulder to check how Xavier was going. If he needed help to hold off the bugs, he'd say something. The fire was roaring, and the air was heating. If they didn't leave soon, they'd be cooked in their stolen armor.

He needed to turn the sled on. He tilted his head, then walked around until he was standing at the front as though he was ready to drive off. The bodies piled up around them, and the bugs were clicking. Something was squealing.

At the front were two grooves. He slid his thumbs into them, and the sled began humming and lifted two feet off the ground. "Get on."

Xavier took a couple of steps back, then knelt on the sled. "Let's go."

Josh stood in front of the controls, not sure what was go and what was stop.

"Joshy?"

He didn't even know how to steer. There were three grooves and one button.

Right then. Grooves for go it was.

He slid his left fingers along them slowly, and the sled moved. He needed to turn, and he needed to turn fast, or they were going to crash into a building, thus ending their escape. He placed his palm over the button, and the sled turned. He said a silent prayer of thanks to whomever was watching over them.

They were on their way.

Chapter Twelve

JOSH STRIPPED off his body armor. His skin was clammy, not from sweat but from his damaged body trying to live. All he could do was try to stay hydrated and hope that essential organs weren't shutting down. Some might argue that his brain had shut down years ago. On days like today, he'd agree.

He lay on his uninjured side using the armor to rest his head, making it the most uncomfortable pillow he'd ever experienced, and that said a lot. For the moment, he didn't care. Overhead, the sky was stained with smoke.

"Talk to me so I don't pass out." If he passed out, he wasn't sure he'd wake.

"How bad is it?" Xavier pulled the IV bag out of the medical kit.

"Pretty bad."

"Been awhile since I've done this." He pushed Josh's sleeve up and located the vein.

Josh doubted that one bag of fluids was going to be enough, but he kept quiet while Xavier did what he thought would help. He ignored the small pinch as the needle slid in.

"Shouldn't you be driving?"

"We're going really slowly, and it's flat ground at the moment."
He picked up Josh's hand. Xavier's was warm. "How can you be
cold?"

Josh's lips curved in a grim smile.

Xavier's fingers pressed against his pulse. No good news there
either.

"Is it not-going-to-last-the-night bad?" Xavier's voice caught.

"I don't know." He swallowed around the ache in his throat.

Xavier was silent for several breaths. When he spoke, his voice
was rough, and his eyes were wet. "Do you want me to stop the sled
and find a nice place to watch the stars?"

"No. I want to see the ocean. I want to plan the wedding." He
wanted to live. He'd wanted Xavier to live.

He'd spent the last decade knowing that death was a possibility,
and now that it had come knocking, he wanted to tell it to fuck off.
He wasn't ready. There were things he wanted to do.

Xavier forced a smile. "I'm planning the wedding. Beach or
something flash?"

"You want something flash."

"I did, but that was before. Now I think I like your idea. The
first ship's captain we see can do it. I don't care that I reek of sweat
and smoke and piss."

"To be fair, that's not much different to usual after a job." He
kept a hold of Xavier's hand.

"Good point."

"How the leg?"

"Hideous beneath the bandage. The stitches can't hold what
isn't healing."

"Yeah…and I'm missing a big chunk of flesh. Tell me the truth
this time. How bad is it?"

"It's a mess. It's not just skin, but muscle too." Xavier pressed a
kiss to his cheek. "Drink my water."

"You need it. I have the drip."

Xavier nodded and let go of him. "I need to check we aren't
going to crash."

"Where are we?" How much farther did they have to go?

"Just passed the lake. Do we keep going on the sled or if I see a boat, should we switch?"

"How are we going to get down any waterfalls?" He was sure there were waterfalls, the kind that tourists paid to fly over.

"We'll keep the sled and go around."

"And when it goes flat?" There was too much ground to cover, and while Xavier might make it on his own, he wouldn't make it very far dragging Josh's ass. "You might need to make a run for the coast. You can always come back."

"No. We make it together or not at all. I'm not leaving you."

Josh smiled. He watched the trees flick by in a quickening blur.

Xavier talked about what he was seeing and even though Josh fought the tiredness stalking him, he was taken and swallowed whole by the darkness.

———

XAVIER PUSHED the sled as fast as he thought he could handle without tipping them both out. It rode over undulations and rocks and down sides of hills where the water roared in his ears. He couldn't stop. He had to reach the coast.

Night embraced him and he kept going even though his thigh shook and his back ached. He needed to eat, but he didn't dare slow down. Josh had stopped answering him. Fear that after all of this he'd be alone lodged in his heart like a random bit of frag that no surgeon would ever be able to remove.

The river widened, and he was sure he saw the ocean. He didn't slow the sled in case he was wrong. Then he was gliding over sand, with nothing but the sea in front of him.

"We've made it, Joshy, so you'd better not be dead."

He didn't get an answer.

There wasn't one ship but two on the water. Marsh's stolen pleasure craft and a Navy ship, plus something smaller on the beach.

"Sergeant Xavier Fisher," he shouted. "Don't shoot." The last thing he wanted was a bullet hole because they thought he was an alien.

People spilled out of the boat on the sand. Xavier slowed the sled. They assumed that pressing on the button would stop it, but it hadn't been tested.

"I don't know how to stop. Stay back," he called out the warning.

He pressed the button, and the sled jerked to a halt, almost throwing him off. He grabbed onto the console for balance. Now he was here, he wasn't sure he could stand. His muscles had locked up.

People swarmed the sled, all of them in black, weapons aimed. Xavier put his hands up, though they barely reached his shoulder. He didn't have the strength to lift them any higher.

The soldiers shone lights in his face and asked too many questions.

"You came for us," was all he could say. He'd expected Marsh and had hoped Bird would be able to patch up Josh until they reached Darwin. But this was so much better. His eyes burned.

They rolled Josh onto a stretcher. His limbs flopped, and Xavier couldn't breathe. Was he too late?

He shouldn't have insisted they go to the base. They should've dashed for the boarder. He should've made sure Josh knew how much he loved him. That seeing him after being away, even if it was only for a day, made everything better. They should've gone AWOL instead of fighting aliens. All the things he should've done pressed against him and threatened to choke him.

"Is he alive?" He pushed past the people around him and stumbled onto the sand. His leg gave way. They were taking Josh away without him. "Is he alive?"

If he'd spent their last few minutes together driving and prattling on instead of holding him… He'd wasted so much bloody time thinking his job was more important. That being someone to everyone mattered more than being Josh's boyfriend, lover, husband.

One of the men turned. "He's alive."

Xavier collapsed onto the sand, the waves echoing in his ears.

They'd made it.

Epilogue

JOSH BECAME aware he was awake because he was as uncomfortable as fuck. There was an incessant beeping, and he was cold. He didn't know where he was, which also caused him more than a little concern. He cracked one eye open. The room was sideways. He was on his stomach.

He gave his wrist a test twitch. No restraints.

It took a few more breaths before he realized he was in a hospital. And everything looked familiar and human, not at all alien. He closed his eyes.

A human hospital.

The tension that had built faded but the discomfort and gnawing pain didn't.

"Hey." His voice came out as a croak, like it hadn't been used for a very long time.

Shit. He had no idea what day it was.

What did he know? Name, rank, date of birth. That was a start.

He tried to move his arm, but it didn't want to cooperate. It flopped off the side of the bed, and he was too exhausted to lift it up.

"Hey!" he called out again. Where was everyone? He needed to turn to see the door.

What if they were all dead and he was here alone? Fear kicked his heartbeat up, and the machine beeped accordingly.

That got a reaction. The door swung open, and footsteps raced toward him.

He was helpless, and he couldn't do anything about it. "Who's there?"

"I'm a nurse. Just relax." Her blue scrub coated legs came into view.

"I need to face the door. I need to get up."

"You're not doing anything except lying there." She checked the screens of the machine. "Are you thirsty?"

Now that she mentioned it, he was. "Yes."

"I'll fetch some ice chips." She made some notes on his chart. "How are you feeling?"

"Um…" He couldn't say like shit.

"Are you in pain?"

"Not really. I'm uncomfortable. I want to move. Where am I?"

"Darwin. What do you remember?"

"Is this civilian or military?"

"Civilian."

He closed his eyes. "Too much." And he couldn't tell her any of it. "Where's Xavier? Xavier Fisher, he was with me."

"Would he be the man who refused to stay in bed and spent too much time sitting in here?"

Josh smiled. "Yeah. That sounds like him."

"I'll let him know you're awake."

"How long was I out? I know my side was pretty bad…" He tilted his head as much as he could so he could see her face.

"I'll leave that for the doctor to discuss."

That wasn't good news if he needed a doctor to discuss it with him.

She lifted his hand and put it on the bed. "You're awake. Take it one step at a time."

That really wasn't what he wanted to hear.

"I'll be back with the ice chips."

Her shoes squeaked a little as she left. The door opened and closed, and he was alone again. He closed his eyes and carefully made sure he could feel each finger and toe, giving each one a twitch. The ring was missing. He didn't remember losing it. He'd been wearing gloves. Had it gotten stuck inside one and been left somewhere?

It was hard to concentrate, to remember all the details. He was too drugged up, for which he should be grateful for. Without drugs, he'd probably be howling. He missed the ring's now familiar weight.

The door opened. No squeaky shoes but something else.

He was in a civilian hospital. He was safe, but he couldn't stop himself from going on alert. He didn't call out this time. He cracked his eyes open and waited.

The person walked around the bed. Dark legs stuck out of a hospital gown, bracketed by metal crutches.

Josh opened his eyes fully and lifted his head. "Xavier!"

Xavier freed his hand from the crutches and took the cup out from between his teeth and placed it on the table. Then he leaned over and pressed a kiss to the corner of Josh's lips. His lips lingered there.

"You don't know how bloody glad I am to hear your voice." Xavier kept his cheek against Josh's for a little longer.

Josh wanted to sit up and wrap his arms around him. "You did it."

"Of course I did." He sat on the seat and picked out an ice chip. "Open up."

Josh did. "The nurse won't tell me anything."

"I had to fight her for the ice chips. Something about letting the doc talk to you first."

"Whatever," Josh said around the ice chip. "I'd rather talk to you." The doctor would get to him eventually. "You going to give me an update?"

Xavier lifted the edge of his gown to reveal a bandage around his upper thigh. "They chopped out a chunk and stole some skin from my other leg to cover up the mess. They said it's healing." He lifted his gaze to look at Josh. "They put you in a coma."

"How long?"

"A week. They were worried that you weren't going to wake up. I told them to fuck off and that you didn't need that negativity."

Induced coma. That explained why his throat was sore and why he felt so boneless. He glanced at Xavier's thigh. "So they filleted my back and stuck some stolen skin over?"

"Yeah, but it was a bit more complicated than that." Xavier raked his teeth over his lip. He'd had a shave at some point and was looking clean and civilized. Josh's teeth were fuzzy, and he didn't know if he still had blood and dirt under his nails. "You were half dead. Lost blood and fluids. They wouldn't give me an answer. I think they knocked me out for a couple of days just to have some peace."

Josh almost managed a laugh. "I'm alive. And planning on staying that way."

Xavier crunched on a piece of ice, then offered another one to Josh.

"What about…about the aliens?"

"I got a visit from a general telling me what a good job we did. That your reports have reached his desk. He hinted at medals."

"Have they taken out any other bases?"

"I'm guessing I didn't need to know because he wouldn't tell me. So I watched the news, and it looks like we're clearing them out." He grinned. "We saved the world, Joshy."

But the cost had been high.

Xavier drew in a breath and leaned forward. "While I had his ear, I told him I was getting married."

Josh was sure his heart stopped. "And?"

"And he asked who, and I told him, and he asked if I was on too many drugs."

Of course he had. "We don't need his permission."

"I got a fancy letter the next day. And so did you." Xavier pulled it, and the pearl ring, out of the bedside table. "I didn't open yours, but I'm guessing they are the same, wishing us luck on our lives together."

"Open it and read it already."

Xavier did. He scanned the paper and then nodded, as though satisfied. "The same." He held out the ring. "Do you still want to?"

"Of course I do. Put the ring back on." Xavier slid it onto Josh's finger. It felt right wearing it.

"They have a chapel."

"Not there." The last church they'd been in had been destroyed. "Is there a garden or something?"

"I'll figure it out. Hell, we can do it right here."

"Is this your new mission?"

Xavier smiled. "I've got to have something to do."

But he stayed in the chair until Josh fell asleep.

———

THREE DAYS LATER, Josh was finally allowed out of bed but was still attached to his friendly drug filled drip. About three different doctors had been in to talk to him, and nurses checked on him every few hours like they expected him to suddenly keel over. He'd checked his own chart to see what they were giving him, and it was quite the cocktail.

Still in the gown, a nurse helped him into a wheelchair to take him to the courtyard. He wanted to walk but wasn't allowed. He wanted to blame the drugs or breakfast for the way his stomach was flipping, but that wasn't it. They were actually doing this.

No more hiding.

He didn't want to go back to how things had been. He wanted more than being a bit player in Xavier's life.

Xavier was already in the courtyard and wearing a hospital gown, but he had boxers on beneath, so his ass wasn't hanging out. He was talking to the chaplain but turned as soon as Josh was pushed through the door. The afternoon light was sharp after being inside for days; that's why his eyes were watering.

Xavier grinned. "Damn, we're wearing the same thing." He

held out the edge of the gown with one hand like he was about to curtsey. His other hand was gripping the crutch that was taking the weight off his bad leg. "And look who turned up for the party."

That was when Josh realized that everyone who'd made it was in the courtyard. Marsh, Bird, Fallon, Dave, Clarence, and Kayla. Not everyone had died. They had saved some.

They had survived.

The chaplain glanced at them both. "Ready?"

"Always," Josh said. It felt like he'd been waiting his whole life to be asked. For Xavier to hold his hand and say I do.

Xavier bent down to kiss him. "Mission complete."

"I think we're just beginning."

————

WANT to know what else I'm working on?

Join my newsletter (www.tjnichols-author.com/lp)

Other books by TJ Nichols

Studies in Demonology trilogy

Warlock in Training

Rogue in the Making

Blood for the Spilling

Mytho series

Lust and other Drugs

Greed and other Dangers

Envy and other Cravings

Vanity and other Monsters

Sloth and other Delights

Wrath and other Troubles

Gluttony and other Hungers

Ogres and other Dating Dilemmas

Familiar Mates

The Witch's Familiar

The Vampire's Familiar

The Rock Star's Familiar

The Vet's Christmas Familiar

The Detective's Familiar

The Siren's Familiar

The Soldier's Familiar

The Billionaire's Familiar

The Firefighter's Familiar

The Bodyguard's Familiar

The Spy's Familiar

Outcast Pack (Familiar Mates world)

Wolf Heart

Wolf Blood

Wolf Soul

Wolf Mate

Wolf Lust

Wolf Hunt

A Summer of Smoke and Sin (historical urban fantasy)

Liminality (fantasy)

Captured Earth trilogy

Resist

Regroup

Revolt

Holiday novellas

Elf on the Beach

The Vampire's Dinner

Poison Marked

The Legend of Gentleman John

Silver and Solstice

Solstice Wishes and Christmas Kisses (holiday novella collection)

A Wolf's Resistance

Hood and the Highwaymen

About the Author

TJ Nichols is the author of the Studies in Demonology and Familiar Mates series. They write mostly gay fantasy and paranormal romance, but sometimes gay action/horror as Toby J. Nichols.

After traveling all over the world and Australia, TJ now lives in Perth, Western Australia.

You can connect with TJ at:

Newsletter: http://www.tjnichols-author.com/lp

www.ingramcontent.com/pod-product-compliance
Lightning Source LLC
Chambersburg PA
CBHW061055100726

47911CB00012B/247